THE TATTOOED LADY...

Queen Minerva was a beautiful woman, even without the blue-and-red decorations completely covering her body. She was gazing up at Longarm boldly and hungrily . . .

"Now you've saved my life twice," he said.

"You could . . . repay me . . . if you wanted to," she whispered.

"Seems no more than gentlemanly. We ought to be able to work out something."

She writhed inside her strapless dress and the garment fell away from her. She stood naked before him.

→→ **TABOR EVANS** ←←

LONGARM

AND THE GOLDEN LADY

A JOVE BOOK

First Jove edition published May 1981

First printing

Printed in the United States of America

Jove books are published by Jove Publications, Inc.,
200 Madison Avenue, New York, NY 10016

Chapter 1

The rising sun winced painfully at the brim of the contorted horizon like some hungover eye winking up red and reluctant from the bottom of a whiskey bottle.

Longarm slumped in the government-issue saddle cinched upon an exhausted agency-leased Morgan horse. A tall man, lean and muscular, he let the patient animal trudge at its own gait up the first rise of the timber-fringed slope into Denver, finishing the ten-mile trek from Eldorado Valley at a walk.

It had been a long, sleepless night. He and the horse were bone-tired, but at least they were alive. They had lived through one more night following longlooper tracks, but the man wrapped in a soogan and sagging across the Morgan's rump behind him was dead.

You kill one, Longarm thought, and Texas Bill Wirt recruits three more owlhoots to take his place. They come up like fleas in a buffalo robe, wild-eyed and hotheaded, anxious to make a gun rep and quick bucks with a lawless band of sidewinders.

He tilted his head, raising the flat-brimmed Stetson, snuff-brown and worn dead center, angled slightly forward, cavalry-style. Pink-flushing sunlight touched at his sharp-hewn face, seared and cured to saddle-leather brown by raw sun and cutting winds and ornamented by a drooping longhorn mustache that augmented the hard ferocity of his appearance. His tired eyes shone a gunmetal blue, and his close-cropped hair, showing under his hatbrim, was the color of aged tobacco leaf. He wore skintight brown tweed pants, as snug as his skin, and low-heeled cavalry stovepipe boots, more suited for running than riding. His frock coat was buttoned tightly against the Colorado night chill, and though he'd been eternal hours in the saddle,

1

his string tie was still knotted at the throat of his gray flannel shirt.

He turned easily in the saddle, catlike, and shifted his eyes warily along the narrow street as the first houses hove into sight. He wasn't expecting trouble, but he was prepared for it—out of nowhere, which is where it usually came from. There was nothing in the atmosphere to alarm him; nothing more than his instincts. He was on guard.

He saw no one along the long street, and for this he muttered a silent prayer of thanks. At 5:00 A.M., it was early, even for the good people of Denver, to whom lazing abed past dawn was one of the Seven Deadly Sins. Thank God he had the streets to himself. All he wanted was to get this outlaw's carcass to the sheriff's office as quickly and unobtrusively as possible—and without any accidents.

Longarm kept his coattail pushed back just clear of his cross-draw-holstered Colt .44-40. As tired as he was, as near home as he was, he didn't want any surprises.

He glanced about in the silent morning. He couldn't explain what troubled him. He'd feel fine as hen's teeth, though dog-tired, if only there weren't this inexplicable premonition of wrong, working at the nape of his neck.

He sighed heavily. Accidents. Accidents were mistakes you made when you relaxed and let down your guard. Accidents had a way of happening suddenly. And accidents could be fatal. The fellow yoked across the horse's rump behind him was the victim of such an accident. The outlaw had accidentally drawn on Longarm when he was down, mistakenly thinking him disarmed as well as prostrate.

"We all make mistakes," Longarm allowed across his wide shoulder. "The fewer we make, the longer we last."

Longarm listened to the patient plodding of his horse's hooves on the hardpacked red clay street. Poplars, elms, and cottonwoods lined the quiet yards. He smelled the first promise of breakfast fires, saw the first pale lamps wink to life at curtained windows closed tightly against the threatening night vapors.

He mused on the youth he had slain in the line of duty and who the boy might be. Law enforcement got brutal sometimes, but it was necessary if good people were to live safely among the human wolves. A kid like this—who was he? Where'd he

2

come from? What made him prey on law-abiding people? What made him join a band of rattlers like Texas Bill Wirt's gang of thieves? What made him draw his gun when he had only to go quietly—and live?

Longarm glanced over his shoulder. He'd thought Texas Bill Wirt's killer legion might ride after him last night, but then he'd realized that this kid, dead, meant nothing to the longloopers anymore. Wirt's men had abandoned the kid to slow Longarm down. Now the boy was dead and nobody cared.

Longarm shivered slightly in the morning chill. It was a waste, a hellish waste, that's what it was.

He glanced east, lifting his head enough so the crimson sun turned his dark mustache red.

His horse carried him and his dead captive into town at a plodding walk, knees and hocks bending tiredly, withers quivering. The sun-splotched streets lay empty at this hour. The long trek was almost over. A body delivered, a report made, oats and a rubdown for his horse, and ten hours in the sack for him. He'd earned it.

His first warning of peril was the sudden thud of boots at a run on the red ground behind him. Behind him? Certainly, where else? Trouble never came easy, only fast.

"Longarm!"

The raging baritone voice, pitched low in the chest to give it power and authority, blasted silence out of the morning.

Longarm's nerves twisted, something congealed in the pit of his stomach. He felt the horse shudder under him at the raucous yell, spooked. Longarm used wrists and knees in an automatic gesture, moving the Morgan into a turn in the middle of the street. As his animal sidled, he drew his gun and crabbed from his saddle, landing on his parted feet, legs set, with the horse as his shield.

Longarm stared, angered but not startled. The kid yelling his name looked like any other saddle tramp under twenty, coyote-lean, hungry-eyed, unwashed, frayed and tousled, with an outsized weapon in a tied-down holster low on his hips. The looks of the kid told everything one needed to know about him. Another young hellion on the prod, looking to make a name for himself as the man who killed Custis Long. Only Longarm wasn't ready to go yet.

Longarm stepped from behind his horse, letting the reins

trail. He further demonstrated his contempt by slapping his Colt angrily back into its holster. "What you want, boy?"

"Don't call me boy, you son of a bitch."

"Get back under your rock and I won't call you at all."

They faced each other on the silent street. "Your name Longarm?"

"My friends call me Longarm. You can call me Long. *Mister* Long."

The boy's laughter fluted oddly. It sounded empty-bellied, tense. The kid probably hadn't eaten breakfast, maybe no supper last night. His precarious circumstances made him as edgily dangerous as his motives—whatever in hell they were. "Smart old man, ain't you, Long?"

"Smart enough to stay alive to *get* this old, boy." Longarm shrugged his wide shoulders. "Now if that's all you got to say, I'm in a hurry."

"You stand where you are, rooster." The boy's voice cracked, brittle with rage. "I'll say when you can go."

"I'm gettin' fed up with this, boy."

"I told you, Long. Don't call me boy. You'll know I'm a man before I'm through with you."

Longarm peered through the dazzling dawn light at the scrawny youth, seeing another rootless kid consumed by a terrible pride and driven by some restless compulsion to prove himself to a world that couldn't care less. He shrugged again, turned, and reached down to take up the dangling reins.

"You move and I'll shoot you in the back, you fat son of a bitch," the boy yelled.

Longarm grinned sourly and shook his head. He supposed the underfed kid saw anyone who had eaten even recently as fat. He felt a flaring of pity for the boy, but his pity was marinated in weary irritation—the very worst kind of savage impatience.

"I ask you one more time, boy. What do you want with me?" Longarm jerked his head toward the corpse tied across his horse. "You know this hombre? That what's eatin' you?"

"No. I don't know him. I don't care about him. It's *you* I'm after, Long."

Longarm exhaled heavily, unobtrusively slapping his coat-tail back from his high-belted holster. "You mind saying why?"

4

The boy grinned wolfishly, seeing that Longarm had bared his weapon; this was the kind of respect the boy liked to see; it was too infrequently accorded him. He had no way of knowing Longarm was a cautious lawman. He would have done as much for a sidewinder. The boy shifted his weight on his scuffed boots. "You know Cotton Younger?"

"Cole Younger? Jesse James's cousin?"

"You heard me, old man. Cotton Younger. You know him?"

In the space of a breath, Longarm sorted through the outlaws stored in the files of his mind. Cotton Younger. A brother of Cole Younger and a cousin or something of the James boys. One of the Cole Younger–Jesse James gang who had terrorized the frontier from Minnesota to Missouri. Cotton had escaped the law. He had disappeared completely. He was a hard man to hide because he was named for his sandy eyebrows, faded blue eyes, and pale yellow hair. Besides which, he was almost seven feet tall; he stood out in any crowd. There was nothing Cotton could do about his height, but he had dyed his hair a fierce black with coal tar and had turned up in that disguise in a Wyoming Territory settlement called Crooked Lance. He'd hired on as a rider for the Rocking H Ranch and soon was bossing the outfit. He had fallen in love with a local belle and could have lived out his life respectable and respected, but he got greedy and ended up a corpse roped across his saddle, like this cadaver from Eldorado Valley.

"I recall the gentleman. Why?"

"Because you shot him down in cold blood, you snivelin' bastard."

"In the line of duty, old son. It was my job. Nothing personal."

The boy shivered like a burro chewing briars. "Well, it's personal with me, killer. You spilt my cousin's blood. I can't live till I avenge his dirty murder."

"You best get your head on straight, partner. It wasn't murder when your cousin Cotton died. Not in anybody's book. Cotton was a federal fugitive—with a price on his head."

"And you kilt him—for the re-ward."

"None of your business, sonny, but marshals can't take rewards or bounties. Like I said, it was strictly business. Now get out of here."

"Oh, no, killer. There ain't no re-ward on you, neither. But I'm killin' you, Long. I'm gunnin' you down as a public service—and to avenge my cousin, Cotton Younger."

"You even make a move like you're going for that gun, and you're in trouble, kid."

"I'm going for it, Long." The boy flung his arms wide at his sides, standing tensely on the balls of his feet. "You hear me, Long? I'm giving you your chance to slap leather and that there's all I'm givin' you."

Longarm winced. He stared at the ragged boy, standing scrawny and defiant, barely enough of him to throw a shadow. But old enough to kill. A bullet from that boy's gun was as deadly as one from some grown man's hogleg. But he glimpsed the dead youth strapped across his horse's rump. He'd killed his quota of fryers. He wasn't going to kill another one before breakfast. He was damned if he would.

"Get out of here, kid," he said.

"Go for your gun, you lily-livered bastard," the boy said. His sun-faded blue eyes swirled wildly, shadowed with the lust to kill, a madness that named itself righteous hatred. The boy betrayed his move, as if he'd sent a message by Western Union. His arm snaked out and plunged downward toward the low-slung holster.

As the boy's hand tipped the butt of his tied-down gun, Longarm fired.

He had drawn with such dazzling speed that the youth, stunned, hesitated, incredulous. The kid's face turned deathly white as he realized he was about to be killed—and that he'd asked for it, never even suspecting there were men who drew, not by time at all, but by instinct.

Longarm squeezed the trigger on his Colt .44-40 twice so the blasts were almost simultaneous. He seemed to fire instinctively, but he knew better. He held his gun with icy steadiness; even the muscles in his fingers, hand, wrist, and arm were under control of his mind. He aimed his fire as he never had before. He wasn't going to kill this kid, not for all the provocation in this world. Not if there was any other way.

Longarm's first bullet ripped into the youth's holster, into the gun butt, into the boy's hand where it gripped the handle, paralyzed. The youth managed to jerk his bleeding hand away,

6

screaming, as the second bullet demolished his six gun's walnut grips.

Holding his gun at his side, Longarm walked tiredly toward his would-be killer.

Eyes wide, round, and white-rimmed, the boy watched death stalk inexorably toward him in the misty sunlight. Involuntarily, the boy began to shake his head. He was numb, helpless, in a trance of agony and fear.

The wounded youth managed to clasp the shattered fingers of his right hand with his left. Blood spurted from the bullet-smashed members with every terrified thud of his heart.

Shaking his head, the boy fell to his knees on the hard-packed street, crying. His shadow seemed to crouch in black agony against him. "Don't kill me, mister. Please. Before God, I beg ya, don't kill me."

"You picked a hell of a time to decide you don't want to die," Longarm said.

"I wanna live, mister. Honest to God, I'm scared to die."

"Sure. All you tramps are. Scared to die. All you ain't scared to do is kill."

Sheriff Marvin Cheeseman poked a dull pencil at the notes he'd made. A lard-bellied man with heavy jowls, he was as near to being a Colorado native as a white man could ever be; both his given name and surname belonged to two of Denver's oldest families. Marvin felt secure in his political position, secure in his own estimation of his self-worth and in his status in the community.

He sat behind his cluttered pinewood desk in a crowded but spacious office in the County Building. His digs were less imposing than those of the U.S. marshal in the new federal complex, but as far as Cheeseman was concerned, the feds had much bigger headaches than he had. Let them keep their swank offices and five-dollar-a-day expense accounts; as far as he was concerned, they earned their largesse. He had to keep a tone of satisfaction from his voice. "So you're satisfied Texas Bill Wirt and his men have jumped my county line?"

Longarm shrugged. Chewing an unlit cheroot, he paced the sheriff's office, more aware of his own hunger pangs and his own weariness than of the smug county law official, or of his prisoner, crouched in a chair and nursing his bandaged hand. The doctor had told the kid he wouldn't lose the paw, but he was never going to be a gunslick. The boy had seemed to sink downward inside himself since they'd left the sawbones. He found little to cheer him in the morning. He was still alive and that was about it.

Longarm said, "Whether Wirt's gang crosses a county line or a state line won't stop us."

Cheeseman managed to conceal his smile. "No. Not you *federales*. But it kind of moves him out of *my* bailiwick, no?"

"That's right. This kid is about all you get out of it. They got away with the money—and until we hunt them down, that's the way it is. I'll leave the kid with you."

"This kid?" Cheeseman frowned, staring at the skinny boy huddled in the hardwood chair. "Didn't understand you to say this kid was one of Texas Bill's riders."

"Not this kid. The corpse. The dead boy. He was left behind as lookout for the Wirt camp. I took him, like I told you. But meantime, Wirt broke camp—or never even slowed down to make one. I think he left the kid just to slow me down until he could lose himself in the Black Lake country. As for crossing the state line, I don't think they will. Not for a while."

Sheriff Cheeseman thrust his bulk forward, his chair squealing dryly. "Why not? What do them desperadoes want around here?"

"I don't know. That's what I wanted to find out. I meant to take the kid alive. He wouldn't have it that way. So I ended up with a corpse. Sometimes you just can't get a lot out of cadavers." Longarm shrugged. "Sometimes not even a name."

The sheriff waved aside the matter of the dead outlaw. "What does Wirt want up here in a civilized place like Denver? Hell, this ain't no hole-in-the-wall country. Not anymore."

"Well, he wants something. Bad enough to risk his hide for it."

"Hell, he can't even show his face on Denver streets. Why, we got Wirt's dodgers up in the post office and in barbershops. We'll let him know we mean business in Denver. That ought to scare him off."

Longarm shook his head. "If the stakes are high enough, nothing will scare Texas Bill off—until he gets what he's after."

8

"Dammit, Longarm. They kilt two people in that robbery yesterday. Broad daylight. Downtown Denver. Must be easier places closer to home for Texas Bill to rob. Nossir, it's somethin' else he wants up here."

"I agree with you. But I don't know what it is."

"Well, dammit, that's what I want to know. What's Wirt after? What's his gang doing up this far from the Brazos? What's he want in Denver? What's he looking for?"

Longarm smiled tautly around his cheroot. "A profit. I know that much for sure." He sighed. "We'll do what we can, Sheriff. I know Billy Vail won't give up as long as he's got a man ain't too saddle-weary to ride."

"Well, you tell Marshal Vail we can't sit idle and let Texas Bill Wirt and his thugs terrorize the good people of Denver."

"Why don't *you* tell him?" Longarm asked brusquely. It came out harder-sounding than he'd intended. His personal estimation of Sheriff Cheeseman and his force had nothing to do with it. He had been a long time in the saddle on a futile errand. He'd had to kill a nameless kid who was under twenty—one hell of a lot under. It didn't sit well, and it was unraveling him. Wirt had struck a Denver bank. At least they *thought* it was Texas Bill Wirt—it had all his style and brainless daring—though Texas Bill was reported to be hundreds of miles south in the Texas plains. Wirt was after something bigger than a bank. The people—and a sheriff in an election year—were yelling bloody murder. And he was in the middle. He softened his voice. "We'll do what we can, Sheriff."

"Nossir. That ain't good enough. You feds got to come out from under your own red tape. You don't even know if it *is* Texas Bill Wirt. But whoever it is, it's a murdering gang of desperadoes. They've moved in on us. We want help from you government people. One hell of a lot more'n we're presently gettin'."

Longarm bit down hard on his cigar. "Why don't you write to Washington?" He clamped his hat down, dead center on his crisp brown hair, and strode toward the corridor door.

Sheriff Cheeseman's voice stopped him. "You think I ain't done that? You think I won't—again and again, until I get the support I need? We got big trouble, Long. Bigger than you. Bigger than Vail is willing to admit—"

"And you've got an election coming up—"

"Vail will put more men on this thing, or by God he'll explain to Washington why he don't. I got friends on the Potomac. Don't you people forget it."

"That's between you and Billy Vail, Sheriff." Longarm smiled coldly. "Good morning, sir."

"Just a back-breakin' minute, Longarm. What about this here kid?" The sheriff swiveled his graying head and stared at the shaken youth. "What'd you say your handle was, boy?"

"Jesse Cole, sir." The boy sounded meek. All the starch was sweated out of him. He cradled his painful hand, practically rocking.

"Yeah." The sheriff looked through the boy, nostrils flared. "What you want me to do with this here Jesse Cole, Long?"

Longarm sucked in a deep breath and hesitated, his hand clutching the doorknob. He stared at the boy. It was easy, looking at this scarecrow boy, to forget an arrogant young hellion daring him to draw on that street out there. Hell, this kid was just out of kneepants, just learning to jack off. If he shaved more than twice a week he was wasting lather.

"I'm sorry I tried to draw down on you, Mr. Long. I know you think I'm just sorry because you outdrew me—and could have kilt me. But that ain't it. Not all of it." Jesse Cole tried to smile, looking hound-dog hungry. "I swear, I musta been crazy... I never saw nobody draw like you."

Longarm didn't smile. "You're lucky you lived to see it."

"I know that, sir. Like I know now, you was doing your job—when you shot Cotton Younger, I mean. I was all mixed up."

"You damn kids," the sheriff said. "You shoot a few bottles off a rock, you outdraw your own shadow a few times, and you get biggety ideas. Going up against an armed man ain't the same as shootin' cans or throwin' down on a cactus."

"Nossir. You're right. And I know I'm almighty lucky to be alive." Jesse Cole lowered his eyes. "I know that. I'm plumb thankful to my Maker that Mr. Long is the kinda man he is and all. And I got no right to ask nothing more of either one of you gents. Whatever my medicine is, I'm ready to take it. I've proved I ain't much of a man, but I'm man enough to take my punishment."

Jesse hunched down, turned inward upon himself in remorse and grief, as forlorn as a wet cat.

10

Longarm swore inwardly. He tossed a dollar on the sheriff's desk. "Hell, there ain't any charges. Feed him breakfast, Sheriff, and let him go. Just so he clears out of Denver."

"I will, Mr. Long. I swear I will." The boy looked up, eyes welling tears. He nodded his head rapidly. "I will. You won't see me no more."

"See that I don't," Longarm said. He walked out, closing the door hard behind him. Damn. Two punk kids in one night. One dead. And the other one? Longarm exhaled heavily. He had no illusions about young Jesse Cole. Jesse was contrite now, scared shitless, ready to beg for mercy. But a kid like that forgot fast. He had to prove himself, prove his own manhood. They had a word for it down on the Mexican border. *Machismo.* A young buck had to prove he had *machismo.* Hell, *machismo* killed more men than heart failure, wives' headaches, and scarlet fever combined.

Chapter 2

Longarm went up the marble staircase two steps at a time and ambled along the sun-stippled Federal Courthouse corridor to an imposing oak door on which gold-leaf lettering read UNITED STATES MARSHAL, FIRST DISTRICT COURT OF COLORADO.

Longarm sighed and glanced around, his hand on the brass knob. He felt good and refreshed after a hot lunch yesterday of steak, potatoes, and green beans, followed by a bath and fifteen hours of uninterrupted sleep. Bathed, shaved, fed, wearing clean clothes, he felt almost human again.

He pushed the door open and went inside. He recognized the pink-faced young clerk seated at a rolltop desk in the anteroom. The reception area was well lit, sparsely furnished with polished wood chairs along a wall and wooden filing cabinets. The most interesting item on display was a newfangled typewriter that was hardly broken in.

The clerk's head jerked up from his paperwork and his face flushed red, going abruptly from surprise to anger.

In his early twenties, the youthful office worker wore a celluloid collar buttoned to a blue-striped chambray shirt, which boasted arm-garters at his biceps and inkproof india-rubber cuffs over his wrists. His three-button dark gray worsted coat hung precisely on a hanger, along with his pan-brim soft black hat, at the hat tree in a corner. His trousers converged to peg bottoms at the tops of kangaroo-grain leather, seamless, high-topped brown shoes, which Longarm knew were advertised in downtown emporium windows as "practically indestructible." He smelled more than faintly of vanilla. Sporting striped suspenders, he considered himself a fashion plate, his pale hair neatly parted in the center. His single vice was evidenced by the package of Pennant Brand chewing tobacco closed neatly on his neat desk, and the bespattered spittoon near his polished shoes.

"Marshal Long," he blurted out without preamble, "where in the hell have you been?"

Longarm grinned coldly. "You signing my pay chits now, Frank?"

Frank's head tilted. "We've been looking for you. *I've* been looking for you—on Marshal Vail's orders—for almost two days."

"How in hell you expect to find me, Frank? I figure you have your troubles finding the courthouse every morning."

"You ain't funny, Mr. Long. This has been mighty serious around here. Mighty serious. You mind sayin' where the hell you were?"

"No." Longarm shrugged. "I don't mind, Frank."

Frank peered up at him, frustrated. "All right! Where were you?"

"Why?"

"So I can report why I couldn't find you, though I made every effort—every conscientious effort." He drew a deep breath, paused. "Where were you?"

"You're not going to believe this, Frank."

"Try me, Marshal Long."

"Asleep. I was asleep."

Frank caught his breath, ready to call him a liar. "Asleep? You mind saying where?"

"No, I don't mind saying where."

Frank practically trembled. "Where?"

"In my own bed."

"In your room? If you were, it must have been the sleep of the dead, Marshal."

"I do everything all the way, Frank."

"I knocked on that door. I knocked and I knocked."

"I heard you, Frank."

"And you let me stand there?"

"I figured it was you. And I figured if I waited long enough you'd go away. You're not my type, Frank. You smell good, but I like 'em with tits."

Frank's face flushed redder than ever, to the roots of his neatly parted hair. "You might have cost me my job, Marshal."

14

"I wouldn't want to do that, Frank. I've never even figured out yet what it is you do around here."

"Marshal Vail has been raging, I can tell you that. He's even taken out his rage—against you—on me."

"I'm right sorry to hear that, Frank. On the other hand, you spend your life kissin' asses, sooner or later you're bound to get shit in your mouth."

Longarm rapped on the inner door, opened it gingerly, and went in, outwardly cool, but inwardly on guard.

His superior, Marshal Billy Vail, looked up sourly from behind piles of papers, warrants, writs, and fliers on his flat-topped mahogany desk.

"Well, goddamn," Vail said in mock cordiality. "You decided to show up, huh? Drank all the booze, laid all the dames, lost all your money at poker, Custis?"

Longarm smiled and shrugged. The chewing-out was serious and semi-official, but Billy's using his Christian name took most of the sting from the reprimand.

For another moment, Vail went on scribbling on some yellow legal-sized papers before him. Vail was a man deskridden from every reason but choice. In his heart and imagination he was still the young, hard-bellied, rakehell lawman who shot it out with Comanche, owlhoots, and fast-draws from the Rio Grande north to the Tetons. After a few years chained to a swivel chair, Billy was running to lard and getting that pink, well-fed look of most courthouse politicos. Vail got little physical exercise anymore. He was too busy, too driven, too harried by the blizzard of red tape and paperwork routed through channels to him from the banks of the Potomac. Sometimes he didn't know whom he hated most, the lawbreakers or the law-*makers* in Washington.

Longarm sat down on the rounded arm of the morocco leather chair across the desk from Vail and chewed at his unlit cheroot.

Vail continued to scribble and swear. The banjo clock hanging on the wall to Longarm's right ticked loudly in counterpoint to the chief marshal's muttered plosives. A thirty-eight-star flag hung dusty and motionless on its staff in the corner. From the wall above Vail's bald head, a sober, framed portrait of the President stared mirthlessly down at Longarm.

"Been looking for you," Vail said abruptly. He looked up

from the papers, squinting and massaging his eyes with stubby fingers and thumbs.

"Heard that."

"Got your report on Texas Bill Wirt—through that stupid Sheriff Cheeseman . . ."

"If it *is* Texas Bill Wirt." Longarm studied the hairs on the back of his hand. "Figure I've got to do a sight more than just trail his gang to get him or anything on him. He's too smart for a running fight."

"Who?"

"Texas Bill Wirt. Who the hell else are we talking about?"

"Oh, hell, I already assigned Wallace and Grenoble to the Texas Bill Wirt matter."

Longarm stood up. "Why the hell are you taking me off the case?"

Billy Vail shrugged. "Seemed reasonable to me. I wanted you off it. I got deputies to assign where I need them, not where they might want to go."

"But you assigned me—"

"And I *un*assigned you. Yesterday. Now forget about Wirt."

"Was I moving too slow for you?"

"I told you, something else came up. Something more urgent. Texas Bill was here before Ned Buntline discovered Bill Cody. He'll be here—"

"Murdering and killing, he'll be here. Unless he's stopped. Hell, I could have kept tailing him the other night. I would have, even with a corpse along. But I figured if I was going to catch up with Texas Bill, I had to be at least as smart as he was. I figured it was better to eat the apple one bite at a time."

Vail laughed, shaking his head. "Hell, Longarm. You and that apple. I swear, even eatin' an apple one bite at a time, you must have et up at least a couple thousand apples by now—"

"Still, I don't like 'em taken out of my mouth while I'm still munching."

"We got too many important things to do to waste time worrying about a *bad* apple like Texas Bill Wirt. If it *is* Texas Bill Wirt . . ."

"You know damned well it is Texas Bill Wirt. Why'd you yank me off in the middle—"

"If I got to explain myself—and I sure hell don't—I did it because something important came up."

"You think it's not important to know what the Wirt gang is doing this far north of the Brazos?"

Vail shrugged. "It's of middlin' importance. Do *you* know why?"

"I know that I never will find out now—not with Wallace and Grenoble on the case."

"Good men, both of them. They'll keep after Texas Bill and his boys. And that's all I can expect right now. When I take Texas Bill, I want all the evidence, witnesses, the works. I can wait—and watch Texas Bill. But I needed you on something urgent."

"It must be all-fired urgent, with Texas Bill terrorizing, robbing, raping, killing."

"In my mind it is."

"Jesus, I got to hear this."

"You give me a chance and you will hear about it." Billy Vail shuffled some papers on his desk. "You ever hear of a"— he checked a document before him—"a Princess Danica?"

"Should I?"

"Since she ain't a belly dancer, a fancy lady in some sportin' parlor on Cherry Street, or a so-called actress with loose drawers, I reckon not."

Longarm walked to the window. He stared down at the sunstruck street below, serene with midmorning traffic. Inwardly he seethed, but his voice was calm, soft, deceptively gentle. "What about her? This Princess Danica?"

"Danica—that means Morning Star. It's one of her names. She has a list of monickers as long as your tallywhacker. Named for everybody back to the Virgin Mary. Princess Danica is coming to Colorado as an honored guest of the U.S. Government."

"Shit. You mean you assigned me to wet-nurse some royal pain in the ass?"

"How do you know she's a pain in the ass?"

"Hell, they all are. They're told they're better than ordinary people until they begin to believe that crap themselves. Jesus. Riding herd on a snooty European royalist who likely thinks her shit don't stink."

"Wet-nursing ain't your job, Longarm. Not this time. If you're worth your per diem, you'll be done before she even gets out here."

Longarm exhaled and turned from the window. "Thank God. What *is* my job?"

Vail stared at him. "Find out who wants to kill Princess Danica. Find out how they might be planning to do it. Stop them."

"Why do you think they'll try to kill her in our jurisdiction?"

"Just lucky, I reckon. I don't. It's just that if it's got to happen, by God, I don't want it to happen in the First District of Colorado. I would find that downright em-barrassin', and when I get downright embarrassed, I'm one ornery pissant, and don't you forget it."

"You got any suspects?"

"Sure. Rebel Croats. Rival Serbs. Elements of the old Croatian Peasant Party. Croatian nationalists. Terrorists. Since something called the Illyrian Movement started in the early part of the century, and a Hapsburg authority was set up in Hungary, there's been trouble between the monarchists and the resistance forces. The Ausgleich of 1867—that means 'settlement' or 'compromise' or both—left Croatia a Hungarian kingdom, and a lot of Croatians resent it."

"And somebody wants to kill this Princess Danica?"

"Sometimes it looks as if *everybody* wants to kill Princess Danica—or her family. She's the most vulnerable one, because she shows herself in public the most. She's trying to win over people who won't be won over, and she won't stop trying. You can't help admiring her, but she does make herself a human target most of the time. There have been attempts on her life before. There will be attempts again in the future. We here in the United States can't change what's already happened. We can't help what might happen after Princess Danica leaves America. But the U.S. Government, from President Hayes down, don't want a hair on her pussy mussed whilst she's an honored guest of the U.S. of A. President Hayes is threatening to fire anybody who fouls up. But I go a little beyond that. Firing will just begin what I will personally do if Princess Danica don't come safe to Colorado and leave safe. Savvy?"

"Where do I start?"

Billy Vail winced. "I wish to God I knew. All I do know

is that a group of Croatian anarchists took credit for the violent bombing death of Princess Danica's late uncle, the Grand Duke. The State Department has dossiers on some of the members of a group like that. As far as State Department knows, at least one of them might be in Colorado."

"You got his name?"

"Oh, I got a whole rundown on him. I even know where he is."

"Why don't you arrest him until after the princess leaves Colorado?"

"You know better than that, Longarm. First, we can't arrest an employed, well-behaved nationalist just because we don't like his politics. Second, even if he is planning to assassinate the princess, he wouldn't be in it alone. Third, if he is trying to assassinate the princess, it would be nice to have some kind of evidence against him—evidence that would stand up in court. Fourth, even if we fail at everything else, but prove to our own satisfaction that our man is dangerous, we can arrest him and hold him—but only if we have probable cause. But we want more than that. If there is a plot against the princess while she is here in Colorado, we want to know what it is, when it might take place, who is involved, and where it might happen. That's what I want from you."

"What's this charmer's name?"

"Begovic. Marko Begovic."

"What does our boy Begovic do when he's not plotting assassinations?"

"We don't even know if he does plot assassinations. We want to find out. What Marko Begovic does for a living is lion-taming."

"Lion-taming?"

"Is there an echo in here? That's what I said. Marko Begovic is a lion-tamer with the Baldwin-Naylor Circus and Wild West Show."

"Looks like that's where I ought to start."

"Good thinking."

It was well into the morning of a cold Colorado Saturday when Longarm swung down from a freight train that slowed for water in a town called Medicine Run. He wore battered Levi's, a shabby jacket, turned-over boots, and a two-day beard. At that, he looked a hell of a lot better than Medicine Run. The place looked as if a vengeful God had thrown the settlement together for spite.

Carrying a shabby bindle by a rope loop at his side, Longarm walked through the deep-rutted, sour-watered main street of the town. The midmorning sun braised the crown of his head and the back of his neck. The main thoroughfare boasted half a dozen brick buildings and false-fronts, a hotel, a feed-and-grain store, a smithy, and a weather-battered livery stable barn with a sapling corral in back. Short feeder streets running off both sides of the main thoroughfare were lined with small, ugly, mostly unpainted frame houses. In the distance he could see the open field where the circus had set up, and he headed toward it.

His bedroll bumped his leg. There was nothing much in it: a straight razor, a bar of lye soap, his Colt .44-40, a clean shirt, and a change of underwear. What money he had was tucked in a belt around his flat belly. He traveled light, giving the appearance of a man who evidently hadn't accumulated great stores of goods in the world marketplace—a hobo happy with his lot.

He felt an almost tangible tension in the still, hot atmosphere of the morning. Natives of Medicine Run eyed him suspiciously and coldly. The circus had brought these citizens enough un-savory characters from the outside. Longarm saw that he was one more stranger than these good folks felt they needed.

He kept his head up and his eyes on the tents, pennants, flags, wagons, and gaudy colors of the circus. He passed the local hotel, wishing he could stop for a bath and a brief rest. But a hotel room—even a fleabag ordinary—was a luxury denied him for the foreseeable future. He had to remember that he was, from the moment he'd swung down from that freight train, just what he appeared to be to the unfriendly souls of Medicine Run—a bindlestiff.

Dogs barked tentatively and ran out at him from yards and shady places along the street. They sniffed at his Levi's and retreated. Hell, he knew he didn't smell good to the animals. He didn't smell good to himself.

All roadways and streets were travel-ribbed and worn bald as he neared the circus grounds. It looked as if business had been good for the Baldwin-Naylor Circus and Wild West Show.

Bunches of small boys, truants from the red brick schoolhouse across town, stood awed, fascinated, and practically paralyzed with excitement at the perimeter of the show grounds, eyes round and white-rimmed.

In the pre-noon heat, the circus area looked like an abandoned battlefield. Sawdust covered the entire compound yellowly, from the temporary entrance—strung now with unlit lanterns and gaudy banners—to the animal quarters in the distant rear. It seemed to Longarm that circus sawdust was always sodden, wet with equal parts of dirty rain and elephant piss.

"Where you goin', bub?"

Longarm stopped at the entrance gate. A man about his age, not especially prepossessing, leaned back on the two rear legs of a kitchen chair in the meager shade of the ticket booth.

"Looking for the headman," Longarm said.

The man grinned without warmth. "At this hour of the morning? Show folks stay up late at night, bub. They sleep late in the morning." Then he smiled coldly. "Looking for the boss, eh? Which one? Baldwin? Or Naylor?"

"I don't care. Just tell me where I might find either of them."

The fellow laughed now, enjoying himself. "Well, I think you might find old Justin Baldwin in the federal pen at Kansas City. Serving ten to twenty. You'll find Naylor in a graveyard at Fort Wayne. He's been dead at least fifteen years. Leastways, we hope he's been dead—he's been buried that long."

"Maybe it's just too early in the morning for jokes," Longarm said. "Who do I see about a job?"

"What can you do, bub?"

Longarm shrugged. "Anything that buys a square meal and tobacco."

"Eatin' only makes you fat, bub. And tobacco's a filthy habit."

"You're a real clown."

"Hell, how'd you guess? I *am* a clown—when I ain't roustaboutin' or standin' guard against town kids. No easy jobs 'round here, bub. If I was you. I'd hop the next freight out—east or west."

"I ain't you."

"You ain't Middle European, neither, bub. These people are clannish. They'd hire nobody but their own family if they

21

could. Next, they hire people from their own country. Anyhow, you don't show up on a Saturday morning expecting to hire on a wagon show."

"Why not?"

"Hell, this is our last show in this burg. We strike the tents tonight after the last act. We head out. You got to clear out of these little tank towns before church-time Sundays, or the good Christians are likely to raise up and *run* you out. Shows and show folks are ungodly on the Sabbath."

"All right, Mr. Clown. I've watched you do your act. Very funny. Now where do I find a clown who can hire me?"

"You don't back off easy, do you?"

"That's right. I ate either yesterday or maybe the day before. I can handle ropes and stakes and horses as good as any other man. I ain't asking any favors. All I want is a job—for eatin' money."

The clown shrugged and spread his hands in a gesture right off the Danube. "Hell, it's your funeral, bub. Just walk down the midway there toward the freak shows. You'll see the boss-wagon. He'll tell you the same thing I've told you. Only he won't be nearly as entertaining about it."

"Well, that'll be some improvement, right there."

For the first time, the unshaven, tired-eyed clown actually smiled. Somehow his smile made him look sadder than ever, his mouth contorted out of shape. "Hey, bub."

"Yeah?"

"Stop by the mess tent. It's on your way. Tell 'em Felix said to give you coffee, eggs, and flapjacks. Hell, I been two days hungry myself—more'n once."

"Thanks, Felix."

"See you around, bub."

Somehow the circus looked unreal, like something Longarm had never seen before. He had been to many of these traveling shows—they mushroomed up from under the rocks these days—the truly universal brand of entertainment. Sometimes the arrival of a circus was the biggest event in a town's existence all year. People looked forward in mouth-watering torment to the annual arrival of the big shows. From that moment when advance men raced into town, stepped down from gaudy carriages, and spread posters, one-sheets, and banners promising the play dates, expectancy arose, anticipation built, until the waiting became almost unbearable.

But now there was, for Longarm, an almost nightmarish quality about the dead, damp grounds and the stunned silences broken only by muffled squealing of monkeys, an occasional roar of a lion, the whinny of corralled horses, the silent, wrinkled, and ratty tents; it was a world without any glamour or excitement or pleasure.

The mess tent yawned open, its flaps tied back, its smells pervading the yards. Longarm walked toward it. He placed his bindle at an empty table, aware of flat, sleepy gazes fixed on him. He even detected a faint glimmer of interest in the haggard eyes of some of the women.

Feeling the unpleasant bite of the same brand of tension and mistrust that had been evident in the town of Medicine Run, Longarm walked over to a serving table, behind which a bearded fat man in an incredibly stained, spotted, and soiled apron presided, a spatula in his scarred, festered fist. Thick hair curled along his upper arms and across the bloated shoulders. "What you want, rube?" he asked, his accent as thick as Hungarian goulash. Felix hadn't lied. Even the cook came from the Adriatic.

"Felix said I might get breakfast. I got no money, I tell you that right off."

The cook shrugged. "All right, my boy. What you want?"

"Them eggs and flapjacks look good."

"They *are* good. I cook good. I cook for the show people, not for the rubes, huh?" As he talked, the big man shoveled half a dozen pancakes onto a tin plate, decorated them with thick butter and six slices of bacon, then scooped three eggs, over light, onto a second plate. "Coffee's in the urn, rube. Help yourself."

People sitting in little isolated groups at the pinewood tables fell silent when Longarm approached. They sat unmoving, unbending, taut, until he passed. He carried a mug of steaming coffee to a plank table apart from the circus citizenry, where he sat down and fell to eating. The pancakes were light, the bacon dry and crisp, the eggs hot and delicious, cooked to a turn. He looked up, caught the cook's eye, and waved, smiling his gratitude and approval toward the keg-chested chef. Flat-

23

tered, the stout man grinned faintly and nodded briefly.

As he ate, Longarm studied the circus population—or that sparse segment of it at early breakfast. Seated along one table was a contingent of sideshow freaks: a tall man as thin as a lodgepole pine; a pretty young woman in a low-cut dress, her body blue with tattoos; a being with one full mammary, one flat, muscular chest, half a beard, a muscled bicep and an unmatching slender, feminine arm; another male with the rough, scaly hide of a crocodile; and, in a wheelchair at the head of the table, a grossly fat woman who could barely reach her mouth across the vast expanse of her bosom to feed herself.

The silence and pressure closed in around Longarm. Felix had not exaggerated. These people were clannish, wary, and suspicious of strangers. He'd always known there was an instinctive mistrust between show folks and townies, but hell, this was ridiculous. These people looked as if they'd consider his speaking to them a felony. He suddenly felt as if he were afflicted with leprosy.

As he risked a cautious peek toward one of the prettier young women who'd met his eye with a less than jaundiced gaze, the silence of the grounds was abruptly shattered to smithereens.

Yells, curses, and male screams exploded from the brightly ornamented wagon directly across the midway.

Everybody in the mess tent sat silent, as if in a trance of terror.

Afraid that his delicious meal was going to be momentarily interrupted, Longarm ate swiftly, filling his mouth and chewing as he watched the boss-wagon rock on its thoroughbraces across the sawdust path.

He was the only one staring toward the wagon. Everyone else in the mess tent was looking as if that vehicle didn't even exist.

Suddenly the flimsy door to the traveling office flew open, slamming against the bright facade of the decorated wagon. A man came hurtling out of the opening, his arms flung out helplessly, as if he were trying to break his fall. He landed hard in the thick, wet bed of sawdust and lay still for a split second, trying to suck in a full breath of air. Then he rolled over on his back, his neck stretched long and his face contorted,

24

red, and oxygen-hungry. He raised his knees and arms, crouching behind them to protect himself.

He was none too speedy in setting up his sole defense. Three men—big, ugly brutes, the kind Longarm recognized as hired bully boys, midway bouncers, back-alley thugs— sprang through the doorway and lunged toward the man on the ground like savage dogs springing in for the kill.

The skinny man, groveling in the sawdust, screamed, a high-pitched wail. As he tried to wriggle away, like a beetle on its back, the three bully boys surrounded him. One of them kicked him in the crotch and the man screeched in helpless agony. Now he writhed impotently on the ground.

The midway was suddenly filled with people. They came running from everywhere, half awake, in every stage of dress. They lined both sides of the lane, numb. The people inside the mess tent got up silently and stood at the rim of sunlight. They watched, unspeaking. All of them looked as if they were not only afraid of taking sides, but feared that the very expressions on their faces might betray them.

A burly figure in a burlap-drape jacket of wide stripes and gaudy hues, gray worsted trousers, and brightly polished continental boots, stepped out of the wagon. Tall, thick-shouldered, barrel-chested, and potbellied, the man wore a silk vest with satin lapels, featuring a diamond stickpin and gold watch chain. His hair was coarse and graying, as were his bushy brows. He alighted cautiously, steadying himself and squinting nearsightedly down the metal steps to the ground. His deep, accented voice rode over all other sounds, compelling silence, commanding respect. One needed no score card to recognize him as the owner of this menage.

"Kill him," he growled in a doughy accent. "I want to see you kill him. Twenty dollars to the man who kills him."

He stood, arrogant, dominant, insolent, lord of all he surveyed. Thick legs apart, he cracked his knuckles, the sound like gunshots in the silence that had greeted his arrival.

For a moment longer, Longarm waited for someone to halt the carnage. He watched the circus owner's bully boys manhandle their skinny, screaming victim out there in the merciless sun. Several things became clear to Longarm, but clearest of all was that for reasons unknown to him, these people were going to stand mute and watch that poor devil beaten to death before their eyes.

Longarm warned himself to stay out of an unequal fight that was none of his affair. He knew nothing about it except that it was unequal. He had no idea what had caused this savage altercation. He had come here to infiltrate, to get a job and investigate, not to make enemies on one side or another. But when one of the bully boys kicked the thin man in the face, Longarm got to his feet and stood in a shaft of sunlight streaming through the mess tent flap.

"What's eatin' on you, rube?" the cook said in a quiet voice from behind Longarm.

"I don't like the odds."

"Nobody does. But you smart, you stand steady, rube. You live longer like that."

Longarm shrugged. "There's more to living than watching some poor devil get his guts kicked out through his eyes."

The hairy cook spread his hands. Longarm pushed his way through the knot of freaks at the rim of shadow. He stepped out into the sunlight, blinking against the fiery blaze.

He ran across the open path, counting on surprise to favor him. The plug-ugly nearest him was bent over the prostrate man, beating his bloodied face with his knotted, blood-spattered fist.

Longarm swore under his breath. He no longer cared who was right or wrong.

He caught the thug by the collar, yanking him up and wheeling him around to face him. As the bruiser turned, Longarm drove his knee into the fellow's groin. The man gasped, retched, and clutched at his crotch with both hands.

Longarm brought his two intertwined fists across the falling man's neck, sending him toppling hard into the sawdust, where he lay inert.

Longarm wasted no time admiring his own handiwork. The fellow standing across his victim's prone body had paused in his brutal assault, his boot drawn back, watching Longarm, his bearded face contorted in surprise.

Suddenly he growled in incomprehensible, heavily accented outrage. He leaped across his victim's shattered form and lunged toward Longarm.

Longarm used the forward thrust of the brute's attack against

26

Chapter 3

The circus people parted, making a small path for Longarm, a narrow fissure in the wall of intractable, malevolent faces. Longarm hesitated a moment. He dragged his gaze along that phalanx of unforgiving, unyielding countenances. The short hairs rose along the nape of his neck. He felt a hot spot, like the bright red bullseye, burning between his shoulder blades.

Exhaling, he walked through the broken passageway. He heard the circus owner's snarling intake of breath behind him. Instinctively setting himself for trouble, he kept walking.

"Look out!" The cry came from the tattooed lady, standing directly in front of him and staring wild-eyed at something across his shoulder.

Longarm swung around, poised on the balls of his feet, ready to spring like a panther in any direction. He registered a dozen unrelated images at once, all adding up to peril. The circus owner stood braced, heavy legs apart, squinting, cracking his knuckles, his nearsighted eyes glittering. On the ground, the beaten thin man sat up, groggy, shaking his head, blood spattering around him like water off a spaniel's back. Sun glinted on bright steel. A heavyset man, knife poised, lumbered toward him, growling insensately. The circus people retreated, pressing into each other. Their faces remained bleak and implacable, but their eyes reflected their horror.

The sun glittered on the white knife blade, thrust forward in the man's hand. Longarm recognized the burly plug-ugly who had run from a fair fight. Now, armed, he had returned, ready to do battle against an unarmed opponent. Clearly, he realized that either he fought here, or found a new job somewhere else.

29

The bully boy lunged toward Longarm. He brought the knife slashing upward, expertly, going for the gut. But he was heavy-footed, leaden-legged, fat-assed, clumsy, and muscle bound, and a knife is a thin man's weapon.

The blade hissed upward through the air as Longarm pirouetted aside, a toreador eluding the onrushing bull. The cutting edge of the knife sliced through his coat sleeve, searing his arm with its fiery sting, but the weapon lodged for one split second in the fabric.

Before the knifer could jerk his weapon free, Longarm snagged his wrist, twisting with strength born of outrage. The big man bellowed like a stabbed steer. His paralyzed fingers released the knife. The hasp dangled from Longarm's sleeve.

The circus owner yelled. "Bronisaca! Bronisaca! Get the goddamn law!"

Even while he was still twisting the attacker's wrist like a corkscrew, Longarm's mind was leaping ahead. Local police. The last thing he wanted. It was either go to jail or reveal his true identity, neither of which he could afford to do. There remained that single alternative, which is known as the better part of valor—getting the hell out of here while he still could.

The big man had been brought to his knees, almost as if he were being screwed into the ground. Longarm kept twisting relentlessly at the wrist until the man's bowed head was slumped deep between his knees, his arm straight up, awkward and unnatural, like a broken wing in Longarm's savage and unyielding grasp.

"Stay where you are," Longarm ordered, and a small, taut-faced man paused at the rim of the unmoving crowd. "All you people, stand easy." He stared straight into the circus owner's nearsighted eyes. "You stop your man, or I jerk this coyote's paw from its socket and hand it to you. It's up to you, mister."

On his knees, the knifer wailed in anguish. The circus owner nodded coldly and Longarm released the bully boy, who sagged to the ground, his forehead pressed into the wet sawdust, his right arm hanging loosely.

Cold with rage, Longarm caught the knife hasp and drew it from his sleeve. Some of the people close around him sucked in their breath. He didn't look at them. He felt blood trickling hotly down his arm and dripping along his palm.

"You're bleeding," the tattooed girl said. "You better—"

Longarm shrugged, too taut with anger to trust himself to speak. He stared at the five-inch steel blade and its leather-wrapped handle, then turned and hurled the knife as far as he could.

He pushed his way through the barrier of human beings, returning to the mess tent, where he had left his bindle.

The chef and the clown, Felix, leaned against the serving table. Neither of them smiled, but if their immobile faces revealed anything, it was faint and grudging admiration.

"For a bum who ain't et in three days," Felix said, "you fight pretty good."

"Two days." Longarm spoke between his teeth. "I told you two days." He bent down and took up his bindle.

"Anyhow he ate my eggs, bacon, and flapjacks," the cook said.

The clown laughed. "Yeah, but so did Josip's bully boys."

"It ain't the same," the cook said.

Longarm straightened. The clown watched him, smiling faintly. "You wouldn't take my advice, would you?"

"I'm smarter now."

"Yeah. But you're bleedin' now."

"You got a lot of inhospitable people here."

"You best let me put some iodine and clean rags on that cut," the chef said.

Longarm shook his head. "Wouldn't want to queer you with your boss—God Almighty out there." Longarm inclined his head toward the gaudy wagon where the big man stood taut, watching him.

"You think maybe Master Josip Barac ain't God Almighty?" Felix said.

"I know he *thinks* he is. A vengeful God." He grinned coldly. "Hope he won't visit you with a plague for speaking to me."

"We'll be all right," Felix said. "We know where the bodies are buried."

Longarm nodded toward the chef, smiling. "Thanks for the food. You cook mighty good—for some mighty low-lifers."

"They ain't all that bad, my boy," the chef said, "when you get to know them."

"They don't make that real easy to do."

"They got to live, like you and me. And they got to live in Master Josip Barac's world. They just know which side of their flapjacks is buttered, that's all."

Longarm nodded and exhaled heavily. He saw that none of the people crowding the midway lane had moved. He could feel Josip Barac's malevolent gaze biting into him like some kind of corrosive acid.

Longarm hefted his bindle in his bloody hand and walked out of the mess tent. He paused, glanced over his shoulder, and spoke to Felix. "Where does this show go from here?"

Felix paused, then grinned. "Place called Black Lake, I think."

Longarm touched blood-splotched fingers to his forehead in a little mocking salute. "I'll see you there."

The chef shook his head. "You a glutton for punishment, boy?"

"I like your pancakes," Longarm told him.

Shoulders sagging, Longarm headed toward the front exit of the circus grounds. Somewhere, a steam-operated calliope wheezed a fast-tempoed polka. The bright music seemed almost to mock him. He was aware of the pain burning in his slashed bicep, the blood leaking in hot droplets from his fingers, the bedroll banging against his leg. He was most conscious of failure. He'd lost round one. He'd taken one giant step forward and fallen flat on his face.

"Mister. Hey, mister."

The voice, thin and high-pitched, yet not unfriendly, caught at Longarm and slowed him on the sun-blasted sawdust lane.

He turned, his eyes widening. Two men loped toward him. One was the skinny little fellow who'd recently been battered to a bloody pulp by Master Josip Barac's bully boys. Through the battered contusions of his ferret's face, he was smiling.

The other man was the real shocker. He was the seven-foot-tall human skeleton Longarm had seen eating breakfast with the freaks at the mess tent.

His head, bouncing and bobbling oddly atop his pipestem throat, featured a short forehead, black brows, beady, close-set eyes on each side of a Roman nose, a tight, pinched mouth, and a receding chin. His Adam's apple jutted almost as prominently as his proboscis. His arms looked rubbery, incredibly long, almost touching his bony knees. His hands were practically as translucent as papyrus, his fragile fingers like a bird's feet. His wobbling walk had earned him fame as the Giraffe Man.

With one long, stringy arm, the Giraffe Man supported his smaller companion as they ran after Longarm.

He paused, waiting. Behind them the polka tooted, mocking in its merry, bright tones.

The bloody little man widened his smile like something pasted haphazardly over a broken plate. He stuck out his hand, timidly. "Name's Slimer, friend. Cy Slimer. Wanted to thank you. You saved my life."

Longarm smiled and shook the bony hand, realizing with a start that Cy had only a thumb and pinky left on his right hand. Slimer quickly jerked his mutilated hand away. "My pleasure," Longarm said.

The Giraffe Man laughed from above them. "Our pleasure too, seeing old Josip's bullies taken down to size." He shook his head. "You made it look so easy."

"You really saved my bacon," Slimer said. The head bobbed and the smile persisted. "I think you said you was looking for work. I think I heard you say you wanted a job, but I'm not real sure of anything after those boys threw me out of Josip's wagon. My head. Kinda mushy. But Ljubo here says you did say you wanted a job."

"Not much chance of that now," Longarm said. "Master Barac would rather kill me than hire me. Much rather."

"Not work for Barac," Ljubo said in his alien, distant, reedy voice. "Work for our boss."

"Our boss will hire you," Slimer said.

"Why?"

"Because you stood up to Barac's bouncers."

"Barac wouldn't let me work on his grounds."

"Barac, he owns the goddamn circus, most of the midway, and the Wild West Show. He don't own us freaks," Ljubo said in the Middle European accent that was already becoming familiar to Longarm in this place. Hell, they were all Croats. Might make his whole job easier. Just arrest the entire shebang until after Princess Danica paid her visit. On the other hand,

33

it didn't make it any easier to find a guilty Hungarian in this stew of Baltic accents.

Longarm stood agog. First, the exotic design and furnishings of this coach confounded him—silks, satins, paintings of pink-fleshed nudes, as well as rich couches and deep plush chairs—but then the young woman appeared and he forgot the luxurious backdrop, forgot Cy Slimer at his side. Struck dumb with surprise and amazement, he could only shake his head and gaze incredulously at the perfection of the tiny female in her trailing silk gown, her rich brown-and-gold hair piled on the crown of her head, a lovely little head, set upon the exquisitely miniature perfection of her slender golden shoulders. She was a showman's embodiment of beauty and shock value.

"Starin' is not real polite," she said in a throaty, accented, and yet softly musical voice.

He peered at this perfectly formed woman—an ideally formed female in every way, except that she was well under five feet tall, even atop the three-inch heels of her satin slippers.

When Longarm remained unable to speak, this wondrous little person laughed lightly and said, "Go ahead and stare. I'm used to it by now."

"I'm sorry," Longarm said at last, his own voice sounding odd in his ears. "I can't stop staring. I never saw anyone like you before."

She laughed, entirely at ease. "Of course you haven't, Mr. Long. That's because there has never been anyone like me before. Maybe one every few hundred years. Sure, I'm a midget—on display as a freak. A pygmy. A dwarf. An elf. I'm forty-eight inches tall. But look at me. Every dwarf you ever saw looked like a prune, something shrunken, whose skin didn't even fit. Right?"

Amazed at even the pure quality of her voice, Longarm could only nod. Wee Vingie Vinson was a knockout, beautifully formed, with the smooth, clear complexion of any goddess. Everything about her was perfect, only done in miniature, lovingly.

At first, when she walked in from her bedroom, he had thought she was a ten-year-old child, a pretty, precocious little girl who was already beginning to blossom, with lemony little

34

tits and rounded hips, a cute little figure, as if she weren't quite ready yet, but if you could wait around for fifteen minutes or so, she'd likely bloom into a lush and lovely heartbreaker. She looked like a prepubescent female playing dress-up in her mama's clothes. One had to look twice to be sure she *wasn't* a child. Yet, all the while, there was about her an indefinable something that guaranteed you would look again—and again— even if it certified you a dirty old man.

While he gazed in awe at her, Vingie looked him over. She seemed pleased with what Cy Slimer had reported. Evidently, she was the one being on the grounds who had not gone running when the lopsided fight started. She touched Cy's face gently and said, "I'm sorry I sent you up there, Cy."

"Somebody had to go," he said between broken teeth.

"No. I should have known better. And so this fellow took them apart. All three of them?" She laughed in vengeful delight. "I think Cy is right, Mr. Long. I think you're just what I've been looking for."

"Thank you," Longarm managed to say. In his mind he was comparing Vingie with the loveliest goddesses who graced the Opera House in Denver—to their loss.

A knock on the wagon door rattled the small, fragile china statuettes on Vingie's shelves. Longarm heard Cy Slimer catch his breath, a man who lived in fear but could not, or would not, run away. The battered man watched Vingie as though he were enslaved. Longarm could see how that could be. Now, Slimer was shaken, but Vingie remained at ease. "Answer the door, Cy."

Slimer limped across the carpeting and opened the door. Josip Barac pushed through without even glancing toward the man he'd ordered beaten.

Like a massive bear, huge and ungainly, he stood in the middle of the Persian rug, out of place and uncomfortable in this exotic atmosphere. He drew his gaze from Vingie's lovely little face, to Longarm's and back.

"Goddamn," Josip Barac said. "Goddamn. Might have known I'd find this killer here."

Vingie smiled and nodded. "You may as well get used to it, Joe. You'll see him here often—whenever you dare to come near me. Mr. Long is going to work for me now."

"Work for you? Doing what? Killing goddamn people?"

"If goddamn people deserve killing," she replied with a gently taunting smile.

"Goddamn, Vingie. Why you do this to me?" He cracked his knuckles loudly in the silent room and then belched loudly. "Now you got me sick on my goddamn stomach."

"Don't blame me, Joe. You eat that rich goulash. Roast duckling with all that grease. You know what the doctor told you."

"Goddamn doctor." Josip swung his arm. "What does he know?"

Vingie shrugged.

Josip shook his head, with its thick mat of black hair. "It's you that's killing me, Vingie. You. Goddamn. Everything to make trouble between us. You do it. Calling me a crook. Sending this Slimer to call me a crook..."

"You *are* a crook," she said in a mild tone, as one might observe the sun's appearance in the morning.

"Now this—this goddamn killer." He gestured vaguely with a meaty hand.

Vingie smiled sweetly. "You got your killers, Joe. Now I got me one."

He shook his head, refusing to accept it. "You got *trouble*, that's what you got. You're just buying yourself more goddamn trouble, trying to fight me."

She shrugged her exquisite little shoulders. "Maybe, Joe. Maybe. But now I got me a man you won't be able to kick around."

The huge man stood helplessly before the miniature beauty, seemingly torn between conflicting urges to sob or to curse. He did neither. Instead, he jerked his large head around and stared at Longarm, his nearsighted eyes squinting. "There are many ways to get rid of goddamn men you don't want around, and don't you forget it. I got a show to run here, and I won't stand you gettin' in my way. You hear that? You hear that?"

He turned on his continental boot heels and strode from the wagon, leaving the door opened. Cy Slimer moved to close it, but Vingie's musical voice stopped him. "Why don't you find Mr. Long a place to stay, Cy? Let him stash his bindle—and get a bath." Her gaze moved across Longarm slowly. "And you might want to shave. I'd like to see what you look like behind that ugly bush."

Cy plodded beside Longarm, toward the men's tent at the rear of the grounds.

Cy didn't speak. He walked with shoulders hunched, arms at his sides, his face set and dark. It was as if he had exhausted his meager supply of hospitality and now shriveled back inside his own depressed loner's mind.

Longarm didn't press him. Cy had been friendly; he might be again. He didn't know what was eating at Cy Slimer, only that *something* was. But he had his own woes.

It was a considerable hike to the freaks' living quarters at the rear of the circus grounds. These unusual people inhabited a district near the tarp-shielded latrines, the horse corrals, and the animal wagons. The air was heavy and humid and fetid back here. It was enough to depress any man.

As they had crossed the concession midway, Cy jerked his head toward a medium-sized blue tent, off at an angle from the main entrance to the huge canvas spread of the big show.

"There," Cy muttered. "There's our show. Miss Vingie's side show."

"Quite a layout," Longarm said. Across the upper facade of the long pine-plank platform that fronted the blue sideshow tent, the sun glistened on the gaudy banners: *LUBO* (without the "j") *the Giraffe Man! See the Human Skeleton! Count His Bones!... QUEEN MINERVA, the Tattooed Lady! Go 'Round the World Never Leaving the Comfort of Queen Minerva's Lovely Body!... JO-JO, the Crocodile Boy! Body of a Man, Skin of a Snake, Molars of a Mad 'Gator. You'll Shudder! You'll Tremble! But You'll Never See Again Anything like Jo-Jo!... FATIMA, the World's Fattest Lady! So Huge She Can't Stand Alone! Seventy-Five-Inch Bust! Scientific! Educational! Unbelievable! See Her! Touch Her! You Won't Believe Your Own Eyes!... CARLO-CARLOTTA! Half-Man! Half-Woman! Two of Everything! Scientific! Sensational!*

Longarm paused. Centering all these canvas sheets was a poorly painted portrait of Wee Vingie Vinson—in a revealing evening gown, with plunging bodice and slit from ankle to hip. *See the Tiny Golden Girl! Only 48 Inches! But Every Inch*

37

Longarm grinned. The World's Most Perfect Little Lady. He'd drink to that. Hyperbole was the lifeblood of the circus world, but they had not exaggerated in designating Vingie as the perfect beauty in miniature. Little Vingie was perfectly sculpted, like the Dresden china statuettes she collected and hoarded in her incense-laden parlor.

Like the most gape-mouthed, fly-swallowing rube, Longarm stared up at that gaudy canvas banner, seeing the real Vingie Vinson on the stereopticon behind his eyes. He had never seen a being like her; in fact, he'd encountered only a few "little people." The only person he could even equate Vingie with was the dwarf Cedric Hanks. Cedric Hanks? The name, the image, and the ugly associations dredged up by the memory swarmed up into Longarm's mind. He remembered the first time he'd encountered Cedric Hanks, on a train heading into Wyoming. He'd thought Cedric was a prissy little boy, with long blond curls, wearing a velvet Little Lord Fauntleroy suit, and traveling with his good-looking blond "mommy," who wore black widow's weeds. But it had all been nightmare. Cedric had proved to be nothing he seemed to be—except dwarfed in body. The woman Cedric traveled with was his full-grown wife, and Cedric turned out to be thirty-five years old, a vicious, depraved, gun-wielding, thirty-five-year-old midget. Longarm remembered his confrontation with Cedric by that mountain creek, and then shook the pint-sized fiend and all the hell Cedric had raised from his conscious mind.

Hell, Vingie was as lovely as Cedric Hanks had been ugly.

"Seen enough?" Cy Slimer's voice was brusque, chilled.

Longarm shrugged. Walking with Cy, he glimpsed Josip Barac's three bully boys lounging in a tight knot near the lion cages. They stared at him, unblinking, as he passed. Longarm waved and smiled.

"They don't mean to let up on you," Slimer said.

"I reckon not."

"They'll drive you away if they can."

"Don't sound as if that would make you real sad, Cy."

"No. You are wrong. I am pleased you are here—to help Miss Vingie. She needs help. But they will kill you if they can. They won't stop, you can be sure of that. Josip Barac wouldn't let them stop, even if they wanted to."

Longarm was enveloped in the thick and humid odors compounded of animal quarters, corrals, latrines, and the damp, sour interior of the male freaks' living area.

The tent was sparsely furnished. The less a man spread around, the less he had to pack, late on Saturday night. A few mirrors were set on makeup tables. Clothes hung on pegs driven into the tent uprights. They walked between the two rows of iron cots, with small footlockers at the end of each. The place was vacated for the moment except for Jo-Jo the Crocodile Boy, who slept in a drunken stupor. Sprawled on his back, the youth clutched an empty wine bottle in his scaly hand. He breathed loudly, his cheeks filling, his lips puffing as he exhaled, blowing past long, pointed molars and disturbing swarms of flies.

Cy nodded toward an unused bunk near the rear of the tent. "You can camp there," he said. "It was Lujac's bed. He's not with us anymore."

"Why not?"

"Dead. He was called the Lion-Faced Man. In Vingie's freak show. Turned out to be leprosy."

Longarm had hefted his bindle to toss it on the khaki-blanketed cot. When he hesitated, Slimer laughed. "It's all right. We burned Lujac's bed clothes. Besides, you get leprosy from the touch. Or in open cuts—like on your shoulder." He stood grinning at Longarm.

Longarm exhaled and tossed his bindle on the cot. He had stepped into an unknown world, there was no denying that.

"About time for lunch," Cy said. "We have to get in there and eat fast. The rubes start showing early for the Saturday matinee. Last day. Everything half-price—and all the midway games twice as crooked."

A soft feminine voice called from the sun-rimmed entrance. "May I come in?"

"Sure, Minerva," Slimer said.

The tattooed lady moved nicely, sauntering along the aisle between the cots. A shapely young woman, she carried a roll of gauze and a small brown bottle. "I was worried about that cut on your arm." She smiled up at Longarm and shivered slightly, her hips wriggling. "I declare, you were so brave out there."

Queen Minerva was a beautiful woman, even with the blue-

39

and-red decorations completely covering the planes and curves of her body like so many distracting pictures of faraway places. She was gazing up at Longarm boldly and hungrily, appraisingly. Her dark eyes devoured him and her full-lipped mouth seemed almost to be watering in anticipation.

Longarm smiled down at her. He saw that her need at this moment was great, and he remembered he had read or heard somewhere that violence was the most powerful aphrodisiac of all.

"Take off that coat and your shirt," Minerva said. "Let me look at—at that cut. You could get blood poisoning if you're not careful, you know."

Cy Slimer's face darkened. He looked more morose and depressed than ever. "Reckon I'll just mosey to the mess tent," he said to no one in particular.

"Yes, Cy," Minerva said, without even looking at the battered little man. "Why don't you do that?"

"I'm beat to hell, and nobody gives a shit," Cy muttered.

Minerva didn't take her fascinated gaze from Longarm. "Oh, Cy, that's not true. But we don't worry about you. You're a survivor, Cy. All you've lived through. You're like a lizard. You survive—even if you get your tail cut off." Minerva laughed at the double meaning of her words.

Red-faced, his split-lipped mouth taut, Cy heeled around and clumped out of the tent.

Longarm removed his shabby worsted coat and then let Minerva unbutton his plain blue work shirt. He peeled the garment away and stood barechested before her. Minerva licked at her lips and her intricately decorated hands trembled. But she managed to smile.

She probed at the blood coagulated on his shoulder. "That cut is bad," she said in a breathless tone. The long, narrow gash in his upper arm had begun to crust over and blacken. Minerva washed the wound. Longarm bit back a yell of agony as she dabbed at the open slash with iodine. The sharp bite of the antiseptic bounced against the top of his skull and curled his toes.

Minerva covered the wound with gauze and then tied it as best she could. "It ought to be all right now," she said. "If you keep it clean."

"Now you've saved my life twice."

She touched his corded chest with the flat of her cool palms. Breathing oddly, she massaged his chest muscles. "You could...repay me...if you wanted to," she whispered.

"Seems no more than gentlemanly. We ought to be able to work out something."

"Yes. Lie down. I ache...I need you to stop the ache." She slid her hand across the flat plane of his belly to the buckle of his belt, and below, clutching at him with her blue fist.

"In broad daylight?"

"Nobody will come in here. They're all at lunch. Then they go to the sideshow tent."

"What about Jo-Jo?" Longarm nodded toward the alligator-skinned man sleeping lustily a few cots away in the swarm of sweet flies. "What if he wakes up?"

Minerva shrugged. "What if he does? He won't know what we're doing. Or care. Along with all his other troubles, he's got the mind of a three-year-old."

She was massaging at his fly with abandon, in heated urgency. She writhed inside her strapless dress and the muslin garment fell away from her in a bundle about her feet.

"With pictures and everything," he said, gazing at her.

"I want it so bad...so good..." she whispered, drawing him down to the cot with her.

She found his fly and loosened it, jerking urgently at the buttons. "I've been so crazy for it," she gasped, her breath shallow and rapid. "Ever since I saw you out there...I knew I had to have it...in me...inside me...deep inside me." She caught his hardness in her hand, gasping in delight. "Oh, it's as big as I knew it would be. Bigger. Give it to me, honey. Give it all to me." She exhaled in pleasure. "I'll take you into Rome," she promised, spreading her painted legs wide. "Just follow the roads, honey...you know...all roads lead to Rome."

Chapter 4

Longarm felt something hard and cold pressed cruelly against his lips. Instinctively, he ground his jaw shut tight and opened his eyes wide.

His heart hammering crazily, he stared up into some kind of insanely grinning mask, the ugliest face he'd ever seen on a human being—if this *was* a human being. That grin was nothing to be shared. It was like all the mindless leers dredged up from all the snakepits beyond hell. Though it was bright daylight, with the sun radiant atop the canvas and splashing around the sides of the tent, he was certain he was still enmeshed in the clutches of nightmare.

Nightmare wasn't only the easiest explanation, it was the only rational way to account for the outsized head floating close above him, the wild mop of pink hair fringing the monk's-cap bald spot, the green, elevated, arched brows, the blue-ringed eyes, the red, bulbous nose, the vast, contorted mouth and black, gaping holes among the yellowed teeth. A clown's face. A monstrous clown. A nightmare clown in broad daylight. But a clown.

Longarm exhaled heavily and slapped the gun barrel away from his face with his left hand as he might swat a pesky deerfly. "Is that you, Felix?" He tried to sit up. "This your idea of some kind of stupid joke?"

"Not Felix. No joke." The gun sprang back into position under Longarm's nose, thrusting his head back on the straw pillow where Queen Minerva had left him after their quick, violent journey into Rome.

"You stay here, hon," Minerva had whispered, "while I sneak out of here. Be a lot less trouble like that."

Exhausted, Longarm had agreed. Minerva was as hot, exciting, and violent as the tattoos littering her lush body. Though her body felt strangely cool to the touch, heat rose from it like smoke from a chimney. She'd been passionately aroused and she had punished him beautifully. Along the row of cots, Jo-Jo the Crocodile Boy still slept the sleep of angels—drunken angels. Minerva had dropped her muslin wrap over her head and disappeared.

Longarm had plunged into exhausted sleep before the tattooed lady cleared the tent. Now, staring up into the grotesque clown's face above him, he had no way of knowing if Minerva had been gone hours or moments.

Turning his head as far as the gun barrel would permit, he saw that Jo-Jo was gone from his cot.

"Lay still," the thick voice ordered. "Or I blow your head off."

"Fuck you," Longarm said. "You talk big, but if you'd meant to blow my head off, you wouldn't have woke me up to tell me about it."

"You wake now," said the heavily accented voice. The tone was murderous, but the milk-white face went on grinning hideously. Only the small black eyes, deep under layers of bright paint, were as dead and empty as rattlesnake eyes. "So. I tell you. You clear out. You want to live? Healthy? You clear out. Now. Today."

It was hard to talk with the gun muzzle pressed unrelentingly under his nose, but Longarm managed to mutter, "And if I don't?"

The hammer clicked back on the gun in the big fist, the sound exaggeratedly loud in the silent tent. It was as if he and the malevolent clown were alone in their own hell. The noise of the horses, the wild animals in their cages, and the voices of other human beings sounded distant and remote.

"You don't and accident happen to you. Bad accident. Plenty fatal accident," said the grinning face.

"Accidents have a way of happening two ways."

The clown face twisted grotesquely and the guttural voice laughed grittily. "You don't know my face—my real face. I can find you in a crowd, but you can't find me."

"Your breath, bully boy. I'll never forget your breath."

"Have your jokes, tough man. But get out. Get out now and alive. Or else." The gun trembled in the big, scarred hand.

44

"I better warn you," Longarm said in a conversational tone, "even if you pull that trigger, dog-breath, you're getting it too."

The black eyes flinched. But the deep, accented voice brazened it out. "You make some big bluff even now, huh, friend?"

"Think so?" Longarm suddenly brought his right hand from beneath the scratchy khaki blanket. He shoved his double-barreled derringer with fearful force into the clown's crotch.

The huge clown caught his breath, a sharp gasping sound, and staggered back.

"Like I said," Longarm told him, "you can kill me. You can still kill me. Right now. But even if you do, I'm going to blast your nuts off."

For a tense moment the clown face hung there, suspended in doubt. The heavy-shouldered man crouched over Longarm, but the gun remained pressed relentlessly into his crotch. The thought of having his testicles shot off was even more horrifying than death.

The clown face went on smiling, but the clown backed off. His voice raged, but he let the hammer down slowly and harmlessly on his weapon. "You won't always be ready—you won't get no more warnings—and you won't know who I am. Or where I'll strike from. We gave you just this one chance. We don't give you no more. Get out of here. Get out of here now."

Longarm sighed heavily. "Sorry, ugly. Tell your boss I ain't leaving."

"Oh, you're leaving, smart man. One way or another. On your feet, if you are smart. Or in a box. That's up to you."

Longarm sat up. He held the brass derringer negligently in his fist. "I been trying to think of some polite way to say this, latrine-breath, but I don't know the right words. The nearest I can come up with is, fuck you—and your boss—and your boss's wife."

The clown retreated slowly, warily, backing away along the rows of cots. Longarm sat unmoving—and unnerved—for some moments after the attacker was gone. The sidewinder had rattled its warning, he couldn't deny that. Somebody wanted him out of this circus, and they didn't even know yet why he was here. Maybe it was the fact that they were convinced that he was no ordinary bindlestiff. This meant he had

45

some other motive for joining the circus, and he was too old to be running away from home for the big thrill. They didn't trust him. They didn't want him, and they would kill him at the first opportunity. He didn't doubt this. He was smart enough to take a man like Josip Barac seriously. He took all threats seriously. That was one reason he had lived so long.

He shoved the derringer back under his belt and got up from the cot. His legs felt as weak and shaky as a newborn colt's; he didn't know whether to credit it to Minerva's pleasure or the clown's threats.

A washbasin and a full pitcher were on a crate next to the cot. He scrubbed his face and hands with lye soap, then he stood for a moment gazing at his reflection in the wavy mirror on a makeup table. The bearded face staring back at him looked haggard. It wasn't easy walking into an alien world, screwing women with strange pictures inked into their chilled flesh, and waking up to guns poked in one's mouth. A weird place, unlike anything he'd ever encountered.

He sighed out heavily and walked through the sun toward the mess tent. Cy Slimer was right: the townspeople of Medicine Run were straggling in early—at least two hours before the matinee showtime. All the lanterns were lit along the midway, but they gleamed weakly, like wan, lost stars in the blaze of afternoon sunlight.

The flap of the mess tent was down to close out the curious gaze of the passing rubes. Some of the freaks were still at one of the plank tables, Minerva among them.

Longarm walked tentatively toward the freaks' table. He wasn't hungry, but after the threat from the clown, the idea of people being around, people—even strange and contorted people—was inviting.

He felt the atmosphere chill noticeably as he approached the table. The freaks stopped eating, laying down their utensils. They stopped smiling. They ceased talking, even to each other. They sat rigidly, staring down at the plates before them. It was as if they thrust a huge sign up into his face. He was not wanted.

He shrugged and walked past them. He carried a plate of barbecued beef, beans, and German potato salad to an empty table. Gradually the freaks relaxed, picking up broken threads

46

of conversation and pretending the stranger did not exist.

Longarm sat down and pushed his food around on his plate. What the hell? These Middle Europeans were clannish, the freaks were aloof and remote to all who were unlike them. They wore their coolness like armor. But he wasn't here to win any popularity contests.

"Care if I join you?"

Longarm looked up. Cy Slimer was bathed and cleaned up, but still looked pretty battered.

Longarm grinned. "Thanks, Cy."

Cy sat down, still smiling through the swollen face. "How was it with the Queen?"

"Don't you know?"

"Not for a long time. I follow orders."

Longarm waited, but Cy added no more and Longarm didn't prod him. After a moment, Ljubo the Giraffe Man came over with a mug of coffee and joined them, wavering like a reed over the table. Then Minerva joined them. She sat in the chair next to Longarm's and massaged his upper leg with her knee. Her tired, pretty face remained immobile.

Bearing a coffee mug, Felix the clown sat down with them. He was not yet in costume. Longarm found himself eyeing Felix suspiciously. It was a hazard of his trade to trust no one. But he was certain of one thing: Felix was not the clown who had threatened him. Felix's hands were too small, and Felix himself was not a huge bull of a man. But that left him where he had been all along—with no idea who had been behind that hideous, grinning mask.

Felix watched Longarm pour pepper sauce on his baked beans. "You going to eat that stuff?" he asked incredulously.

Longarm grinned. "I like my beans with some sass."

Felix shook his head. "Man, you eat that stuff, you goin' to be shootin' Indians all night."

Longarm shrugged. "My grandma always said there's more room outside than in."

"You tellin' me ladies know about fartin'?" Felix taunted.

"I do," Minerva said.

"I'm talking about *ladies,* Minerva," Felix said, and they all laughed, even Minerva. Longarm noticed that the freaks were watching them covertly.

"You can't eat this food without gettin' some kind of relief," Minerva said. "You ask Mr. Long's grandma. The old girl was right."

"My grandma was an expert on the subject," Longarm said. "Besides, who the hell said my grandma was a lady—me bein' from West-by-God Virginia and all."

The men at the table laughed and Minerva smiled, but Cy protested. "Man, you'd kill another man for sayin' that about your grandma."

Longarm grinned and nodded. "And don't you forget it."

"You from West Virginia, Long?" Felix said.

"That's right."

"I had a dog once. From West Virginia," Felix said.

"Might of been related to me," Longarm agreed. "I had a hell of a dog when I was a kid back home in West Virginia. But I had to get rid of him. That dog could smell a female in heat two miles away. Lot of the old boys from West Virginia were like that, too."

The people at the table laughed. By now the freaks were glancing at each other and grinning.

Longarm felt the tension inside him relax slightly. It wouldn't be a piece of cake, but the freaks would thaw. Minerva and Ljubo's acceptance of him helped. He wouldn't push it, but he felt it was going to be all right between him and the special people at that other table.

"With that accent, I know by God you're not from West Virginia, Felix," Longarm said.

"Never said I was, bub. Said my *dog* came from West Virginia. Used him in my act. When he died, I was heartbroken. Decided never to have another dog. Hurts too damn much when the poor little creatures die. Reckon I'm a one-dog man."

"You might like women if you ever tried 'em," Minerva said.

"You're the only woman I ever wanted, Minerva," Felix said in that teasing voice.

"Why, that's very nice of you, Felix," she said.

"I'd of been after you too," Felix teased, "but when I had to stand in lines back in Hungary to get bread, I swore I'd never stand in line again—for anything."

"Go to hell, Felix," Minerva said.

Longarm tried to keep his voice casual. He said, "You from

Hungary, Felix? I read somewhere that your Princess Danica is coming over here for a state visit."

Chilled silence spread across the table, wiping out the last vestige of a smile. Felix said only, "She ain't *my* Princess Danica."

After that, the lunch sort of dissolved and unraveled. Longarm realized he had learned at least one lesson, but that particular lesson might prove to be as valuable as hell.

The direct approach wasn't going to buy him anything at all in this place. He could make book on that.

Wagons crowded the fields and roadways outside the circus grounds when Longarm left the mess tent. People streamed in at the main gate, buying a ticket to the main attraction as the price of admission. It cost adults twenty-five cents to get into the grounds and into the big tent; children were admitted for a nickel. Vingie Vinson's sideshow and everything along the concession midway cost extra. It looked like a big Saturday for the Baldwin-Naylor Circus and Wild West show.

A laughing, milling, shoving crowd on the midway slowed him down and he paused, able to see over the heads of the growing mob. In the center of the gaggle of shouting people, a skinny, slovenly, bearded wreck of a middle-aged man stood, grasping a live rooster by its neck. He gripped it tightly in his quivering fist, as if the fowl were the straw that would save him from purgatory. The chicken squawked and fluttered and kicked wildly. The tramp had placed a battered felt hat on the ground at his feet and was grinning vacuously, prodding, pleading, and heckling the spectators into throwing coins into the hat.

His whiskey-roughened voice battered at them. "You want to see me bite off this rooster's head, mister?" The geek peered at a farmer in the front row. "You ever seed a man bite off a live rooster head, mister?" the geek whined. The farmer shook his head. "Ought to be worth a dime. One dime, duke? You wanta see a man bite a rooster's head off or you wouldn't be takin' up room right here in the front row. A live, kickin' rooster. Bite its head right off for you. But it's got to cost you, hunt-stumper, you can see that. Hell, man, the roosters cost me plenty. I can't steal 'em every time."

Repelled, fascinated, Longarm stared at the geek. It was

incredible to him that such men actually existed, that a man could sink so low, but he knew that such human flotsam did find their way into this hell.

Around him, the crowd urged the geek on. There were many farmers and townspeople, but most of the crowd was made up of the roustabouts, hostlers, and circus laborers. They shouted and laughed and dared the geek to perform.

Finally someone threw a silver dollar into the black hat. Along with the change already collected, the geek decided he'd made his nut for the afternoon. He grabbed up the hat, caught the money in his hand, slapped the hat on his matted lice-ridden head and shook the squawking rooster high. He began to prance around the circle, swinging the rooster, clumsy and awkward, but grinning like a being possessed, yelling mumbo-jumbo incantations.

Suddenly the geek thrust the rooster's head into his mouth and clamped his jaws shut, muscles working along the sides of his skull.

Blood spurted from his lips. Men gagged. Women screamed and turned away, watching through splayed fingers. The mob scattered from around him, staring at the geek. The man went on grinding his teeth together until the fowl's neck snapped, parted, and broke free, bloody feathers spilling from his mouth.

Oh, Jesus, Longarm thought. Killing a princess would be easy for these people.

Crowds gathered outside the blue tent of the sideshow. His battered face heavily painted with brown makeup to conceal the contusions and bruises, Cy Slimer stood in the open-topped ticket booth to the left of the stage outside the tent. He harangued the crowd while Queen Minerva, Ljubo, and Carlo-Carlotta made brief, tantalizing appearances, designed to whet unsophisticated appetites.

It worked. Farmers and their families lined up eagerly to buy the "special ticket . . . today only . . . this show only . . . special . . . one price for all, a family ticket to the greatest sideshow of freaks on earth."

When the buying slowed, Cy sudenly waved his hat, calling all the people on the midway in closer to the stage. "Tell you folks what we might be able to do—you and me—if we really try . . . The very top attraction of our educational, scientific,

50

and thrilling entertainment is our own Miss Vingie Vinson, the World's Most Perfect Little Lady. How'd you like one quick look at *her*, ladies and gentlemen? Maybe we can coax her out here where you can get a good look at her. For free. For nothing. Absolutely won't cost you a penny. Now move in closer, let everybody have a fair chance to see Miss Vingie. Come in closer, folks. You can't see from where you are, and you won't want to miss this treat . . . the most exciting vision you'll have for years to come. You can tell your grandchildren about how you saw the one, the only, the beautiful little Miss Vingie, in person."

As he shouted, Cy pointed his cane toward the gaudy banner topping all the other freak attractions and featuring Miss Vingie Vinson—The World's Most Perfect Little Lady.

"Come on, you people. It's all up to you," Cy shouted. "You want just a peek at what you'll see inside this tent—on our stages—for one quarter? One-price ticket for all, this afternoon only. One ticket per family? Let's bring Miss Vingie out here. Let's bring out the most beautiful little creature on God's green earth . . . Folks, you never in your life saw forty-eight inches of such creamy perfection anywhere . . . Call her out here, folks. She'll come out here, if you make her know you want to see her bad enough! Come on! Clap! Clap them hands so she can hear you in that tent. Cheer! Applaud if you want to see Miss Vingie . . . in person . . . on this stage . . . for free!"

A calliope burst into swift-tempoed music from within the blue tent. The crowd, worked into a frenzy and led by Cy Slimer, went wild, applauding, whistling, cheering, screaming, pleading, yelling her name in the sultry afternoon.

Longarm grinned. Sure enough, the applause of the crowd won the heart of Miss Vingie Vinson. She could not resist their pleading.

A man opened the flap in the backdrop. The music rose. The man hurled out a length of red carpeting, and after a breathless moment the doll-like beauty walked regally out upon the center of the stage.

The crowd was struck dumb. The people pressed forward as one, gawking, gaping, openmouthed, and incredulous. Never had they seen anything like this before. Miss Vingie Vinson in the flesh was even more astounding than Cy Slimer had promised. Women gasped at her fragile beauty, so radiant as to seem unreal. Men licked at their dry lips. Some shook their heads, as if they'd like to disbelieve she was real, but could not doubt their own eyes.

Miss Vingie was as gracious as she was lovely, but she did not remain long in the blazing sun. She wore a fragile picture hat and a lime-green lace gown, slit revealingly from ankle to thigh. Her perfect, delicately rounded legs were enclosed in pink tights to give an illusion of nakedness without incurring the wrath of the local authorities.

Then Miss Vingie graced the rabble with the loveliest smile most of them would encounter in their deprived lives this side of the Pearly Gates. Fascinated, they wailed, clapped, and cheered her again—cleverly led by Cy Slimer.

Her silvery little voice, delightfully accented, chided them through her smiling. "Well, don't just stand there in this sun, dear people . . ." She gazed down directly into male eyes. "You can't see what I'm really like—unless you come inside."

Ninety-eight percent of the people outside the blue tent followed Miss Vingie into it, buying their tickets from Cy Slimer. Amazed and delighted with Miss Vingie, her beauty and her showmanship, Longarm stood across the sawdust path, watching from the shade of an awning on a stand that sold hot corn on the cob.

The moment the last of the crowd bought tickets and pressed through the entrance into the blue tent, two of Josip Barac's bully boys appeared, practically on the run. They closed in on the open-topped ticket booth.

For the first time Longarm noticed that Cy had been working frantically, in a panic, scooping the admission receipts into a cloth money sack. But when Barac's men appeared on each side of the booth, Cy stopped working abruptly and sagged against the wall of the cage, defeated.

Longarm didn't have to hear the bouncers to know they were after the gate receipts. Cy chewed at his broken mouth, but did not protest aloud.

Longarm strode across the midway, moving in fast. He pushed between the two bully boys, grinning at Cy. "Anything wrong, Slimer?"

Cy shook his head, afraid to speak.

One of the bully boys reached for the money sack. Longarm

snagged his wrist. "Hold it, friend," he said. "What is this? A robbery in broad daylight?"

"You stay out of this," one of the bouncers said, close against Longarm's face. His breath smelled offensive, but not familiar.

"I work for Miss Vingie now," Longarm said in that same pleasant and unruffled tone. "If you're going to take her show receipts, I got to know why."

For a moment the two thugs stared at each other, then one of them nodded his head toward Slimer. "Why don't you tell him, Cy?"

Slimer exhaled heavily. "Barac's orders."

"That's right. Josip Barac's orders," one of the men said amiably.

"For Miss Vingie's own protection," the other plug-ugly contributed. "We pick up all big cash receipts. We stack them in Mr. Barac's safe, where Miss Vingie can have them anytime she wants them."

"We do it to protect her. Some of these country boobs get ideas of quick cash withdrawals."

"Especially on Saturdays. On our last day."

Longarm stared at Slimer. "That right, Cy?"

Finally, Cy nodded. At last he said, "That's the way we always do it." He looked ill, ready to throw up his lunch.

Longarm nodded. Satisfied, the two bully boys wired the top of the cloth bag shut. "You see, we're wirin' it shut," one of the men said to Longarm. "It'll be wired shut when Miss Vingie picks it up."

One of the big men took the bag of cash and strode away through the crowds toward Josip Barac's wagon. The other man convoyed him, his holstered A. J. Aubrey "hammerless" revolver in plain view.

Longarm exhaled heavily. He stared at Cy. "You let them rob you."

Slimer looked ready to cry, but his voice was hard. "My face got prettied up like this when I raised hell about being robbed."

"You went to them about the way they rob you—and they beat you?"

Slimer laughed ruefully. "I didn't go willingly. Miss Vingie sent me." He laughed emptily. "I reckon they'd of killed me—they were having so much fun—if you hadn't come along." He shook his head. "I'll wait till my face clears up before I say anything again."

Longarm whistled. "Barac's robbing Vingie like this—every show?"

Slimer merely nodded.

"What's this about you gettin' wired-shut sacks when Miss Vingie sends you to pick them up?"

"Oh, they're wired shut. With new wire. And eighty percent of the gross take gone."

"Son of a bitch."

"That's what I said. And look at my face."

Longarm walked slowly through the noisy, dusty midway toward the male freaks' tent at the rear of the grounds.

He passed the entrance to the main show. People were going in to get the best seats for the afternoon performance. He wanted to get a look at Marko Begovic, the lion-tamer, at work. Marko was the big reason he was here. A canvas banner near the entrance of the circus tent promised: *"Extra! Wild West Show! Greatest bronc riding—six-shooting—roping—exhibition on Earth! See Bronco Bob Kidd—The Shootin' Kid From the Lone Star State!"*

Longarm grinned tautly. Getting to know as much about Begovic as he could was the reason he was here, and seeing the Texan was a challenge. But he couldn't figure this bold way Barac robbed Miss Vingie—under the self-righteous pretense of protecting her. It didn't sit right. It churned in his stomach along with the baked beans and barbecued beef. Seemed he ought to talk to Miss Vingie about it.

Smiling, he remembered that Miss Vingie had told him to bathe and shave before she saw him again. He shrugged. Anything for a lady.

He found a pink envelope tip peeking from the edge of his pillow. It was a note from Minerva. The tattooed lady wrote in an alien, spidery hand, but there was no doubt about the intent of her message: *"Meet me at suppertime. I'd rather eat you than Cookie's baked beans. Excited. Minnie."*

He returned the note to the envelope and reached for his bindle, which he had stashed beside his cot.

He stopped, hand in midair. He didn't have to touch the bedroll to know it had been opened and hastily retied. He never had tied a granny knot in his life.

He found nothing missing. Still, it enraged him that somebody had gone through his possibles. There was nothing to identify him, but he was cold with anger anyhow. Somebody was really after him.

He walked out to the men's wash tent, carrying a towel, soap and a razor, and fresh underwear. He poured buckets of well water into the public bathing trough and climbed in, biting back a yell at the chill.

By the time he'd soaped and rinsed, the water was tepid, almost body temperature. He hadn't realized he was so tired. He shaved and then lay back in the water and closed his eyes.

Something disturbed him and he jerked his head up, eyes wide. His clothes, money belt, and derringer were just out of reach.

Then he saw a woman's breast at the edge of the tarp partition, full, pink, bare, and rounded. At first he thought he'd gotten in the woman's showers, but then he saw a hairy arm, a muscled chest. Exhaling, he recognized Carlo-Carlotta, the half-man, half-woman.

"Been watching you," Carlo said in a sweet, sensuous voice.

Longarm felt hackles at the nape of his neck. "Oh? Why?"

"Why, dear boy? You look good to me. To half of me you look simply ravishing. Why fool around with that Minnie and her ugly tattoos? I'm more fun. Twice the fixtures, twice the fun."

Carlo-Carlotta looked ready to join Longarm in the water. Longarm got up hastily from the oaken trough and jerked the plug. He gathered up his clothes and belongings, heading out of the tent, soaking wet.

"Don't run away, dear boy," Carlo said, simpering. "If you want something really different, I'm available. I've got everything Minnie has—and more..."

"I'll keep it in mind," Longarm said, and kept walking.

Naked, he ran across the narrow open ground to the tent. Dripping, he went between the rows of cots, toweling himself haphazardly. Jesus. Looked like everybody was after him. For one reason or another.

Chapter 5

Longarm lay on a folded cot and mattress atop an open dray wagon. He listened to the plodding of the huge hooves of the fat horses, to the lulling whisper of greased wheels on the trail, and to the pounding of his own heart. He had never been so tired in his life, too tired even to sleep.

The long caravan of circus wagons stretched as far as he could see in both directions. The people, animals, and vehicles moved like an army, a well-disciplined, silent cavalry.

The moment the last paying customer had departed the grounds, every able-bodied person and animal in the compound leaped to work. Every horse, mule, elephant was pressed silently and immediately into service. Even the little gray jackasses, which the clowns used to frustrate and defeat themselves in the center ring, suddenly lost their stubbornness and worked intelligently. Like pieces on a giant board, the booths, tents, and platforms were dismantled and stowed neatly and compactly. The huge main tent was collapsed. The stakes, poles, and lines were stacked, and forty men lined up to fold the canvas as smoothly as an oversized blanket.

The incredible column of vans, coaches, and wagons lined up and headed west out of Medicine Run, almost stealthily, a little after 2:00 A.M. that morning. The field where the magic had existed for a week was suddenly a barren, pocked, and cratered eyesore, without even a memory of the eye-widening, mind-boggling delights. To Longarm, it seemed the circus had moved out in record-breaking time. He had worked as hard as any man in the crew. The head roustabout had congratulated him, and soon the other laborers accepted him as one of them. He ached in every fiber and every tendon. Muscles stung and burned that he hadn't even known he owned. His hands were raw and torn.

The sky stretched a star-bedecked black tent above the slow-rolling procession. Things had gone well. At least, he couldn't swear that any of Josip Barac's bully boys had tried to kill him. A falling thousand-pound pack of canvas that just missed him when he leaped away from the wagon could have been an accident. For the moment, overwhelmed with fatigue, he was willing to mark it down as an accident and let it go at that. He fell asleep, lulled by the motion of the wagon.

The blaze of sunlight awakened him. His hands still burned and his body ached, but he felt better. He watched the fir-trimmed foothills drift past against a faint blue, cloud-pocked sky. The day had a chill in its thinning atmosphere. The caravan was climbing toward the Divide country. He could see the higher ranges crowding up in broken lines, shouldering off the world beyond, vast hills lost among hills, wild and lonely high country.

The caravans took a two-hour break along the shaded banks of a white-water mountain stream. The freaks gathered off to themselves. The circus stars—Marko Begovic, Bronco Bob Kidd, Miss Vingie—as well as Barac, did not mingle, or show themselves from their well-equipped vans. Minerva kept signaling Longarm with her eyebrows to join her for a quick hike into the rocky underbrush, but, exhausted, Longarm pretended to misunderstand her. He relaxed in the shade, listening to the cook and some of the clowns and hostlers, talking quietly over bottles of warm beer.

He had just sagged into a full-bellied nap when the call came along the line, "Load 'em up. Head 'em out."

His body protesting, he climbed back to his cot on the wagon. He moved to fall into it when he saw Minerva lying there in all her pictorial nudity. "We've got a nice, long, beautiful time together."

He was too beat to protest, and protests would have availed him nothing. Minerva seethed with desire, and when he didn't respond fast enough to her stroking fist, she fell upon him, nursing furiously until he forgot all the other muscles of his body and mounted her feveredly. "Oh, I want it so bad," she whispered in agony of delight. "You drive me so crazy, just looking at you."

"You're the one with pictures," he teased.

She flung herself across him, as if astride a bucking pony, abandoned and naked and indifferent to any prying gazes along the column. Luckily, only trees and hilltops reared above the slow-plodding wagon, because public cohabitation and fornication were on the lawbooks as felonies—and what she did to him with her mouth was considered a crime against nature, even between consenting adults. As far as the lawmakers were concerned, adults could consent only to wedded copulation, behind locked doors, with shades drawn and in one position— the missionary. Anything else was ruled "lewd and lascivious." And that was Minerva all right—lewd and lascivious. Even the Leaning Tower of Pisa across her high-standing left breast quivered and threatened to tumble into the sea beside the Merrimac and the Monitor on her rounded little belly. At times like this, Longarm was glad that none of this activity was a *federal* crime; it would have been embarrassing as hell to have to arrest Minerva—and turn himself in as an accessory before, after, and *during* the fact.

It was almost dusk before she sagged, sated, beside him and would release him from the fury of her passionate attack. Still, even lying beside him, she clung to his sagging, sodden member, clutching it hotly in her fist. "I'll bet you think I'm cock-crazy," she whispered against his face.

"Now where would I ever get an idea like that?"

"Maybe I am," Minerva said. "Sometimes I think maybe it was the way I was raised. You know? I was born on a farm near Mezokovesd."

"In Hungary?" Longarm came awake slightly, alert.

"Yes. Hungary. On the plains of Hungary." She settled upon him, massaging him almost unconsciously. "A farm. There were twelve children. Eight girls. I felt lost. Nobody ever looked at me. If I was dead, nobody would know or care. It got so all I wanted was *attention*. Oh, I wanted somebody to *look* at me. To know I was alive. I was alive. Then, when I was a young girl, and walking around wanting a man—or a horse, a dog, a donkey, *anything!*—I saw this woman in the open-air marketplace at Mezokovesd. She had tattoos on her forehead. And everybody looked at her, they noticed her. I was very young, very impressionable. I found a man who would tattoo me. When my family saw the tattoo, they threw

59

me out of the house. I had disgraced them. I found a wandering circus and got more tattoos. I got my whole body tattooed. And people looked at me. They noticed *me*. I had part of what I wanted. But this I want more. I stay hungry for *this*—all the time."

The circus equipage rolled into Black Lake settlement after midnight Monday morning. Only dogs ran out to bark as the columns rattled through the streets and out to the grounds. Black Lake township wasn't much larger than Medicine Run, and it was even uglier and older—an aging trail town trying to survive after the hundred-tentacled railroads had made trail towns obsolete.

By one-thirty, the wagons were lined up inside the new circus area. Though it was six hours until daylight, all hands fell to, setting up tents, booths, and concessions by the light of bonfires, lanterns, and torches. All equipment was laid out smoothly and in place. Historians praised the ancient Roman legions for building precise and well-engineered camps, even after interminable forced marches or day-long battles. These men drew from that same well of energy. They labored in the fire-illumined darkness, and by eight o'clock that morning every tent and booth and stall was in place, and a corral had been constructed for the horses.

In the early pink daylight, Longarm stood exhausted and stared at the circus compound. He shook his head, astounded. The Baldwin-Naylor Circus and Wild West Show was set up in a new town, but in layout and design, it stood exactly as it had the first moment he walked into it. Magic waiting for the rubes.

A rumbling in the earth brought Longarm to the newly constructed corral. Dirty and dusty horse-herders brought in half a dozen wild ponies caught on the plains south of the Divide.

Longarm watched Bronco Bob Kidd standing at one side of the corral, tallying the new shipment of unbroken animals. When the wild-eyed, frantic ponies were inside the pen, Bronco Bob jerked his head toward his handlers. One of them cut out one of the mustangs, and roped and snubbed him. A bridle was thrust between his teeth and over his head, a light saddle cinched to his back. The animal quivered, shaken and terrorized, as it was hazed, slapped, and driven to the fence where Bronco Bob waited to mount.

The circus star slid into the saddle and the handlers leaped away. The pony was small and shaggy, but it was all heart and terror. It seemed to stand on its rear hooves and lunge toward the sun, twisting and turning like a ballet dancer. It came down, braced on four stiff legs, and crow-hopped like that around the corral. It smashed itself against the sapling fence, trying to get rid of that hated burden on its back. It clawed at the sky and tried to climb the corral rails. It did everything but roll over on its back.

Longarm held his breath, watching the way Bronco Bob tormented the terrorized animal. He kept taking in rein to force the horse's head down, to break his fierce pride and humble him. The harder the horse fought, the more Bronco Bob savaged the reins. He used his fist, beating the horse on the side of the head, yelling at it, spurring it when it slowed. The little animal slavered, insane and confused, driven, wanting to quit, but it was not allowed to.

The handlers rushed in long before the horse was broken. They roped him, and snubbed him against a fencepost. Bronco Bob leaped free. The saddle and bridle were removed and the lathered, agonized horse whinnied and pawed at the air. The handlers had already moved to cut out a second pony.

"Jesus," Longarm said to the man standing beside him. "He's not even breaking those ponies."

"Hell, no," the man said. "He don't want 'em full broke. He knows what he's doing."

"That horse never will be any good for riding now."

"That ain't what Bronco Bob wants, fellow. He wants those ponies to be savaged. They'll fight when the saddle is put on them in the show ring, and they'll fight him when he mounts up, but he has taught them to submit to him—when he's ready—or he'll rip their mouths open."

Bronco Bob was savaging the second of his new shipment of ponies. Longarm shook his head, watching. "The son of a bitch," he said. "I figured he was the kids' hero. 'The Shootin' Kid from the Lone Star State.' Clean living, clean shooting, clean riding . . . What part of Texas is he from?"

The man laughed. "From the Ukraine part, I think. He's a real what you call a Magyar—a gypsy Hungarian. You can't really tell, what with the bleached-out hair. But he knows horses."

"The hell he does. He doesn't know a damn thing but cruelty."

The man shrugged. "It's what the people pay to see, bub."

Longarm shook his head. "Even the Texas cowpokes in this circus are from Transylvania or some other damn place."

"Hell, everybody out here is from somewhere else, bub. Except the Indians—and every Indian I ever saw looks just like the deer-herders from Siberia."

Longarm shook his head. He had seen enough of Bronco Bob for one morning. But as he turned to leave, Bronco Bob leaped from the saddle of his third half-broken, half-crazed pony. He landed a few feet from where Longarm stood. He laughed and puffed his chest out in pure vanity.

"You think you could ride like that, hombre?" Bronco Bob asked in a heavily accented voice. He was tall and slender, wearing a flat-crowned black hat, a black shirt, a fringed leather jacket, and Levi's stuffed into calf-high boots. He smelled like horse sweat. He was in his middle thirties, though, and with his shoulder-length peroxide-yellow hair and sharp features, he resembled a young General Custer from a distance.

"I *wouldn't* ride a horse like that, *hombre*," Longarm said. "Nobody would who gives a goddamn for horseflesh."

Bronco Bob laughed gutturally. "What the hell, hombre? These cayuses will be food for Marko's lions after my shows this week."

"Well, you're doing a great job of breaking them for lions' food," Longarm said.

He turned away, but Bronco Bob caught his arm. "You got a burr under your tail, hombre?"

"Nothing that would make sense to you, Bronco."

The lean, hard hand tightened, viselike, on Longarm's arm. "I'll tell you what *does* make sense to me, tramp. See that white gelding? That's my show horse. She needs to be cooled off, watered, and rubbed down."

Longarm met the strange black eyes and muttered, "You'll have plenty of time to cool her off as soon as you've ripped open a couple more ponies."

Longarm tried to turn away again, but the rodeo star stiffened and swung him back to face him. His obsidian eyes flared with rage; his face went deathly pale, his nostrils were pinched, and his mouth was gray.

"You want to go on working around here, stumblebum, you'll walk my horse cool, you'll give him water, and you'll rub him down. And you'll do it now."

He gave Longarm another hard look and then walked past him, bumping him aside with his shoulder. Longarm stood where he was, staring at the star's broad back, but still seeing the expression of merciless, overweening arrogance glittering in Bronco Bob Kidd's strange gypsy eyes. The man standing next to Longarm whistled through his teeth. "I swear, bub. You independent rich or something? Ain't you got any sense a-tall, crossing Bronco like that, and in front of his own people?"

Longarm exhaled heavily. The man made sense. It wasn't going to buy him anything to make another powerful enemy in this circus. Quietly, he took the white horse's bridle and walked it slowly under a blanket. Then he returned to the stall and rubbed the gelding down, placing a dry blanket over it as it drank. One fact remained. Bronco Bob knew enough to take care of his own mount. Stiff tendons cramping up had put more good horses out of action than broken legs, blind trots, or screw worms.

When he returned the gelding to its stall, Bronco Bob stood near the gate with half a dozen of his retinue. He didn't bother thanking Longarm. He did say, in contempt, "Well, saddle tramp, I see you do know a little about horses."

Longarm nodded. He returned Bronco Bob's contempt in spades. He hated what the so-called Shootin' Kid was doing in breaking those wild ponies. Only what Bronco was doing was not breaking them at all. He was only tormenting them into a frenzy so they would be wild and fractious the next time somebody threw a saddle on one of them in the show ring. They'd make Bronco Bob look good for a little while, and then they would be fed to the lions. But this had been going on before he got here. It would continue after he was gone. He just didn't have to watch.

"You know about taking care of them," Bronco said, his nostrils flaring. "So take care of them. There's horseshit in Whitey's stall. Clean it up before you put him in there."

Longarm bit back the rage that welled up in him. He led

Whitey out of the stall and found a shovel. He stared at Bronco Bob bleakly. There were some men he just couldn't get along with, no matter what he did.

Longarm came out of Whitey's stall. He saw with relief that Bronco Bob was standing in a crowd of his aides, hostlers, and hangers-on. He was not looking his way. For this, Longarm was thankful. Cleaning horse stalls was not his chore; he worked for Vingie Vinson's sideshow, not Barac's circus. But he wanted no trouble with the Shootin' Kid; he would disappear as quietly and quickly as possible.

A burst of laughter stopped and turned him. Near the corrals, Bronco Bob had leaped into the saddle of a paint pony, and his cheering friends were yelling him on.

Riding with reins laid over his little finger, Bronco was playing out a riata, forming a lasso. Then Longarm saw the object of Bronco's chase.

Ljubo the Giraffe Man had come out of the latrine, tall as a pine and waddling along like a big, helpless, and ungainly bird. Bronco Bob shouted Ljubo's name and the human skelton turned his head, glancing over his shoulder. His face went bleak with terror.

Ljubo wheeled around and ran toward the freaks' tent. But with Bronco Bob mounted and twirling a widening loop over his head, Ljubo was never going to make it.

Longarm didn't hesitate to consider any possible outcomes. He grabbed up one of Bronco's own lariats and leaped into a saddle. He cut at an angle across the field. Ahead of him, the ungainly Ljubo ran for his life. If he were jerked to the ground, his fragile bones would snap. Covering his head with his long arms, Ljubo ran screeching for cover.

Raging with laughter, Bronco Bob rode in pursuit. Longarm cut him off at an angle, letting out his own lasso. Somebody yelled a warning and Bronco turned his head just as Longarm threw his rope.

Bronco's face contorted. He jerked his horse around as the lasso settled around him, and Longarm yanked him from the saddle. By this time, Ljubo had reached the safety of the freaks' tent.

Bronco Bob landed hard in the dirt. Seeing that Ljubo was safe, Longarm released the lariat, letting it fall to the ground.

Bronco Bob leaped to his feet, cursing, raging. Longarm

stared down at him for a moment, then turned, walked his horse back near the corral, slipped from the saddle, and strode away toward the freaks' tent.

Bronco Bob jerked the rope off himself and ran toward Longarm. Half a dozen men grabbed the circus star. He stood trembling as Longarm walked away.

One of the hostlers stared at Longarm and whistled through his teeth. "Damn, I'd rather be standing in three feet of shit than be in your boots right now."

Longarm shrugged and kept walking.

When he entered the mess tent, the people at the freaks' table smiled, called his name, and motioned to him, inviting him to join them for breakfast. Grinning, Longarm nodded. He got plates of eggs and beans and a mug of coffee, and went to the long table, where the freaks greeted him warmly, as if he were one of them.

Ljubo got up from his bench with tears in his eyes. He embraced Longarm fiercely. "If that . . . that man . . . breaks my bones," he said, "I am a dead freak."

"Bronco Bob is not a bad kid," Longarm said, grinning. "He's just got sawdust for brains."

"He's begun to believe he's a wild cowboy," Fatima said.

"If his talent was one-third the size of his head," Longarm said, "he would be a fair horseman."

Ljubo laughed. "If he ever hears that you said that, he will kill you."

Longarm sat down at the table. Beside him, Minerva writhed excitedly. More violence, more passionately aroused need. Minerva was practically drooling. She massaged him fiercely with her hand under the table. Longarm tried to ignore her ministrations, but he was pretty sure everybody at the table— including Jo-Jo, who was fed with a bib under his throat— knew what the tattooed lady was doing.

Longarm tried to eat. He was tired, hungry, and sore. Also, he felt rage turned against himself. It wasn't going to help his investigation to make a mortal enemy of a money-making star like Bronco Bob. Personally, the Shootin' Kid might be an empty-headed bastard, but the public didn't know—and didn't care. Bronco Bob gave them what they wanted, and fighting him wasn't going to help turn up answers. He needed to get in these peoples' confidence, not on their shit list.

He shook his head. So far, the only person he could really talk to was Minerva, but she didn't want to waste time talking. Her hand moved on him, faster and tighter, the friction burning deep into his loins.

Cy Slimer entered the tent. He paused just inside the open flap, surveying the faces of the people at the tables. He found Longarm and walked toward him, not smiling. This was one hell of an omen, because, for Cy Slimer, a smile was the first answer to every problem.

"Trouble," Minerva whispered.

"I will tell them," Ljubo said. "You saved my life. I will tell them."

Longarm grinned at the human skeleton. "It's all right, Ljubo. Don't make them hate you too. I can handle it."

Cy paused beside Longarm. "It's Miss Vingie," Cy said. His voice sounded tight. "She wants to see you—as soon as you've bathed and shaved." Coldly, Minerva jerked her hand away from Longarm's crotch.

"Kiidislenco wants you fired," Vingie said when Longarm entered her wagon, shaved, bathed, shined, in fresh clothes and cleaned boots.

Longarm smiled. It was easy to smile at the tiny, elfin woman. She looked pink and doll-like in a wraparound silk lounging robe. The soft fabric seemed to be all Vingie was wearing, except for those high heels that only accentuated her small stature. "What the hell is a Kiidislenco?"

"You know what I'm saying to you. Janos Kiidislenco. All right, Bronco Bob, if you insist on playing games. This is a serious thing. I need you, I thought I told you that. There are pressures—big pressures—on me to fire you. Bronco Bob says he will kill you if I don't fire you."

"And what do you say?"

The tiny girl elevated herself into a chair with a motionless pirouette perfected through long practice in a world never made for the comfort and convenience of little people.

She sat staring at Longarm. "What do I tell them?"

"That's up to you." Longarm went on standing there in the exotically furnished room. He had never been in the boudoir of Turkish royalty, but he imagined such a place must resemble this room, down to the incense lightly tickling his nostrils.

"You have no contrite—for what you have done?"

"I have no contrite," Longarm teased her gently. "I thought I worked for you. I thought Ljubo the Human Skeleton was a valuable property. I thought I ought to protect him."

"Kiidislenco said he was just having a little fun."

"That's right. But if he roped Ljubo and jerked him down, he would have cracked his bones like kindling."

"He says he never meant to rope him, only to make him run because he looks so funny."

"Sorry, I missed the joke."

"Then what do I say to Barac, who is foaming at the mouth? Barac is happy to have this excuse to get rid of you. You do not make it easy for me with Barac."

"What *could* make it easy for you with Barac, except to tell him you have fired me?"

"I don't want to do that."

"What do you want?"

Her almond-shaped eyes grazed across him and she shrugged faintly. "I will tell you how we could settle the entire matter."

"I'm listening."

"For you to make apology to Kiidislenco."

Longarm drew in a long breath, held it. "All right."

"A public apology. In front of people. In front of those people that Bronco keeps around him to worship him. He wants an apology from you—in front of them."

Longarm exhaled, and nodded. After a moment, he said, "Is that all you wanted to see me about?"

Wee Vingie's gaze impaled him. "I hear you have been screwing Minerva, the tattooed bitch."

Longarm shrugged.

The little head jerked up. "What is that supposed to mean?"

"That it's none of your business, I reckon."

"Well, it is my business. I make it my business. You screw with that one and you'll get more than you want. A lot more. There is no cure for what you can get from such a one."

Longarm grinned faintly. "You take a chance every time you drink water."

"Not such a chance as you take with that one. You are screwing her and I want it stopped. Bad as I need you, I cannot endure that you should screw with her."

"If I sign on to work for you, that don't mean I take you as my mother."

"It means you do what I tell you."

"Maybe I won't screw her as much. Maybe I won't put it all the way in."

"You won't put it in at all to her—if you want to stay with this circus."

Longarm stared at Vingie, the determined little chin, the hard, taut line of her mouth, the way her eyes narrowed sometimes, even when she smiled. And right now she wasn't smiling.

Longarm spoke coldly. "You going to tell her, or do I have to do that too? You want it in public—or can I just tell her in private?"

"You need tell her nothing in private. I will get the word to her."

Longarm shrugged. "Is there anything else?"

She sat forward on the big chair. The soft fabric whispered away from her thigh. It was not like looking at a little girl's upper leg, nothing at all like it. Longarm forced his gaze away. "Are you in such a rush to escape me, then?"

Longarm spread his hands and waited, watching her. After a moment she drew a small pattern on her silk gown with her index finger, sighed, and looked up, meeting his gaze. "I went through your bindle," she said.

His mouth gaped open. "You?"

"I wanted to know about you."

"Well, if you want me to stay around here working for you and not screwing Minerva, you'll have to stop going through my things."

"Why?"

"Because you don't know how to tie anything but granny knots."

Vingie laughed suddenly, startled and pleased. "I like you, Long. Not only do I admire you and respect you. I like you."

"You don't know anything about me."

"Perhaps I know more than you think."

"You didn't learn much, going through my bindle."

She smiled oddly, her eyes glittering. "Perhaps I learned more than you think."

Longarm grinned at her. "What could you learn? I shave. I change my underwear and I carry a gun."

"Ah. But that's the secret."

"You want to share it with me?"

"It's your gun, Long. It give you away. You are not what you want people to think. You are not some bindlestiff down on his luck. Not by a million years."

His heart quickened. He said, "Why do you say that?"

"Why? Because it is true. Look at you. You are the best-looking male specimen I have seen. Ever. Anywhere. And I have seen many men, I promise you. Men in show business. Men who take care of themselves because in show business, their bodies are their fortune—men like Marko Begovic and Bronco Kiidislenco. They are nothing beside you. No, Long. You take care of your gun. You take care of your body. Your gun and your body. They told me what I needed to know. You are no bindlestiff."

"No? What do you think I am?"

"I don't think," she said in a flat tone. "I know. You are a lawman of some kind."

Was it lettered on his forehead? Did the size of his feet give him away? Or was Wee Vingie Vinson simply more astute than other, larger people? God knew, he hoped so. He tried to laugh and tried to keep his voice level, but failed in both attempts. "Me? A lawman? I could have stolen the gun."

She held his gaze levelly. "You could have. But you did not. You are not having to lie to me, Long. You are a lawman."

"Am I? Do I make much money? Is it a good job?"

"Making the jokes don't change nothing. A lawman."

"What kind of lawman am I?" He tried to sound amused, but this was less than successful too.

She gestured with her trim, delicate little hand. "You can fool the others. They are fools. Like that cow Minerva. With her sexy cities painted on her ugly body. If I had such a great ugly body, I too might paint it up. The peasant! You can fool the peasants, with their Grand Forks, and their Bangkoks. Such silly names for towns! Did she show you French Lick?"

He grinned, glad to get off the subject. "I think we got off the road somewhere there."

"You think I brought up Minerva for some reason than that I know you to be a lawman. Well, I didn't."

Longarm smiled faintly. There was no second *d* in Vingie's *didn't*s. She said "dint." But even at that, she handled English a hell of a lot better than he could have managed the strange language of the Magyars. "You could have fooled me," he said.

"You are a lawman. You are here for a purpose. I want above all for that purpose to achieve. You fool around with cows like Minerva, you will be revealed. Milk is not all that cow gives away."

"You hate good."

"I do everything good, Long. With all my heart. With all my soul. That's why I own my own freak show when I could have been just another helpless freak—like Jo-Jo and Fatima and the others. But I have built of my life something good. I want to keep it. I think you and I want the same thing."

"Are we still talking about the law?"

Vingie put her head back. There was a sudden, strange recklessness in her laughter. But her chilled words denied it all. She was coldly, deadly serious, all business.

"We are still talking about *you*," Vingie said. "And you are the law. I know this. And I welcome you here. I have known for a long time that someone from the law would turn up on this midway. I could see it coming. I am not blind, as Barac thinks. I am not stupid, as Barac thinks. I have been telling Barac, warning him. People complain in every town we play. There is trouble in every town. With people. With the law. The night before you joined us in Medicine Run, there was almost a riot when some young cowmen thought they had been robbed by Barac's concession people. And they had been."

"So he runs a crooked midway?"

She gave him a taunting smile. "You play the innocent with me. But I know. You *know* his midway is crooked. Every wheel is fixed, every game is a lie, the cards are marked, the dice are almost alive. He thinks he can get away with it."

"You're right. Enough complaints, they'll shut him down in one of these towns. They'll confiscate everything. Impound it."

"This is what I know! This is what I try to tell the fat fool. He is thick in the head as well as the chest. To nobody will he listen. He thinks because he cheats us and exploits us and

70

gets away with it, that we are stupid and don't know what we are talking about."

"I agree with you—he's heading for trouble."

"I try to tell him. He has pickpockets that work the crowds. Yes! Yes! It is more than that he allows these crooked men to work his midway. He hires them! It is not enough to cheat on the wheels and games and overcharge for everything! He wants the last penny in a poor man's wallet. He is greedy. He is consumed with greed."

"I saw his men take your gross receipts Saturday afternoon."

"Cy told me how you tried to stop them. I thank you. He has been cheating me for a long time. I know he takes eighty percent of my gross. Can you believe such a thing? He leave me twenty percent to pay and feed my people, and to pay him for the right to put up my blue tent on his midway! He keeps me in debt to him, when I could be rich. For this I can never forgive him. But even this, this is not the worst."

"Sounds pretty bad. What's the worst?"

She stirred uncomfortably on her chair. "That he is so greedy that he cheats the customers in every town. He is bold about it. He is a fool. He acts like nobody is smart in the head but him. Well, I knew all along the law had to step in. He will ruin his own show, and it does make money! Not the kind of wealth that Barac wants—but a good living for us all! If only he didn't spoil it with his brazen robberies of the customers. He will bankrupt us. What will I have when I lose my blue tent and my freaks?"

Longarm exhaled. "You're right. That's the worst."

"No." Vingie shook her lovely dark-blonde head sharply. "That we are bankrupt, ruined, that is bad. But that we are destroyed is worse."

"I'm not sure I know what you mean."

"I mean you have come here. A lawman. You represent the law. The smell of Barac is so bad that the law can no longer ignore him and his stench. That is the worst, that he has ruined the last place for some of these poor people to hide."

"Hide?"

"You must know. We are a European show. It was not always so. I was with the show when Baldwin and Naylor actually ran it. They were crooks. Like Barac. One is in prison.

71

The other lies dead—from bullet wounds. But it is of the little people I talk. Some of the people have not joined the circus because it is a good life; it is not. It is a hard life. Lonely. Ugly. Dirty. And it is hard work. But it is the only place for some of them. They have run from trouble. Maybe they have change their name. Maybe too change—what you say?—identity. They are hiding from something, from somebody in a bad past. Or a sad past. Or a troubled one. They have hidden here in the circus. They don't want the law on them."

Longarm drew a deep breath, then cast out his line cautiously. "Like Marko Begovic?"

Vingie stared at him, completely puzzled and confused. She shook her head. "What about Marko?"

Longarm backed off. He had gotten no glimmer of the response he'd hoped for. He shook his head. "Nothing. I just picked a name. I thought maybe you meant him. What do you mean? These people might be scared of the law?"

"Not scared. That's not the word. Except in a way. It is not that they have done something criminal. It's just they don't want the law digging in and turning them up, even accidentally."

"What would they be hiding from?"

She spread her lovely little hands. "I would not know. Only that some of them *are* hiding. Like Cy Slimer."

Longarm said nothing, recalling Cy Slimer's mutilated right hand. Obviously, Vingie's chief aide had not spent his life in a cloistered monastery.

"People like poor Cy. He has been hurt. Trouble, in the old country. You know. Nothing, perhaps. But one has run away. He has changed his name."

"Slimer is not his name?"

"Slimer?" Vingie laughed. "This is a name for a Magyar? No it is not his name, but you need not ask me for his real name. I do not know. He has been with me many years. I have not stuck in my nose. You see? I do not pry what is his real name. Who knows? Maybe he doesn't even remember. I do not say he has done a wrong. Or broken a law. But he does not for some reason want to be found. There are many like him, who do not wish the law to hound them."

"And this is the worst thing about Barac's crookedness and greed bringing in the law?"

"I see it as the worst. Because it can destroy our show. It can scatter our people. It can ruin us, for no good reason that will be served."

Longarm sighed. "And you think I've been sent here—by the law—to check on Barac's crookedness?"

She met his gaze levelly. "I would bet my cherry on it."

He laughed. "Your last cherry?"

"My *only* cherry."

Chapter 6

For some moments a taut silence settled in the brocaded, velvet-draped room. Longarm tried to keep his eyes off the compact perfection of Vingie's lovely little body. Her vented robe, exposing a perfect leg in miniature, fascinated him. He couldn't go on standing there, and the little doll seemed lost in thought, as if she had put him from her mind. At last he cleared his throat. "Is *that* all you wanted to see me about?"

Her lovely little head jerked up. "Isn't that enough? But no, that is not all. There is more. Much I must say. And yet, I seek for the right words to make you believe me."

"I haven't doubted anything you've said yet."

"You've had no reason to—so far. I have said nothing I can't prove. Barac is a crook. Cy is in hiding under an alias. Minerva Jo Hinkey is a tattooed cow. What is to doubt?"

Longarm grinned. "But now you're afraid I won't believe you?"

Vingie hesitated. She sat a moment, her featherlike hand pressed to her shapely little breast. She gazed at Longarm as if trying to see past his eyes, his guard, to look inside him.

Then, abruptly, she leaned forward in the oversized chair and extended her hand to him. Longarm was afraid to touch it for fear it might break. She gestured impatiently and he frowned. He didn't know whether she expected him to kiss it or simply admire it, since she gazed at it, fixedly.

"Go on. Touch my hand," Vingie said at last. "Hold it. See how cold it is. Like ice. Because I am in terror. Because I live in terror."

She made him feel huge and clumsy and awkward. "I would have said you weren't afraid of anything, not Barac or the devil."

She almost smiled. "I do not fear Barac—or the devil. Nor do I fear anything I can see or know. I fear the unknown, Long. And I need your help."

"You've hired me. You've got it." He went on holding the tiny hand.

"I don't mean to protect me from Barac's cheating and greed and his exploiting me and my people, although I hope you can do that. I hope you can stop Barac in his greed before he ruins and destroys us all. But I am not talking about that now." She drew a deep breath. "I am in mortal danger."

His brow tilted. "From what?"

"Oh, I see, you are about to laugh. Even Cy would laugh at me, if he dared. If he laughed at me, I would kill him. If you laugh at me, I will kill you."

"You haven't left me a smile to my name."

"There have been attempts on my life," she said. "Subtle attempts—things happen that look so accidental they could not possibly be accidental. Somebody is trying to kill me."

Longarm bit back a smile. "Why would anybody want to kill you?"

"Save the cute and cuddly routine, Long. I know I look like a doll. But I am not a doll. I am a living, breathing, adult human being—in a small package. But I am serious. Somebody is trying to get rid of me."

There was no doubt about her genuine concern. Longarm stopped smiling. He said, "You want to tell me about it?"

"No. But I guess I'll have to. There was one time on the midway. A horse and buggy almost ran me down. It barely missed me. I was too shaken, too terrified to move. I stood there, with people running toward me and screaming. Suddenly the carriage wheeled around, and came back directly toward me. Someone knocked me aside—or I would have been killed."

"Who was driving the carriage?"

"That's it, Long. That is what I am telling you. There was nobody holding the reins. Nobody headed that horse toward me. Nobody turned it back on me. And yet it almost killed me, twice."

"The midway was full of people. They all saw it. Who owned the cart? What did they say?"

She stared at him, eyes bleak and face gray. "They said it was an accident. That was the only way it could be explained.

The man who owned the carriage was a local man. I had never seen him. He said he parked the carriage. Something must have startled the horse and it ran along the midway—just in time to almost kill me. I am seldom on the midway. But I cross it, at almost the same hour every day, to get to the freaks' tent."

"Nobody at the reins? And yet they made another run at you?"

"They all said this was most accidental of all. The people, running and screaming, they frightened the horse. They turned it, and it ran back as it had come."

"Makes some sense. As much as any of the rest of it."

"And yet why would that horse run directly at me a second time?"

He said nothing.

Her lovely mouth twisted. "You have it all figured out. The run at me the first time was a mistake—as was the second time. That explains it so neatly, doesn't it?"

"It's about the only explanation."

"And a rifle fired at me—from the target concession? I was across the grounds, in the opposite direction of the targets. The man who ran the concession said it was a kid who had grabbed up a gun, fired it, and then run away."

"Another accident."

"Yes. At the exact moment I walked out on that stage in front of the blue tent. There have been other attempts, but I see you marking them all down as accidental. A stair on the stage that gives way under my weight, yet has supported men bigger than Cy. Someone does want to kill me. Someone does want me out of the way."

Longarm nodded. "That I can buy. Does Barac want your freak concession?"

"In the worst way. He tries to buy me out. But I refuse to sell. Still, he does not have to kill me. If he goes on cheating me, I will be so far in his debt that he can simply take over everything I have. No. I don't believe it is Barac. He is greedy, arrogant, domineering. But he is not that smart. Not that subtle."

"Who do you suspect?"

She shook her head, trembling. "I don't suspect anybody— and I suspect everybody. Don't you see, it takes almost more courage than I have to cross the midway. It is torture to walk out on that stage in front of my blue tent and try to smile at the people—when I know somebody out there is trying to kill me."

"Has anybody threatened you?"

"In words?" She shook her head. "No. They are too clever, too subtle for this, Long. I tell you it is unknown forces."

Suddenly, Vingie burst into tears. She cried helplessly, tears streaming down her face. She seemed in that moment no longer a miniature goddess, a fingerling fantasy, but a terrified, mortal woman caught in the webbing of some waking nightmare.

"It's all right," he said. "It's all right."

The kindness in his tone only made her weep louder. He bent down and took her up in his arms. She was light; she weighed nowhere near a hundred pounds, though she was solidly put together and firm.

Still sobbing, Vingie put her arms around his neck and clung to him. She had existed alone in her dark terror as long as she could stand it. She buried her face against his throat, crying, her hot tears searing him. It was as if she'd lived with her terror as long as she could endure it. She had kept her unprovable fears and her growing horror of the "unknown forces," which she was convinced threatened her life, bottled up inside herself. Now, the very act of talking about it was like letting down the floodgates. All her dread and anxieties and misery spilled out of her.

He sat down in the chair, holding her, trying to reassure her. He pressed his lips against the faintly scented tendrils of hair at her forehead. "It's all right," he kept whispering.

"You will help me?" she whispered against his throat, her tear-damp breath hot.

"I'll do whatever I can. Whoever is behind this, I'll try to find them."

She gasped for breath. "You don't believe it's . . . unknown forces . . . do you?"

"I don't have to believe that to believe you're scared," he said. "Somebody scared you. If I can find out who it is, I'll stop them."

"I feel safe," she whispered. "For the first time in God knows how long, I feel safe."

He loosened his arms to permit her to move away, but she

pressed closer. "Hold me," she said. "Please hold me. I've been in hell for so long . . . I've been so afraid."

She lay there for a long time. Gradually her tears subsided. She nestled closer, pressing her hot, parted lips against his throat. "You shouldn't be doing that," he teased. "Even if you were a big girl."

She writhed on his lap. "You think I'm not a big girl?"

"Not for what I'm talking about," he said.

She tilted her head back, staring up at him. "What a fool you are," she said. "You are such a strong man, and so smart— and such a fool."

He grinned. "Well, we all have our weaknesses."

She smiled, her swollen lips turning up beautifully. "But you would not be so weak as to . . . touch a little girl, would you?"

"Not as long as there are big girls . . ."

"Like that cow Minerva?"

"Little girls are called 'penitentiary pullets' in this country, honey. A man can spend his life in jail or be hanged for touching one. Even if it was fun it wouldn't be worth it."

"Do you think I am a . . . 'penitentiary pullet'?"

He laughed. "To tell you the God's truth, I'm doing my best not to think of you at all right now."

"Why? Are you afraid of me?"

"I don't think afraid's the word."

She twisted on his legs. "Would you like for me to sit across your lap? Isn't that what little girls do for their doting uncles?"

"I don't know. How did we get in this conversation, anyway?"

She seemed not to have moved at all, yet suddenly she had twisted inside his arms until she was straddling him, sitting with her legs on each side of his hips. She worked her trim little hips up and down upon him. He felt himself respond. This was ridiculous, but he was only human. In fact, he was as human as hell.

"What are you trying to do?" he asked.

She worked her hips seductively. "I'm trying to make you feel good."

"I think this feeling good could get out of hand."

"Do you?"

"Don't you?"

"You want me. Say it," she teased. "You want me to lie with you."

"You're unlike any other woman, that's the truth."

"Also is the truth how bad you want me. Oh, you do want me, Long. You would like to make love to me? No? With your great thing into me? You are stirred inside as to what this might be. No? You need not answer. I can look at you and see this truth." She squirmed her heated thighs upon his lap. "I can *feel* how much you want me."

He shook his head. "It *would* be different..."

"You don't know how different." She laughed. "Not like with a fat tattooed cow."

"I'm going to think you're jealous."

"Me, Vingie Vinson, jealous? Of a cow? Never. First I better teach you a lesson. There is something you need to know about me."

"I already know. You're full of hell."

She shrugged. "There is something else. I want you to understand, I am held only if I wish to be held. I am caught only if I want to be caught."

"Oh?"

"You doubt this? You think any man—*any* man—could hold me against my will? Hold me. Go on. I sit across your lap like a little tart. Try to keep me there," she challenged him.

Laughing, admitting he was far more aroused by this tiny charmer than made good sense, Longarm tightened his hands at her waist.

It was grabbing quicksilver. It was holding lightning in your hand. Before his fingers could close on her waist, she had sprung lightly upward, eluding him. She was gone before he could close his hands, even on her feet.

She stood three feet from him, laughing at him, taunting him. "You think perhaps this was a trick? I surprised you? Wait. I will do it again."

She danced lightly into his lap. "Hold me," she whispered, teasing him. "Put your arms around me. Hold me tight against your great thing. You don't want to let me go, do you?"

He closed his arms, but she was gone. This time she placed her tiny feet against his belt and leaped outward as if from a trampoline. She did a triple somerset in the air and landed on her feet.

"Catch me," she dared him. "Catch me, Long, and you can have me."

He hesitated, then grabbed for her. But she was not there. It was like trapping a hummingbird, or catching a firefly. She danced about him, moving gracefully, with blinding speed. She put herself into his hands and before he could close them, she escaped.

She leaned against a velvet drape across the narrow carpeting from him, and looked at him in sympathy. "My poor great big thing. Perhaps sometime I will let you catch me."

"No." He shook his head. "I'll never chase you. You'll come to me—or you'll keep all those cherries."

"Oh, my poor great baby, I treat you so badly, no? I'll be nice to you . . ." She let her gaze rake him, from his eyes to the bulge at his crotch. "Would you like to look at me . . . naked?"

"Certainly. You're beautiful. Perfect. I'm human."

"All right. I don't mind. Sit there. It does not matter, you could not catch me anyway, unless I will it so. I will do my show for you. The one I used to do—but no longer. Once I used to strip down in my act—on the stage in front of the farmers—to give the rubes a treat." She laughed. "We called it scientific and educational—seeing the perfect adult woman, in miniature."

"But you don't do that act anymore?"

"Undress? Onstage? Not for pay. No more. Now I do it only to amaze my friends and amuse myself." Her teasing laughter raked at him. "I'm so pretty it's even fun for me . . . I'll maybe . . . maybe show you sometime, eh?"

"I hope I live to that supreme moment."

"I hope you do."

What may have happened, Longarm didn't get to find out. Vingie was teasing him, tormenting and tantalizing him, but she was also guaranteeing that he would stay near her; he would come back, and keep coming back. But as he sat there watching her draw her hands along the silken robe, someone knocked on the wagon door.

Longarm jumped as if caught in the act of some crime against nature.

Vingie laughed at him and called over her shoulder, "What do you want, Cy?"

The front door was opened and Cy stood there. He looked physically ill, a man consumed with jealousy. He was almost astonished to find Longarm and Vingie fully dressed. He tried to smile, but could not do it. He was dressed in his barker's suit and straw hat. "Time for the matinee show, Vingie," he said.

Vingie thanked Cy and then forgot him with the casual cruelty of the truly beautiful woman—a women who accepted homage from all men simply as her due, even the sick jealousy of a slave.

Vingie looked at Longarm and laughed. "You will come back to see me again, won't you? I wouldn't think of leaving you like this, but you know the old adage—the show must go on." She started toward her dressing room, paused and glanced over her shoulder. "Oh, did I forget to tell you how pretty you look, shaved and bathed? You must try it again sometime."

Longarm stood up and crossed the narrow room to the front door. Cy stepped down to the ground to let him pass. Longarm felt honest pity for Cy. The man was in hell. He said, "We talked business, Cy."

"I know. You've been cut off at Minerva's Pass."

Longarm met his gaze. "Like you, I follow orders."

Chapter 7

To Longarm's surprise, Minerva sat perched on his cot in the male freaks' tent. She wore the revealing costume from her act, and her dark hair was piled and brushed atop her head and secured with a tiara. She watched him come along the row of cots toward her, and she didn't bother to smile. There was no doubt about it; Minerva had gotten the word from Wee Vingie. Stay away from Long.

He would rather have told Minerva himself. Still, she didn't look offended. On the other hand, she didn't look very happy, either. He forced a grin, hoping it looked natural. "What are you doing here? Isn't it showtime?"

"I thought we could take a little quick run to Italy." She smiled with her lips only, watching him with flat, hurt eyes.

"Sounds good to me," Longarm said. "But it will just get you in trouble with the tiny terror."

"How about you?" Minerva said. "She's warned you to stay away from me, hasn't she?"

He bit at his underlip. There was no easy way to handle this. "She did say something about it."

"She can't run our lives."

"She can fire us."

"Damn little bitch. She's jealous. She wants you for herself. She wants everything for herself."

"Still, she is the boss."

"She's a bitch, that's what she is. Let me tell you something. You better stay away from *her*. You fool around with Vingie, you'll get something hot all right."

He shook his head. "You two girls shouldn't hate so deeply."

"That little half-pint bitch. I can't see what any grown man

83

would want to mess with her for. Screwing that midget must be like playing with yourself."

"Oh, it's got to be better. At least you got somebody to talk to."

Her eyes glittered. "Are you trying to make me mad?" Then she smiled. "I'm sorry, Long. That little bitch will fire us, but couldn't we have a last one for the road? The road to Rome, that is?"

Longarm didn't think it would be polite to say no. So he kept his mouth shut and she accepted this as agreement. She stood up, shaking the loose, low-cut gown from her body. Her breathing was shallow and rapid. She reached down and jerked the buttons loose at his fly. He was still half-tumescent from holding Wee Vingie across his lap. Minerva's knowing hand soon had him pulsing and rigid.

Longarm ran his hands down her bare shoulders, along the small of her trim back to her generous, painted hips. He kissed her and for a long moment they stood in the brilliant daylight inside the breathless tent, unaware of the heat, except in their own bodies as they tried to melt into one another.

He lifted Minerva up in his arms and laid her down on his cot. She was already spreading her legs wide and guiding his chariot toward its arena. She went wild, her hips thrusting like a piston, even before he penetrated her.

"Oh, it's so good," she whispered. "Because you've got what I need—and I know what you like about me."

"Rome?"

"You'll like Paris even better. I'll go down there on the way back..."

The main-attraction tent was crowded, loud with smells, sounds, and dust. The small brass band played at its highest pitch, making up in decibels for what it lacked in quality.

Longarm stood at one side, watching the clowns. These men were truly funny, trying to douse a fire in a clown hotel with little gray jackasses and jennies to pull their fire engine. The animals seemed smarter than the men. They would rush forward long enough that the clowns grew hopeful, then they balked, refusing to go nearer the fire. They even turned their heads and looked at the clowns as if to say, "Me, go in that fire? I'm a jackass, not crazy."

84

The large crowd loved the clowns; they were simple, direct, easy to understand, and everything was overstated. Longarm let his gaze move over the farmers gathered on the tiers of plank seats, laughing happily. He didn't know what a big first-day matinee crowd should be, but it looked as if the take here in Black Lake should have satisfied even the greedy Barac. Strange that a man would get so consumed with greed that there wasn't enough money for him, as long as he had to share it; he had to have it all, or he had nothing. . . .

The clowns managed to burn the clown hotel to the ground, to haze and bully, push and pull the little donkeys off the ground. The band struck up a fanfare. The tall master of ceremonies, in his red clawhammer coat, black boots, and stovepipe black hat, ran out into the center ring with his huge megaphone.

"Ladies and gentlemen, I call your kind attention to the lion cages. In one moment, huge African lions will enter that cage through that chute. There is nothing to fear—for yourselves. Those iron bars are strong and there are men standing by with powerful rifles in case of any accident. Only one man in this great arena will be in jeopardy this afternoon. Marko Begovic. The world's greatest animal trainer. The Great Begovic will enter that cage, armed only with a small whip. You will see that, unlike other animal trainers, The Great Begovic carries no holstered gun, no weapon of any kind. The small whip is used only to direct his magnificent animals through their paces, for your delight and edification.

"Ladies and gentlemen, the management of Baldwin-Naylor Combined Circuses and Wild West Show takes great pride in introducing the star of our internationally acclaimed show— Mr. Marko Begovic."

The band struck up a noisy march and Marko Begovic strode out into the center tent. He was indeed imposing, stately, and dignified, and though well past forty, he maintained a muscular youthfulness, a classic handsomeness and arrogance.

His graying blond hair looked as if it were sculpted to his romanesque head. He wore a flowing red cape as he strode, head up and arms outstretched, into the center ring. He threw off the cape. A young woman in a tutu ran out to retrieve it from the sawdust. Longarm had been near enough the animal trainer to know that Begovic hid hideous scars under the red leotard that was cinched at his flat waist by a wide black leather belt and a glittering silver buckle.

He paraded around the ring, cracking the small whip. At this moment, lions were emerging from the chute, crouching for a moment, and then, prodded, running out into the cage and circling it, growling. Begovic put on a breathtaking spectacle of a performance. His lions looked and sounded vigorous and healthy and unmanageable as they raced about the cage, swatting at each other and roaring defiance. But Begovic was truly a remarkable personality. Despite the action in the cage, few took their eyes off the man striding about the ring. His eyes were steel-blue, piercing. When he shouted at the lions, his accent was thick, his basso profundo voice hard and uncompromising. He walked on the balls of his feet, balanced on his toes, constantly alert, always ready to move in any direction.

The band broke off abruptly. The sudden silence seemed exaggerated, as if everyone in the big top were holding his breath.

"Ladies and gentlemen," the master of ceremonies said in a low tone, "I ask for quiet. These are young cats, easily alarmed. Marko Begovic is putting his life on the line to entertain you as he enters this cage without a weapon of any kind—to force these magnificent animals to do his bidding."

He need not have asked for quiet. Nobody spoke. Far across the tent a baby yelped once, the sound loud in the tense stillness. People laughed in relief, and fell silent again, watching the lone man in that cage walk among his lions, force each of them to sit on colored stools, to leap through hoops, to stand with his paws on his shoulders.

The place went wild when Begovic finally had the animals lined up and marching in a quiet parade to the chute—and out through it. Longarm stared at that man in the cage. It was hard to hate a man who had such incredible courage. An anarchist he might be, but he was brave.

Still, Begovic was the State Department's prime suspect. It was Longarm's job to stop him. . . .

The lion act was the climax of the circus show. It was followed by the appearance of a dozen or so buckskin-clad cowboys and bare-chested roustabouts pretending to be Indians. They rode up and down the length of the arena, shooting at each other, taking spills, making running leaps from the ground to the backs of racing horses.

The crowd went wild. One could look at them and believe they had never seen cowboys and Indians—though they lived in what remained of the wildest part of the frontier. They loved this show. Watching the cowboys ride, they even forgot the peril and thrill of the lions.

Finally the horsemen formed an honor guard in two lines near the center of the tent. The master of ceremonies mounted a podium. "And now, here he is, ladies and gentlemen—the star of the West, the man you have been waiting for, the greatest sixgun artist, the world's supreme horseman, the finest roper in the universe. Bronco Bob Kidd—your own Shootin' Kid from the Lone Star State!"

Resplendent in silver and white, his golden mane flying in the wind, Bronco Bob rode his white gelding into the ring. He stood the beautiful horse on its hind legs and walked it almost all the way around the ring like that. The mob roared, yelling, whistling, shouting his name.

Someone tossed Bronco Bob a rifle and he shot almost anything that moved and made a direct hit every time. Indians raced past on their ponies, carrying pennants aloft on staffs, and Bronco shot the pennants loose. He broke balloons at the top of the tent. He shot cans, coins, and bottles. When it seemed he would go on shooting forever, from one position or another, and never missing, Bronco suddenly hurled the gun over his shoulder—and there was a flunky there to grab it in midair. The enthused crowd even applauded this performance.

Bronco Bob's next act was with three ropes. He lassoed racing horses, running women, squealing calves, and finally threw a loop over six horsemen riding side by side, carrying an American flag. The crowd went hysterical in its applause. Many women were openly weeping. In that moment Bronco Bob could have been elected President.

As he rode up and down the length of the tent, leaping off and on his pony, riding under its belly and even sidesaddle to the wild cheering of the crowd, tall fences were placed, creating a corral into which the half-broken mustangs were hazed.

Longarm winced. It was easy to fall under the spell of Bronco Bob's charm and expertise, and his bright smiling— he loved himself almost as much as his audience loved him.

He loved himself so intensely that he engendered love in those watching him.

Longarm shook his head as Bronco Bob spurred and savaged one of the squealing, bucking, sunfishing little ponies about the corral until its mouth split and blood spurted from the rowel ruts in its flanks.

"The hell with him," Longarm said under his breath. "He's a son of a bitch and I've got to apologize to him because he *is* a son of a bitch—or I lose my job."

Longarm waited beside the outer corral when the applause finally died and the adoring fans allowed Bronco Bob to leave the arena. Bob's hired hands saw Longarm, recognized him, knew why he was there. They looked at each other, grinned, and delayed their chores as they awaited the arrival of the Shootin' Kid for the confrontation at the circus corral.

At last Bronco Bob did ride out of the big tent, still waving his white hat and bowing, his thin face wreathed in a self-adoring smile. He was all glittering teeth, gleaming eyes and squared shoulders. He sat tall in his saddle. He was almost to the corral before the pleasure of his triumph thinned enough that he became aware of the tension in the faces of his waiting men. Then he glimpsed Longarm standing alone beside the pole gate of the corral.

Bronco jerked his head straight so that he did not fully recognize Longarm or admit that he was present. The star laughed and yelled something to his men. He disregarded Longarm, didn't even bother to toss him a look of contempt. Bronco was riding high on his euphoria and he didn't want the petty malice of a hostler to spoil his gratification.

"What a show," Bronco shouted, swinging down from the saddle and tossing reins to a hostler. "Right, hombre?" He slapped one of his stunt riders on the shoulder joyfully.

He let Longarm wait. He ordered his white gelding watered, walked, cooled, curried, covered with a blanket, and secured in its stall. There was a crust of rough camaraderie and joking, but underneath it was a thick and cold silence that spread out to where Longarm stood. The onlookers stayed tense, waiting for the moment when the top rider would finally notice the tall man standing patiently, waiting humbly for the star to notice him.

At last, when his animals and gear were secured, Bronco Bob stalked toward Longarm. He walked tall, the black hat slanted forward just slightly over his forehead, his sweat-matted, bleached curls hanging sodden to his shoulders. His face was streaked with dust and caked with mud, but Bronco Bob presented a beautiful picture and no one was anymore aware of it than the Shootin' Kid himself.

Bronco Bob was almost as tall as Longarm, but to himself and to his silent cohorts watching, Bob gave the impression that he loomed over the tall lawman. His eyes narrowed and his mouth thinned out. He paused, facing Longarm, and casually shook out makings into paper and rolled himself a smoke. He said, "You waitin' to talk to me, hombre?"

"Yes."

Bronco's tight eyes glinted. "Yes, what?"

Longarm kept his tongue out of his cheek, but even the vainly smiling Kid could see Longarm was anything but humble. "Yes, sir. Mr. Kiidislenco."

Bronco's head jerked up. "What is this here Kiidislenco?"

"Oh? That's not your name?"

"My name is Kidd." Bronco spelled it out. "I am American citizen. As much as you, maybe. More, maybe. I respect the flag. I protect womanhood. I have pass my citizenship test. My name is Robert Kidd." He tilted his head and gave Longarm a vain, cold smile. "You will call me Mr. Kidd." Then he took a long drag on his cigarette and exhaled a cloud of smoke in Longarm's face. "That is, you will call me Mr. Kidd—if you wish to talk to me—for as long as it pleases me to talk with you, hombre."

The onlookers nudged each other. Longarm suddenly realized this business of apology was going to be even tougher than he'd imagined. It would be as difficult as Bronco Bob Kidd wanted to make it.

He drew a deep breath. The hell with him. "What I have to say to you won't take long."

"You saw my performance in there?" Filled with his success, arrogant in his strength, Bronco demanded his due. "I was pretty good."

In a way he knew would infuriate Kidd, Longarm smiled thinly. "Yes. You were pretty good. In there."

"What does this mean, hombre?" Kidd's mud-flaked face

reddened. "I was damned good in there. Did you hear them cheer? Did you hear them yell? Did you see them standing up as I rode past?"

"I saw all that."

"And yet you—a nobody, a bum working as a hostler—you dare to say I was pretty good."

Now Longarm did thrust his tongue into his cheek. He could not resist the temptation. "I thought you *were* pretty good."

Bronco Bob clutched his fists tight, crushing his cigarette without even realizing he was doing it. "Do you say that I am less than the greatest? I am the best horseman, the best roper, the best gunman in the world. Even a stupid like you must see that."

Longarm nodded and kicked at a horse apple with his toe. "I'm sorry, Mr. Kidd. I better not say anything more. I've already stepped out of line with you once before."

"You sure as hell did. I could have killed you for yanking me off my horse."

"Yessir, I reckon you could. And I want to apologize. I didn't realize you were just having a little fun, giving the good old boys a laugh. I was afraid you would kill that poor helpless bastard. I'm sorry."

"Yeah. I reckon you ought to be. Sorry and thankful."

"Thankful, Mr. Kidd?"

"Thankful you are still alive. Thankful I let you live to apologize," Kidd said loudly enough so that all his silent, watching riders could hear.

Longarm nodded, taking this. He supposed Kidd had this much coming.

Longarm drew a deep breath. "All right," he said. "Now I've done it. You got my apology. We wipe the slate clean." He started to turn away.

Bronco stepped forward, caught Longarm's arm, and jerked him back around. "Don't you walk away from me, hombre. I'll let you know when I'm finished with you."

"I've said I'm sorry," Longarm said between his teeth. "Don't push it—*hombre*."

"I want to know what you thought of my work?"

"What do you care? I'm just a bum. All your paying customers loved you. Your riders bow and jump when you say froggy—what the hell you want from me?"

"I tell you goddamn it what I want. What I want from you. I want to know what was wrong with my show?"

"How the hell do I know?"

"You *don't* know." Bob's guttural voice lashed him, carrying across the field. "That's what I'm telling you. You don't know a goddamn thing. But you act like you're so high and mighty. Like you know something I don't know. I want to hear from you. What's wrong with my goddamn show?"

"Nothing."

Bronco's voice shook. "Either you tell me where I fail, or by damn you tell all my men that I am the greatest—the best you ever saw."

"Not by a country mile."

For a moment Bronco Bob Kidd was struck dumb. His face flushed red to the brim of his black hat. His clenched fists quivered at his sides.

"You don't like my shooting, eh? You saw me miss, eh? When did I miss, hombre? Tell me once that I missed."

"I ain't about to tell you any such thing," Longarm replied. "You couldn't very well miss. I've seen it done before, though, by a gent who called himself Colonel Comanche John. You might be able to fool all those folks, but you and I both know you ain't going to risk slinging forty-five-caliber bullets around in there—you hit some kid, and that'd fry your bacon good and proper. You got those sixguns loaded special with birdshot. The way it spreads out guarantees you won't miss, and even if you hit someone accidental, it won't do any damage that a payoff on the q.t. won't smooth over. Be a horse of a different color, though, was someone shootin' back at you."

Bronco looked as though he might erupt, but he didn't contradict Longarm, since of course everyone listening was in on the trick. "And my roping?" he persisted. "You have seen better, hombre? Six riders in one loop?"

Longarm drew a deep breath. "If you think I'm going to say you're better than a pretty good stunt roper and gun handler, we'll be here until Christmas, Mr. Kidd."

"You son of a bitch. You could do better?"

Longarm shrugged. "The place went wild for you. What do you care what I think?"

91

"Because I care. I want to know. You have not mentioned the horses. That's what rakes your coals, ain't it, hombre? The horses."

"I think you're a vicious son of a bitch when it comes to horses," Longarm said in the mildest tone he could manage.

The onlookers caught their breath, but Bronco Bob did not. He did not breathe. That the apology had degenerated into name-calling did not concern him. He had called Longarm a son of a bitch; Longarm had returned the compliment. Bronco knew the code of the West demanded reprisal for such an insult, but he was struck where he lived—in his vanity, his ego, his self-confidence. The world told him he was the greatest. This bastard stood insolently before him—in front of all his people—and told him he was a no-good with horses.

Bronco Bob's voice shook. "You could do better?"

"I just wouldn't do it. I wouldn't drive a poor, scared, wild pony into insanity and then rake his guts open and tear his mouth, just to make a lot of damn fools yell for me. So what the hell. Let it go at that."

Again, Longarm turned to walk away. This infuriated Bronco Bob beyond all limits of reason. "Goddamn you," he said, "you try to walk away from me one more time before I tell you, I'll kill you."

Longarm shrugged, and leaned against a corral upright. He calmly removed a cheroot from his pocket. He offered a small cigar to Bronco Bob, but the Shootin' Kid was too enraged to notice the gesture. Longarm's calm angered the man as much as his insults. More, because that air of calm carried with it the certainty of truth.

Longarm lighted the cheroot, drew on it, and waited, watching Bronco through the haze of smoke.

Bronco lowered his rasping voice. "You think I got no talent, huh, hombre?"

"I didn't say that."

Bronco didn't even hear him. "You think I got just the big head, huh, hombre?"

"I might have said that."

"Damn you. Goddamn you."

"If I didn't say it, I might of thought it." Longarm blew out a cloud of gray smoke. "My apologies, Mr. Kidd."

"Don't you try to be nice to me, you hombre bastard. You tell me I can't ride wild horses—"

"Hell, I never said that. I said you kill 'em. But who gives a shit? Your audience don't. Your riders don't. Marko's lions don't. You sure as hell don't."

"But you—you care, huh?"

Longarm shrugged. "You just don't prove nothing, riding a half-broke, half-crazed mustang, wearing spurs and a bit that cuts its mouth."

"You would do better?"

"If I couldn't, I wouldn't do it."

"Tell me, you smart-talk bastard, before I break your face—how would you do it?"

Longarm grinned coldly. "Before I advertised myself as the greatest wild horse rider in the world—even in Texas—I would try to *be* that."

"By God, I am. Before God I am."

"Then what are we arguing about?"

"You. I tell you this. You ride a horse wilder than I do—better than I do—and I kiss your bare ass on that midway."

His riders laughed at that and shoved each other.

Longarm exhaled a cloud of smoke. "I might just take you up on that, Kid. But new rules."

"You name the rules, you bastard hombre."

"Sure. You get the mustangs in. You leave 'em wild. You don't put any saddle on them—or half-break them—or touch them—until you bring them into that ring. Then you put on a light saddle, with no pommel to grab, and a single-rope rein, like the Apaches use."

"You stupid son."

"All right. Forget it." He grinned coldly. "Can I go now, Mr. Kidd?"

"No. You can't go—because by God I accept your challenge. On Wednesday we got fresh horses coming. We got Buffalo Bill Cody going to be in the audience. Buffalo Bill himself. Buffalo Bill is going to start a Western show and he wants me to join him, as a star rider. I put my whole career—my whole life—on the line, you smart-talk bastard hombre. We ride—rope bridle, first one to grab leather loses. Right, hombre?"

Longarm stared at the vain, handsome cowboy for a long moment, impressed despite himself. After a moment, he extended his hand. "I still think you are a son of a bitch, Kid, but you're a better grade son than I gave you credit for."

Bronco Bob Kidd stared at the extended hand a moment. Something happened in his face; he almost softened, almost smiled. Instead, he steeled himself and shook his head. "About this shaking hands, hombre. We'll see about that. On Wednesday. After *you* have kiss *my* ass—on the midway."

He roared with laughter suddenly, all the malice washed away. He had what he wanted: a contest, a chance to prove himself as he had done a hundred times before.

The blast of gunfire shattered the quiet around the corral. There was one shot, followed almost immediately by another. Then Cy Slimer came running around the main tent and across the torn-up ground.

Cy staggered, his arm extended. "Long!" he shouted. "Long. Mounted men. Six. Holding up Barac's pay wagon."

Cy's legs buckled under him and he fell. Longarm ran to him. There was a bullet hole in Cy's side, and a bad slash along his thigh. He had taken both bullets. He whispered. "They warned everybody to stand still. I ran . . . one of them chased me on his horse . . . shot me."

"Get a doctor!" Longarm yelled. Bronco Bob repeated the order and a youthful hostler jumped on a pony and rode fast across the field toward the town.

"There's gunmen mounted on horses out there, men," Bronco shouted. "Three of you fellows go left, three to the right, three take the front gate. Old hombre-bastard here and me will go in from back here." He jerked his head around, his gaze insolent. "Unless you ain't got the guts, Long."

"I better warn you—those are real bullets in their guns," Longarm said.

"So are these, hombre." Bronco threw open a chest, grabbed up a revolver, and threw it toward Longarm. "Let's go have some fun, bigmouth."

Chapter 8

Longarm caught the pistol and stood for a moment in the thick dust that clouded the corral and swept across them, motes of dust glinting in the sunlight. Three men knelt over Cy Slimer. Longarm warned them not to try to move Cy until the doctor came. Then he turned around, finding Bronco Bob at the hitching rail.

Bronco Bob jerked up the lines and swung into the saddle of the nearest horse. He jerked its head around and then hesitated, glancing toward Longarm. "You comin', bigmouth?"

Longarm laughed at him, striding toward the string of ponies lining the railing. "You're in such an all-fired hurry to get killed, you go ahead and start without me, *hombre*."

Bronco Bob waited only until Longarm had swung up into the saddle. Then he spurred his horse, riding between the tents and guy ropes toward the midway.

As Longarm rode behind Bronco Bob, his gun at his side, something flashed through his mind. It wheeled and buzzed there like a hornet for a moment before he could isolate it in the chaos and dust. It was something about Black Lake, the Black Lake country. Abruptly, it hit him. Texas Bill Wirt's gang was supposed to be holing up in the Black Lake country. He had followed them up this way, getting all the way to Eldorado Valley before that unknown youngster ambushed him and bought Wirt and his men time to elude him. He yelled, "Hey, Kid. Hold it up a minute."

Impatiently, the Shootin' Kid reined in between the tents and turned in the saddle. "You tryin' to give them a chance to get away, hombre?"

"I'm tryin' to keep you from gettin' your fool head blown

off. I figure that might be Texas Bill Wirt and his gang hitting the pay wagon, and—"

"Texas Bill Wirt? Who is this Texas Bill Wirt?" Bronco looked ready to spur his pony forward.

"Railroad and bank holdup men. They never pull a job that they don't stake it out with hidden lookouts. Texas Bill has his own way of mapping out these jobs. And like you, he's pretty good at what he does."

Bronco laughed savagely. "But not the greatest, eh?"

"Not the greatest," Longarm agreed. "Let's ride easy to the end of this here tent and take a look-see. Ain't a damn bit of sense in ridin' into a crossfire—not if we can help it."

"I'll drink with you at that," Bronco said.

"Good. That's a sensible old Texas saying," Longarm said.

"It is?" Bronco grinned, pleased.

They eased to the brink of sunlight at the edge of the midway. They could see all the way to the entrance of the circus park.

There was nothing reassuring in what lay before them. "Looks like a Texas Bill Wirt job, all right," Longarm whispered.

"You just find me an ambusher and don't palaver so much, hombre."

Longarm grinned in spite of himself. Either Bronco Bob had the kind of foolhardy courage that characterized his compatriot Marko Begovic, or he was a kid looking for excitement—and shooting was a game, even with real bullets and real outlaws shooting back at you. It was hard to tell about the Shootin' Kid.

"You stand steady a moment, mister. Let me get a look at this. I got one skin, I want to take care of it."

Bronco stared at him pityingly, holding the reins tightly, ready to release them and spur his horse into that open midway.

To Longarm, it looked like a no-man's-land. As far as he could see, six riders had taken over. There was no way of knowing how many were hidden, standing back in reserve, the way Bill Wirt worked his armed robberies.

All the circus customers—those stragglers, who had not yet departed the premises after Bronco Bob's Wild West exhibition—had been forced to lie down in the dust, with their arms and legs outspread. This was a Texas Bill Wirt trademark. He

96

made witnesses lie with their faces in the dirt, and the first one fool enough to lift his head got it shot off. It made a lot of sense too. It took extra seconds for a man to pull his legs in and brace his arms to rise from a prostrate position, and sometimes seconds meant the difference between a successful and a failed operation.

This flashed through Longarm's mind too swiftly even to be considered a rational thought. The ideas rattled inside his head as he searched for hidden gunmen, or for any riders in ambush.

Two horses were ground-tied outside the open door of Barac's pay wagon. This meant they had made it in time. Two of Wirt's men were inside the wagon. The others, with shotguns across their arms, were lined up along the midway, alert and wary.

"See any hiders-out?" Bronco whispered.

"If they're there, they're hidden," Longarm said. "Your men are ready to come in behind them anyway. Pick yourself a target, Mr. Kidd—and let's ride out there."

Before Bronco could move to spur his horse, the two robbers dashed out of the door of Barac's brightly painted wagon. The one in front didn't bother with the metal steps. He leaped outward, carrying pouches across his shoulder and a sixgun in his hand. The second thug scrambled out behind him. They had made a haul that would equal the best of Texas Bill Wirt's takes.

"Get them hombres!" Bronco yelled, spurring his horse and leaping out of the shelter of the tents.

For a moment the outlaws seemed to freeze, staring at Bronco Bob and Longarm riding, guns ablaze, into the sun-struck midway. People on the ground leaped up to their knees and crawled under the nearest protection.

Riding directly toward Barac's pay wagon, Bronco Bob leaned forward against his horse's mane. Longarm swore. The bastard made one hell of an impressive-looking rider racing to the rescue. Bronco fired, exactly as he might in the circus arena, on the run. And he was as accurate as he had been there, even with real bullets.

The biggest of the two men carrying the money pouches threw his pouch over the rump of his horse and then grabbed at the reins.

That was when Bronco shot him. The big man went dancing and sprawling back from his spooked horse.

From every side, guns firing, Bronco's men rode into the midway. Bill Wirt's men panicked. Whatever contingencies Wirt had prepared them for, this was not one of them.

The riders holding the people at bay spurred their horses between the tents, making for open country. They rode low to their horses, faces buried in manes, and they trampled anything in their paths.

Longarm fired at the fleeing targets. He hoped he could just wound one of them; a winged outlaw could be made to talk—about Bill Wirt and whatever in hell Wirt was doing up here in Colorado.

Suddenly his gun's hammer clicked on an empty chamber—and clicked again. He stood in the middle of the midway, unarmed.

He saw Bronco Bob still riding in on the robbers at the pay wagon. The Shootin' Kid was a man with one thought on his mind. The big outlaw was sprawled on the ground. Bronco put another bullet into him. The owlhoot shuddered and sprawled forward. Longarm didn't have to count pulses to know the robber was dead.

The others had broken and run, with Bronco's men in pursuit. The only one left in sight was directly in front of Bronco Bob and as good as dead. He was a small, thin man, in Mexican sombrero and leather chaps. He seemed to be calm, but he was unwilling to release either his gun or the pouch of money bags, and he was fighting to mount his frightened horse.

Bronco straightened in his saddle and yelled at the Mexican, but the little man didn't even bother to look up at him.

Longarm yelled, "Bronco! Kid! Don't!"

But he may as well have been talking to himself. The Mexican finally was able to shove his boot into a stirrup. He had just swung himself upward toward his saddle, his right leg hoisted high in the air.

Bronco fired and fired again. He could have saved the second bullet. His first struck the Mexican in the middle of his chest and the little thug died in that instant. But for a moment his body went on fighting to escape. With the horse bucking, he hung for a frozen instant in time, his leg up, his grimy fist gripping the pommel and clutching at gun and money pouches, then he fell back into the sawdust and his horse galloped off.

Bronco took a satisfied leer at his handiwork, then he gave a banshee yell and rode off like a Comanche after his men.

"Longarm!"

Longarm tensed as though someone had shot at him, instead of calling him by a name unknown in this circus.

He swung down from his horse, looking around. Across the runway, near the freaks' tent, he saw a riderless horse, reins dragging in the sawdust.

Holding his useless gun at his side, Longarm looked around.

"Longarm!" the voice shouted again. That voice was somehow familiar, a raging baritone that he had heard somewhere before, and pitched low in the diaphragm to give it a ring of authority. "I'm over here, Longarm."

Longarm turned around in the midway. He saw the boy then, and in that moment recognized Jesse Cole. Unarmed people stood, repelled, fascinated, cowed in the shadows.

Jesse Cole was wedged between the open-topped ticket booth and the heavy framing of the stage outside the freaks' blue tent. Cole had put his back to the planking so no one could come in behind him. He could have ridden away with the others of the Bill Wirt gang, but he must have seen Longarm ride out from between those tents.

"What are you doing here, boy?" Longarm said.

Jesse crouched low. He held his revolver extended before him in both hands, taking no chances on missing this time.

"Come to kill you. Just like I said that day in Denver. Joined up with ol' Bill Wirt. I seen you, and I recognized you. And I waited—'cause you're what I come for. I come all this way to kill you, law-dog—and this time I don't miss."

"You still ain't smart," Longarm taunted. "You should've shot at me and run, Cole."

"Oh, no. I wanted you to see me, law-dog. I wanted you to know when you got to hell that it was me—me, Jesse Cole—that sent you there."

The gun trembled, coming up slightly in Jesse Cole's clenched fists. Longarm almost felt he could see the boy's finger tightening on that trigger.

Suddenly the blast of gunfire broke the stillness. But the sound came from the tent flap behind Jesse Cole.

Struck in the back, the gunman pitched forward into the

sawdust, on his face. His gun went flying through the air under the impact of the bullet that knocked Jesse off his feet.

Longarm strode across the open midway and took up Jesse's pistol. Then he walked to where Jesse lay, facedown. The boy was dead. Longarm turned him over and hunkered there, staring at the youthful face, the tousled hair, the dirty fingernails, the letter jutting from his pocket. These damned punk kids. You gave them a second chance, and they used it, all right, trying one more time to kill you.

He lifted his gaze and found Wee Vingie Vinson standing in a pale blue gown on the center of the stage. She held a revolver in both her hands. With the little beauty holding it, the gun looked like a howitzer.

"You saved my life," Longarm said.

She smiled. "And I was right about you. You are a lawman. *Longarm*. The long arm of the law . . ."

"I can't ever thank you," Longarm said.

She laughed. "Oh, I think you can. We'll work out something. But what you can't do is change the subject. I knew all along. You are a lawman."

Longarm straightened in the street as people came out of hiding. They crowded around him. Damn that Jesse Cole. He hadn't killed him, but he had sure hell blown his cover.

Barac staggered out of his wagon. Blood leaked from a savage gash in his forehead. His thick hair was matted with blood. He was beaten, bruised, and bleeding. Barac had been hit where he lived. He had put up one hell of a fight for the only thing on earth he would fight for—his money.

Barac leaned against the doorjamb. He squinted his near-sighted eyes and warily came down the metal steps.

Longarm and Vingie crossed the midway to where Barac wavered like a great and rootless old oak. He was barely conscious after the brutal pistol-whipping he'd absorbed.

"Barac," Vingie said. "Josip. Are you all right?"

The thickset man was barely aware of the curious onlookers crowding around them. He had not yet seen the riderless horse, or the two men sprawled dead in the sawdust near his wagon.

"They got my goddamn money," Barac said. His groan sounded as much like a growl. "They got all my money."

Longarm gathered up the saddle pouches stuffed with cloth money bags. He held them for a moment where the nearsighted, bloody man could see them. Then he tossed them through the open door to the wagon floor.

"The money is there, Barac," he said. "Your money is all right. You can thank Bronco Bob for that."

The onlookers standing in a circle around them cheered and cried out, applauding as if all this were part of Bronco Bob's act. Longarm grinned helplessly. Hell, maybe it was.

As if the applause of the farmers were the cue Bronco Bob Kidd had been awaiting in the wings, he suddenly appeared, coming through the lantern-hung front entrance at the head of his riders.

Longarm shook his head in admiration. The Kid was a showman to his toenails. It was almost as if the scurvy circus band were unseen somewhere playing a fanfare for Kidd.

Bronco and his riders came along the midway. In his white hat, his blond hair slapping like a mane in the wind, the Kid rode like Caesar at the head of his conquering legions.

A cheer went up from the people gathered along the tents. Even the show people applauded. They were out en masse now, as if to pay homage to the returning hero.

Bronco Bob took the cheering as his due. His head tilted, he sat straighter in his saddle, and even the pony he rode appeared to prance haughtily.

Bronco rode close to where Longarm and Vingie stood with the pistol-whipped circus owner. Bronco swung down from the saddle. With a grin of satisfaction and his chest outthrust smartly, he checked the two dead outlaws. "Well, these hombres won't rob no more honest folks," he announced. And everybody cheered.

Bronco turned and raked Longarm with his glance. "Well, hombre, what do you say now? Am I not the greatest? You ready to kiss my bare ass in front of all these people?"

Longarm grinned. "You're good at what you do all right, Kid."

Bronco laughed at him. "How many did you get, hombre? I count two that I cut down with my flaming sixguns. They were the hombres with the stolen money—money they can't spend in hell."

Longarm exhaled heavily. Bronco sounded exactly like something right out of the pages of Ned Buntline. "Buffalo Bill Cody is going to love you," was all he said.

"You damn better believe it," the Shootin' Kid said. "I reckon even you got to admit Bronco Bob is pretty good—and better than pretty good."

Barac shook himself and swung a bloody arm, indicating Longarm. "This fellow is a goddamn lawman."

Bronco Bob sucked in a deep breath. His mouth thinned out and his wild eyes narrowed. "Son of a bitch," was all he said. He stared at Longarm for another moment, shrugged, and then turned and walked away. His riders followed.

Longarm found Cy Slimer on a cot in the first-aid tent, where he had been moved on a stretcher. A doctor was with him.

Cy looked as if he were asleep. His face was tortured with pain and he whimpered involuntarily. "Will he make it, doc?" Longarm said.

The doctor stood up. He was a tall, slender man—almost six feet tall, but spare and lean, with the look of the totally exhausted, overworked man. His sun-faded blue eyes were tired, the corners of his wide-lipped mouth drooped down, his wide thin shoulders sagged. He looked as though the act of speaking required more energy than was left to him. "I'm from Black Lake," he said in a gray, tired voice. "Name of Lawson Bennett. Dr. Bennett."

"Good to know you, Dr. Bennett. It was neighborly of you to come out when we needed you."

The fatigued man smiled. "It's all right," he said. "Folks here have been nice. They gave me a pass—good for my whole family—for any show."

Longarm smiled, liking the aging medic. "Well, you can't hardly beat that," he said.

"That's what I told them," Dr. Bennett said. He nodded toward Slimer, asleep on the cot. "I figure he'll pull through. Nothing vital hit by that bullet, and I was able to get it out in one piece. Gave him some laudanum. For the pain. Help him sleep. With enough rest, he ought to make it."

Longarm grinned, thanking him. "With some rest, I figure *you* might make it too, doc."

The doctor yawned helplessly. "No chance for me to get that kind of rest, friend."

Longarm turned to leave the first-aid tent. Minerva entered as he reached the door. The tattooed girl's face went taut and

102

she turned quickly away rather than face him.

Longarm shrugged and walked out of the tent into the waning afternoon sunlight. Minerva's avoiding him had nothing to do with Vingie's orders for him to stay away from her. He saw contempt in her face. He was the law to her now, and like most of the show people, she despised the law.

He walked back along the midway, feeling a sense of isolation that was sharper and more clearly defined than when he'd joined the show in Medicine Run. Then, he'd been only a stranger regarded with suspicion like every stranger. Now he was hated.

Exhaling heavily, Longarm turned between two closely staked tents, heading for the male freaks' tent.

Suddenly a scarred fist, as big as a ham, reached out from a tent flap and caught his arm. He stared at that hand, remembering he had seen it somewhere before.

"Hold it, lawman," a gravelly voice said from the darkened tent. "I want to parley with you a minute."

The man pushed the tent flap back. It was the circus cook. Startled, Longarm stared again at that battered hand grasping his arm.

"You," Longarm said. "You were dressed up in that clown face."

The cook looked shamefaced. "That's what I wanted to talk to you about. I'm sorry what I did—the gun in your face and all."

Longarm had some difficulty concealing his astonishment.

"I didn't know you were a lawman," the cook went on. "I mean—they told me to try to scare you away. That's all it was. I swear. I had nothing against you then. I got nothing against you now. I didn't mean to hurt you. I just meant to scare you out. I was just following orders, that was all."

"Sure," Longarm said evenly. "A lot of that going around."

Chapter 9

Longarm shook his head at the big cook and tried to smile.
"We all got our problems," he said. "It doesn't matter."

"I want no trouble with the law."

"If you mean me, you got none."

The cook caught Longarm's hand in both of his own and
wrung it passionately. Longarm withdrew and walked tiredly
toward the male freaks' tent. There was no chance that he
could hide his identity any longer. That meant there was no
chance to find any anarchists among the circus people. His
cover was blown; nobody wanted to come near him, much less
confide in him. It looked as though, as far as carrying out the
job he had come here to do, he was finished, up that well-
known creek without a paddle.

He walked into the tent and struck a wall of silence that
was almost tangible. The male freaks didn't speak to him or
look directly at him. He was back where he had started with
these people—a non-person. He didn't exist. Not in their
world. They wouldn't let him. It was bitterly comical that he
occupied the leper's bed, only he didn't feel like laughing.

They stepped aside when he passed, but they didn't look
at him. Only Ljubo suffered an anguished conscience. Ljubo's
problem was that if he treated Longarm civilly, he himself
would be ostracized too, by his fellow freaks. And the freaks
didn't have that many friends. Still, Ljubo was at war inside
himself. Longarm had saved his life, been kind to him, and
the poor Giraffe Man could not forget his debt to his outsider
friend, even if he had been revealed as part of the hated and
oppressive law of the outside world.

Ljubo waddled like an ungainly ostrich along the row of
cots. He stood gazing down at Longarm, who had sat down

on his mattress. Ljubo tried to smile. "It is more than you saved my life, Mr. Long. I can never forget that. Never repay you."

"It's all right, Ljubo. You owe me nothing."

"That's not it. It is not owe. I have liked you. From the very first. You must admit that I was not like the others. I smiled and spoke to you from the first. Almost from the first, eh?"

"I appreciated it, Ljubo."

"No. What I try to say, I wanted you to be my friend. You see?" Ljubo looked wounded, as if Longarm had somehow betrayed him.

"I didn't mean to hide from you who I was," Longarm said. He smiled. "I just had a job to do, Ljubo. I couldn't tell anybody."

Ljubo nodded. "That's it, my friend. I understand. I do not hold it against you that you hid your identity." He shook his small head atop his long, thin body. "If we did that here, we would hate everybody—almost everybody. We all hide something in this place. Sometimes our true identity is the least of our secrets. No. That you were not what you seemed does not distress me. That is a way of life here."

"It's all right."

"No. It is not all right. Not all right at all. These people all hide something. Sometimes much more sinister than that one is a . . . a policeman. What hurts is that if I am your friend, I am alone against all these people I must live with."

Longarm nodded. He smiled up at the human skeleton. "I wouldn't want that, Ljubo."

"It cannot be helped. It is a fact."

"I think it *can* be helped. You must live and work among these people. You want to be my friend, and I want you to be my friend, Ljubo. But I want you to be as happy here as you can be. I think we can be friends. Like secret friends, eh? Everybody else has secrets here, that will be ours. We'll be secret friends. Nobody needs to know."

Ljubo hesitated a long time, as if the idea had to crawl slowly up his elongated frame to the top of his head and simmer there for some moments. At last he broke into a smile. He nodded. "That will work," he said. "We will do that. You are a good man, Mr. Long, in your heart."

Longarm grinned crookedly and extended a hand. "My friends call me Longarm," he said.

Longarm toppled back on his cot. He heard the movement inside the tent around him as the freaks gradually resumed talking to each other, going about their interrupted lives. From somewhere, a calliope played. A distant lion roared, horses whinnied in the corral, and a sudden burst of mindless laughter shattered the silence, and was abruptly stilled.

With his hands locked under his head, Longarm stared at the musty roofing of the tent and tried to figure his next move. He should wire Billy Vail at once. The chief marshal in Denver would likely—hell, would *absolutely*—want him out of here and off the case. A state visitor's life was endangered. Time was vital. They needed somebody here who could show results fast. This was no longer Custis Long. But he didn't want to go yet, there was too much unfinished business, too much that troubled him. How could he just walk away and leave all these questions unanswered—even the matter of the threat to Vingie Vinson's life? Nobody else took her seriously, but he did. And now he owed her something. She had saved his life out there by gunning down Jesse Cole. Vingie Vinson had begged him to help her; how could he just walk away from her? Still, staying here like this—unable to do his job—he was obstructing any useful investigation. As much as anyone, he was endangering the life of Princess Danica, the woman he'd been assigned to protect.

He exhaled heavily. His job came first, his obligations and responsibilities as a deputy marshal. Common sense told him to send a report to Billy Vail and allow himself to be removed from the case.

He made up his mind. He would walk into Black Lake township and wire Billy Vail a report on the Texas Bill Wirt raid on Barac's pay wagon and on the fact of his own blown cover.

He was weary; his eyes burned and he shut them. He became aware of a taut silence that spread from the front of the tent, like molasses, seeping back over him like a chill.

He opened his eyes. A beautiful young woman bent over his cot. Her eyes were a gypsy ebony, her thin brows arched, her features elegantly cut, a beauty he had seen somewhere and yet could not place. Then he saw the tutu and remembered: she was Marko Begovic's assistant in his lion act. She never went into the cage, but she kept things moving outside it.

"Hello," he said just as she reached out to shake his shoulder.

She jumped, startled, and then caught herself, smiling at him. "I am Lisa," she said in a low, accented Middle European voice.

Longarm grinned. "You certainly are."

She frowned, puzzled, and then smiled. "You make a joke? No?"

"No." He smiled again, trying to put her at ease. "I was never more serious."

She frowned again, puzzled. "You mean you know I am Lisa, Mr. Marko Begovic's assistant? But how could you know this?"

"I've seen you, Lisa. A man sees you, he doesn't soon forget. You're prettier than Begovic's lions. In fact, you're even prettier than Begovic."

She blushed prettily and smiled. "I am come with a message from Mr. Marko Begovic. A most important message, please."

Longarm sat up and swung his legs off the cot. He was more than startled; he couldn't believe his own ears.

"Mr. Marko Begovic wants to see you," Lisa said. "At your convenience."

Longarm smiled. "That means right now, I reckon."

Lisa smiled and sighed, relieved. "That would be most courteous. What is the old saying? 'There is no time like this present now'?"

"I don't know that one," Longarm said. "I'm still working on the one about an apple a day. . . ."

Longarm entered the gypsy caravan wagon that Marko Begovic called home. Lisa held the front door open for him, and then, at a signal from Begovic, she retreated from the vehicle and closed the door behind her.

Begovic stood tall in the confining quarters of his living room. He seemed to have surrounded himself with old, heavy, and clumsy heirlooms from some half-forgotten past. He was dressed in his red leotard, wide, silver-buckled belt, and glittering boots, ready for his evening performance. He seemed to find it necessary to apologize for his appearance. "I have but one life anymore, Mr. . . . . Mr. Long? That life is my great cats. Between my performances in that center ring I do not live—I merely exist. I now live only for those moments with my great cats."

"You put on an exciting show, Mr. Begovic."

The lion-tamer nodded, then gestured in a sharp, back-handed motion, as if striking big cats across the nose with a short whip. It was the same gesture with which he had dismissed his assistant a moment earlier.

Begovic had that classic handsomeness even up close. The glamour that one saw in his distinguished figure in the center ring glowed around him in his wagon. That graying blond hair was so carefully trimmed and brushed in layers upon his well-shaped skull that it looked unreal, but it was genuine. With his finely chiseled profile, he seemed something sculptured. He said, "Yes. I do have a act that is better than ordinary. It is not yet what I want, but someday perhaps I will succeed in a dream of mine."

"A dream?"

"Yes. Someday, perhaps, trainers like myself will dare to work lions and tigers in the same cage."

"Why in hell would they want to do that?"

"Because that is the ultimate test of skill and courage, Mr. Long. Nobody dares to try it. It is too dangerous. But I shall do it. I shall be the first. That is my ultimate ambition." He made that backhanded gesture again.

"I don't think you need to—I've never seen anyone handle lions the way you do."

"It is not merely a need, Mr. Long. It is a drive, an ambition, a compulsion. It is—how you say—an obsession with me."

Longarm tried to smile. "Seems a mite like suicide to me."

"I can think of no better way for a man like me to die, Mr. Long. It is the only dream I have left."

Longarm shook his head. "Well, it's your lion act. And your life. But it looks to me like you're one of the top performers with big cats. Why not go with success? I know you don't want my advice, but I'd just keep those lions doped and—"

"Doped?" That cutting backhanded gesture again. "Do you believe, Mr. Long, that my beautiful young animals are doped? Is that the way you think I handle them?"

Longarm spread his hands. "I have no wish to offend you, sir. I know nothing about it. It just seemed common sense to me. I'd like lions very doped up if I was alone in a cage with them, without even a handgun."

"A handgun..." Begovic's handsome mouth twisted. "A handgun is no good against a huge lion, Mr. Long. Handguns are used for the noise they make. Some trainers believe they can control the lions by scaring them with the gun-blast in their faces... I find I can crack my whip as loudly and effectively. But... drugged? No. Never, Mr. Long. Perhaps some men may work with such animals. But if they do, they are not worthy of the name of animal trainers.... And as for me, I would never knowingly get in a cage with drugged lions. Cats that are doped can be dangerous without even knowing they are dangerous. They cannot follow orders, or they misunderstand—or simply become wild in a different, uncontrolled way. A doped cat can be far more dangerous than an alert, well-fed animal which has learned two things: trust—as far as it is possible for his instincts to learn trust; and fear—as long as he can remember to be afraid. Those, Mr. Long, are your tools. Your *only* tools in that ring. Either they are enough for you—or they are nothing. That's why I believe one could work as well with lions *and* tigers. Fear and trust. Tigers can be taught this as well as lions."

"I admire you for the work you do," Longarm said. "I admire any man who's the best at his trade—whatever it is."

"Devotion and dedication, Mr. Long. Those are the qualities a man must bring to his... trade. I am sure that's what you have brought to your own career as a lawman."

Longarm chewed at his underlip, finding another ironic twist in the fact that he had come here to invesitgate Marko Begovic, and while he had learned nothing about the lion man except that he was a genius in his profession, Begovic knew his secret.

"I do the best I can," Longarm said. "Sometimes—like on this job—my best wasn't all that great."

"You and our friend Bronco Bob Kidd—you put on as

excellent a show on that midway this afternoon as I ever saw in a circus ring . . . or in a theater. Drama. Conflict. Excitement. Death. Movement."

"Kidd is a good rider and marksman—a hell of a showman."

"Yes. A friend of mine. A good friend, because we respect one the other—in our work."

Longarm said nothing, not sure where this was leading. Obviously, Marko had had some reason for sending for him. Begovic had not summoned him to discuss lions, even though the big cats were the man's entire existence.

Begovic strode back and forth in the small room, as if it were a confining cage, far too small for him. At last he turned, made his characteristic gesture, and said, "What would you say, Mr. Long, if I told you that I planned to use lions and tigers together—for the first time—at the reception for the Princess Danica of Hungary in Golden, Colorado, at the estate of Governor Loving?"

"Jesus . . ." Longarm whispered.

Begovic gave Longarm a strange, puzzling smile. He nodded, as if he were somehow pleased by the lawman's reply. "That is what I thought you would say."

Longarm gazed up at Begovic and waited.

The distinguished-looking man sighed. "For a long time I have been expecting you," he said.

"Me?"

"A man from the law. In my own country, I can tell you, the national law enforcement would have closed in upon me long ago. You see, I know that my reputation—my past—has followed me here to this country, no matter how hard I tried to hide it."

"Your reputation?"

"Don't play cat-and-mouse games with me, Mr. Long. If we are to respect one another, let us begin by being honest. I am trying to be honest with you."

Longarm spread his hands, completely stunned by this turn of events. "Go ahead. I reckon it's only fair that we lay all our cards on the table."

"Thank you. I may as well tell you, I believe that you came to this show—and joined it incognito—because of me. I could expect no less. If I were in the place of your superiors, I would behave no differently toward a man with my reputation, my

111

past, my . . . police record. You admit you know I have a police record in the old country—in my homeland?"

"I know about it."

Begovic sighed heavily. "I am glad that it is almost over."

"*Is* it almost over?"

"That will be up to you—after you hear what I have to say. I hope that you will do me the kindness to listen to what I have to say, though I admit I have no right to ask it. It is your decision to make."

"You invited me here," was all Longarm said.

"Thank you. I hope what I have to say will not bore you. I assure you it is most important to me—and to you, as a lawman seeking the truth about me. And I vow to you that what I say will be as near the truth as I can make it. I will not—at this moment, and in this place—consciously lie to you. The Marko Begovic you are looking for is dead."

"What?"

"Oh. *I* am alive. I am the man who was once a radical student in Buda, before it was united with Pest. A long time ago. I am the man with the criminal record as an anarchist, an enemy of the crown. But the young man—the mind who behaved as I did in those years—is quite dead. I can only say to you, sir, that whatever differences there are between what I am, standing here in America, and what I was when running with the starving radicals in the streets of Buda, are the differences between two men who are strangers one to the other.

"I have no desire to confuse you. I am only trying to say that, whatever mistakes a man makes when he is young, impressionable, hungry, idealistic, driven, he can grow inside. He can change in his heart and in his mind. That is why I say to you, the person I used to be is only a distant and hardly known relative from my past as I stand here. I can tell you, I could have been the featured performer in the circus of Phineas T. Barnum. He offered me the sun and the stars, and piles of gold coins. But I refused because I was afraid to come that far out into the sunlight.

"I know now that I must come out. All the way out. Either you must believe what I tell you, or you must arrest me. I understand that."

Longarm tried to smile. "I ain't quite sure I understand what

112

you are trying to tell me. You are guilty, but you are not guilty. Is that it?"

"Not quite. Am I guilty of the crimes listed in my police dossier of my youth in Hungary? Yes. Most of them. But am I the danger I was to the crown—to Emperor Franz Josef and his family? No. Absolutely, I am not. That is what I am really trying to say." Begovic gave a wry smile. "But of course, any criminal would say as much, eh?"

"I've heard some weird stories in my time."

"Then I shall try to tell you a plain and unadulterated one. Let me go back to my youth in my homeland—before my name was Marko Begovic. Yes, I took the name Marko Begovic from my circus mentor, my teacher, the man who taught me first to respect and handle and then to love the great cats. His lions went berserk. I do not to this day know why. Perhaps for all wild things in captivity, there comes that moment when they can no longer cope—they simply go insane. Perhaps that day will come to me, as it did to the first Marko Begovic, back in Buda.

"But even now, I get ahead of my story. I was born on a farm—the place is undoubtedly listed in the police dossier. My childhood was unhappy only because it was so desperately poor. We lived in grinding poverty. My mother wanted me to escape the rigors of such an ugly life. I can tell you, I wanted to escape. I managed to go to Buda, to the university. As a student I studied to be a veterinarian. I still believed I would return to my native province in Croatia and work among my people, and among the animals I had always loved. But I continued to be hungry, going sometimes for days with nothing to eat, while I tried to work at any job I could find, and while I tried to study. And more often than not I was unable to pay even my lab fees, or for new soles for my shoes.

"I saw, on my empty stomach, the great gulf between people like me and the very rich. The wealthy had everything and they would share nothing. Not even crumbs. There was a radical leader named Deak, and I followed him, along with hundreds of other hungry, idealistic young students. We did not want revolution so much as a full meal. We wanted a democratic-socialistic government—a government where the poor had some chance, and where some of the unequal wealth

113

was shared. We marched in protests, we broke windows, and we swarmed in mobs in the squares. The followers of Deak joined with the disciples of the far more radical Kalman Tiszar to form the great but powerless Liberal Party. That is when we found that bombs were weapons that the wealthy and the influential and the authorities all feared. That is when the crisis climaxed in the bombing death of the nephew of Emperor Franz Josef. I was there in the mob when the Grand Duke Bojdan Kerenski-Cata Cuzane was assassinated—killed by a terrorist bomb.

"I had a police record. I was not a bombing terrorist. But I belonged to them. I hid out. I finally escaped the country, and eventually came here to America under my new name, Marko Begovic.

"Over these years, much has changed in poor, bloody, starving Hungary. Many of those wrongs we fought as student rebels at the time of the assassination of Grand Duke Bojdan have been redressed by the Emperor Franz Josef. Commerce and industry have increased in the country. New railway lines crisscross the kingdom. A new state of prosperity exists. The cities of Buda and Pest were united seven or eight years ago. There have been great strides in wealth among the deprived, in science, and in the arts. It is not yet heaven; I would not have you believe I think it is finally paradise. It is not. But the country has changed over these many, many years. And I have changed."

"And yet you had a police record and you have been expecting to be arrested and returned to Hungary?" Longarm asked.

Begovic shrugged. "I have no great guilt. I did not plant the bomb. I among hundreds of others knew it would be there, but that was all. That was the extent of my guilt. No. It was when we heard that Princess Danica was coming to America that I knew Hungarian nationals would be rounded up and questioned—and detained—if they had anarchist police records."

Longarm sighed. "You've just about stated the case against you, Mr. Begovic. It seems the State Department has no capital offenses against you—but there is the matter of your being an active member of the old radical parties—and you said yourself

114

that you knew, before the fact, about the assassination of Princess Danica's uncle, the Grand Duke."

"Yes. And I anticipated the discovery, and I was quite resigned to that. I have lived free for many years. But then, because I have created something of a sensation as a handler of African lions, I was invited by Governor Loving's staff to appear before Princess Danica at the reception the governor is giving for her at his mansion in Golden. It is quite an honor. As a Hungarian I feel a great pride, a great desire to perform for the princess.

"You see, Mr. Long, I now revere the Emperor Franz Josef. And I respect his family as the rulers of my native country. And I admire him for what he has done for my poor, broken, fragmented country. I am through with hate. I have long been through with hate—which, in my country, was another word for politics. I have no politics anymore, Mr. Long. I will swear to this. I have now only my career. I care only for my animals. It has been like this for a long time. I no longer have any guilt. I now have only one desire, one wish, one obsessive drive, and that is why I asked you here. I want with all my heart to be allowed to perform in Golden for the Princess Danica.

"I hope you can understand my grand desire to do this. The Emperor Franz Josef has accomplished much for our native land. But he is not alone in having made something of himself. I, too, have achieved to a high place. I want to display to the world that I, Marko Begovic of old Buda, too have climbed high with no more than my own talents.

"Perhaps you will understand some of the greatness of the honor being shown me by featuring me at this great state reception for the Princess Danica. Only two people from this circus—from any circus—will be asked by the governor to perform at the Princess Danica's party in Golden."

"And the other performer?"

"My great and longtime friend Kiidislenco—Bob Kidd, or Bronco Bob. We both are being accorded this great honor of entertaining her highness, Princess Danica. In my heart, I must tell you that I feel that I am the more honored by this unique opportunity. Bob Kidd represents something uniquely and totally American—the cowboy. This is something the governor and his people would naturally want to display before the prin-

115

cess. In choosing Bob Kidd, I agree they have chosen the best. But there were many other acts for their choosing, other than that of handling the great cats. But my act was chosen—*I* was chosen, Mr. Long.

"That is why I plan such a thrilling climax for my command performance before Princess Danica. It is there, Mr. Long, that I will, for the very first time, present an act using both lions and tigers, in the same cage, at the same time. They are so honoring me that I wish to honor them by giving them the performance they have never seen—nor dreamed of—before.

"You can understand now, perhaps, a little of how much this appearance in Golden before the Princess Danica would mean to me?"

"I can see that, right enough. But I haven't the authority— even if I take what you say as true—I haven't the authority to agree to your appearing there, or even being allowed within twenty miles."

Marko Begovic looked ill. "Where would I get this permit?"

"I don't know. I reckon from the State Department. I can turn in my report, based on what you have told me, about all these years in which you have taken no part in anarchist movements. But even then, I don't know."

"Is there not some way I might convince them of my honesty, of my sincerity?"

Longarm sat for some moments in silence. "Like I said, I can't speak for the chief marshal, or for the State Department. But I can tell you this. The State Department badly wants to know any names of people who might endanger Princess Danica. If you agreed to give them any such names, and cooperate in any way they ask, they might give you the permit to appear at the reception."

"I have no politics anymore," Marko Begovic whispered. "Informing—that was the way one bought freedom of sorts in the old country, under evil regimes. I don't know. . . ."

"I'm sorry. It's just that I know they'd want your complete cooperation before they'd consider cooperating with you, Mr. Begovic. There are two sides to this thing. All the government is thinking about is the safety of a state guest—Princess Danica."

"I understand that."

Longarm stood up. "Like I said, I can't promise anything,

because I don't have the authority. But I can turn in my report and my recommendation, along with your agreement to cooperate—"

"And name names?"

"They might want you to do that."

Begovic made that sharp gesture again. He appeared to have aged ten years in these last few moments. At last he said only, "Give me a little time, Mr. Long."

"I don't know how long I'll be here with the circus, now that everybody knows I'm a federal marshal. But I'll promise you one thing, Mr. Begovic; I'll see you before I leave. You can give me whatever answer you want me to take back to Denver with me then."

Chapter 10

Longarm walked in the twilight down the incline from the circus grounds into Black Lake township. He found no relief from the suspicion and tension in the settlement. A thick-shouldered man, sitting with half a dozen loungers outside the general store, stood up and blocked the boardwalk. "Hey, fella."

Longarm winced. By now, he could smell trouble halfway across a town as small as Black Lake. "Yeah?"

"You from that circus up yonder?"

"Yeah."

"What you doin' in town? We don't allow chinks, Injuns or carney tramps in this town after dark." He glanced over his shoulder for reinforcement from his silent, grinning friends, sitting watchful and amused.

Longarm felt the anger well up in him. He'd had it up to his ears with prejudice and arrogance. He reminded himself that he had troubles enough; he didn't need more with an intolerant hayseed. "Got business in here," he said.

"That ain't what I said. I said you tramps ain't allowed in here after dark. Maybe you'd like me to run you out."

Longarm gave him a chilled smile. "Yeah. I'd like that."

The fellow's arrogance missed a beat. Something in Longarm's voice dampened his ardor for this fight. He glanced at his friends, but found they'd retreated and were no longer smiling encouragement. He cleared his throat. "You just get your business done and clear out."

Longarm nodded. "Mean to do that." He continued to smile blandly. "I tell you for a fact, I don't know what in hell a Chinaman, an Indian, or a tramp would want in this town—day or night."

"Just get out, or I'll have the sheriff lock you up."

"What about you throwing me out?"

"Just get out—before I *have* to throw you out."

"Don't say anything you can't back up," Longarm advised. He walked forward so suddenly that the big man had to jump out of his way, stumbling slightly. The loiterers laughed, but now their taunts were directed at their townsman.

Longarm continued through the dusk to the railway station. Here he composed a night letter to Billy Vail:

"MARKO BEGOVIC ADMITS TO HUNGARIAN POLICE RECORD STOP NOW SWEARS ALLEGIANCE TO CROWN STOP HE AND BRONCO BOB KIDD ANOTHER HUNGARIAN NATIONAL ASKED TO PERFORM FOR PRINCESS DANICA IN GOLDEN STOP TEXAS BILL WIRT RAIDED CIRCUS PAY WAGON STOP GOT NO MONEY AND MY IDENTITY KNOWN PLS ADVISE STOP LONG"

He smiled, knowing Billy would be pissed at the long-winded wire; even though it was a night letter, it would still be more expensive than the chief marshal liked. And he'd be even more pissed at the message it contained. Longarm reflected with amusement that Frank, Billy's secretary, would likely have a rough day tomorrow. Poor fellow.

He walked back along Main Street, taking his time, but not loitering. It was full dark by the time he reached the crowded circus grounds. The people had turned out for the big first night show. There was a belief in small towns that carnivals, tent shows, chautauquas, and circuses all put on their best shows on Monday night so that word of mouth would sell tickets all week.

The grounds glowed with lanterns and torches, rang with laughter and chatter. Longarm paused a moment to watch the master of ceremonies, substituting for Cy Slimer, telling the crowd there was plenty of time to visit the greatest freak show on earth before the main event of the evening in the big tent. Longarm walked on past.

He ate dinner, silently and alone in the mess tent. No one spoke to him, but they did not threaten him in any way, either.

After he'd eaten barbecued chicken and baked beans, he walked along the lighted midway and entered the main arena, which was already filling with people. He sat on the end of one of the plank tiers near the ring.

The tent filled quickly. This was that unusual and unknown treat these people had been looking forward to for a long time. Expectant adults and children crowded in, chattering and pointing. The place was even more exciting than they'd dreamed.

Clowns seemed everywhere just before showtime. Laughter erupted suddenly in all parts of the tent where the outlandish entertainers played their pranks on a nervously laughing audience. No one knew what to expect. People rocked with laughter. They had never seen anything like this before: flowers sprouting suddenly from shirt fronts; buckets of water thrown in their faces and turning into harmless confetti; candy cartons that became jack-in-the-boxes when opened.

Above them, as the band played and the master of ceremonies urged them to see marvels beyond compare, the aerialists performed on high wires without nets, and clowns followed them, falling, hanging by one hand and sliding down greased poles. There was too much to see, something happened everywhere, one could not see it all. The wonder of it left one breathless. Eyes widened, mouths gaped open as flyers dived outward from the high trapezes, only to be snatched from certain death at the last moment by a catcher, hanging by his heels, and seeming to appear from nowhere.

The stunned crowd grew silent only when the huge, beautiful lions raced, prodded, along the iron-barred ramp and into the center stage.

They applauded, wildly enthusiastic and adoring, when Marko Begovic appeared. Not only had word-of-mouth spread his greatness; he looked as if he'd come down only recently from Olympus.

He threw off his red cape. His lovely assistant, Lisa, retrieved it and draped it across her arm. Begovic prowled, preening and striding, and women held their breaths, gazing at that lithe, lean, and hard-sinewed body.

But despite the way Begovic prowled, lord of all he surveyed, something was wrong. Watching Begovic, Longarm frowned, troubled. He could not say why, but Marko looked far less than his usual arrogant, godly, and unapproachable self.

The crowd neither saw nor sensed anything amiss. They stared agog, fascinated as Marko Begovic strode the arena, cracking that whip, which was to be his sole weaponry against those huge cats snarling and lunging inside that cage.

Longarm could dismiss his concern as imagination. Only he knew that Begovic was at war inside himself, wanting to buy amnesty from the United States government, but unwilling to inform on people he had once fought beside.

Still, it seemed to Longarm that something more than a troubled conscience plagued the lion trainer. Marko did not stride with his usual animation and haughty pride. To Longarm's eyes, it was as if he were looking at a man who had aged twenty years since he'd seen him this afternoon. The man walking in that ring looked like the father of the man who had dominated this place at the matinee performance.

Then, abruptly, Begovic hesitated and glanced around for an instant, as if disoriented.

Longarm sat forward on the edge of his seat.

No one else in the arena seemed aware of anything out of the ordinary. They cheered and whistled, paying homage as they gazed in amazed admiration while Begovic quickly recovered and strode toward the iron gate of the huge circular cage.

Begovic's entering the cage of lions was always a magnificent production orchestrated to the least movement, a matter of tension and excitement. It was no less now.

Uniformed men stood at rigid attention on both sides of the barred gates, armed with Winchesters. The guns were held at the ready across their chests. They gazed with terrible concentration at that gate and at the snarling animals beyond it.

A third man, also armed, and wearing a castle guard's plumage, acted as gatekeeper. Begovic stood, an impervious noble, until the sentinel glanced at him questioningly.

Begovic gestured broadly and nodded disdainfully. He cracked his whip at his side. This always accomplished two things: it brought his cats up for a few seconds—they'd learned to cringe inwardly at the *sound* of the whip—and it focused all attention totally where Begovic wanted it.

The report of the cracking whip was loud in the silence, and the audience reacted, drawing a collective breath.

The gate sentry, with a melodramatic flourish, unlocked the

gate and held it open just enough for Begovic to enter. The gun-bearers came up to ready position, their guns trained on a bare area just inside that portal.

The whole tent waited with bated breath for the master to stride into that cage, but again Begovic hesitated. He looked around, almost as if he didn't know where he was.

The door-guard's head jerked up. He looked as if he might slam the gate shut.

Begovic shook his head, as if clearing away mists that clogged his thinking processes. Then he wiped the back of his hand across his forehead.

Longarm stared at the man pausing before the opened gate. Begovic looked like a man suddenly depleted and unmanned by fear.

Then, as if reacting to some formidable inner will unknown to lesser men, Begovic gathered his wits. He straightened to his full, impressive height and stepped across the threshold.

Instinctively, the animals sensed something wrong. Whatever ailed Begovic, his cats could smell it. They raged, snarling and spitting, setting themselves upon powerful haunches, ready to pounce.

The iron gate slammed loudly behind Begovic. Again, Begovic looked around, troubled.

Sweating, Longarm slid off the plank and stood taut, watching the man wavering reedlike inside that cage.

Begovic lifted his whip, but did not crack it.

The leather stock slipped from his fingers as if they had gone suddenly lifeless. The whip fell to the sawdust.

A cry went up, as if from one vast throat. The crowd gasped, hesitated, and then cheered this newest display of the renowned Begovic's incredible courage.

Longarm took two steps forward involuntarily. He did not believe this was a display of courage, whatever it was. It even occurred to him that Begovic might be staggering drunk.

In the cage, Begovic seemed unaware that he'd dropped his single weapon. The whip lay on the ground near his feet, unnoticed.

He drew his hand across his forehead again in that troubling, confused way. Then, as if acting from old habit, or from that same instinct which impelled his great cats, he took one long step forward.

Begovic's legs crumbled beneath him. He cried out. He fell to his knees. For a moment he tried to recover, but he could not rise. He clutched at his throat with both hands.

He tried again to rise, could not, and pitched forward on his face.

Longarm ran toward the cage. He did not know what he could do, only that he had to do something.

The audience screamed as one. They stood up, gaping, gazes fixed on the unmoving figure in that cage with the snarling, milling lions. Some among the audience applauded and nodded appreciatively. This was heart-stopping melodrama unexpected, unknown, untried—the great Begovic prostrating himself before his wild lions, without even his whip in his hand. No one had ever seen anything like that before.

"Now watch him," they kept saying knowingly among themselves.

Begovic remained sprawled facedown in the sawdust.

"Get those goddamn lions out of that cage," Longarm yelled at the trainers and handlers who stood in stunned confusion, watching the red-suited body, unmoving in that cage.

Longarm's shout galvanized Begovic's assistants into action. They knew what to do as quickly as they recovered from their shock and terror. One of them jerked up the gate to the ramp. Another threw raw meat into the narrow alleyway leading to the cages. Others ran close to the bars, shouting and cracking bullwhips. Men came running with long poles. Thrusting the rods through the bars, they pummeled and turned the animals away from Begovic's prone body and toward the ramp.

As soon as the last lion had leaped into the enclosed runway and the gate had slammed down behind it, Longarm entered the cage and knelt beside the fallen trainer.

Marko did not stir. By now the managers of the show had regained their senses. Clowns came pouring from all sides, some driving small wagons pulled by burros and jackasses. The band struck up a tinny-sounding rendition of "Camptown Races." Shouting through his megaphone, the master of ceremonies ran out into the ring as soon as the cage was dismantled, calling attention to the next attraction, "the greatest Western show on earth."

The show was moving around them. Roustabouts were running everywhere, setting up for Bronco Bob's act. Felix and another clown came in with a stretcher. Felix said, "A doctor is on his way. We'll take him to the first-aid tent."

Longarm looked up into the clown face. "Has this ever happened before?"

"To Marko? Not since I been with the show."

Dr. Lawson Bennett was in the tent when Longarm got there. The tall, rail-thin medic looked wearier than when Longarm had seen him last. He glanced across his shoulder and yawned a greeting.

"Haven't you slept any yet, doc?" Longarm said. He knelt beside the bed where Begovic had been placed, naked, on his back. The man's complexion was colorless.

Dr. Bennett yawned. "Being the only doctor in a town the size of Black Lake ain't real conducive to rest. It's all those house calls. And babies. Those little bastards are the least considerate of all. In my twenty years of doctoring, I've hardly ever had a kid that cleared the chute between nine in the morning and five in the afternoon. Hell, I got so that now I can look at a pregnant woman and know whether she's going to deliver just after I get in bed at night, or around four A.M., when it's too late to go back to sleep by the time I get home again."

"How is he?" Longarm asked.

The doctor looked over his shoulder and frowned. "My God. Didn't you know? He's dead."

For the first time, Longarm looked closely at the still figure on the cot.

"But why? What happened?"

"I don't know what happened. I can only tell you what *didn't* happen. He wasn't shot and didn't die violently at all. Near as I can tell from the only examination I'm able to make is that he was poisoned."

"How do you know that?"

"Burns inside his mouth. His throat is burnt raw, too. Whatever poison was used was deadly and fierce. I can figure such a poison killing a man. What I can't figure is how you get a man to drink it."

Longarm found Lisa in Marko Begovic's caravan wagon. The beautiful girl wore her tutu costume. She wept unconsolably where she had fallen on the floor, her head resting on the brocaded seat of Begovic's built-in divan.

She did not respond to Longarm's knock on the door, nor did she look up when he entered the small living room.

Longarm sat on the edge of the divan beside her. He said, "Lisa."

She looked up, her eyes deep in tears. "He's...dead ...isn't he?"

When Longarm nodded, the girl wept again, burying her face in her arms. Longarm let her cry. He sat quietly. He removed a cheroot from his pocket and chewed on it without lighting it. At last, when her sobbing quieted, he said, "Marko was poisoned."

"When? How?"

"I thought—I hoped—maybe you might have some ideas on that."

She looked up at him, her eyes bleak and red-rimmed. "You don't think I had anything to do with it?"

"I'm sorry if I let you think that. I wasn't trying to blame you. It's just that you're here all the time. I thought you might know who came to see him today."

"You did."

Longarm gave a faint, rueful little laugh. "For now, Lisa, let's clear present company of any guilt. If you're the last person who'd want to see Marko Begovic killed, I've got to be the next to last."

"Who would want to kill him?"

"I have no notion at all, Lisa. That's why I'm here." Longarm touched her rich hair gently. "Maybe if I ask the questions..."

"What would I know?"

"There you go again. Maybe you don't know anything, Lisa. On the other hand, maybe you don't know you know something. Something that might be important to me. Like— let's start easy—who came to see Marko today between shows? Besides me."

"Nobody." Lisa sniffled and drew the back of her hand under her red, swollen nose. Longarm pressed a handkerchief into her hand.

"Nobody at all came here after I left?"

"Nobody who would want to kill Marko Begovic. The only

126

visitor he had was around five this afternoon. The same as every afternoon at five since I have been with him. Either Mr. Bob Kidd comes to Mr. Begovic's wagon for a before-dinner drink, or Mr. Begovic and I walk over to Mr. Kidd's wagon. They have one drink together before dinner. They've been doing it for I don't know how many years. It is a kind of custom between them."

"I see. And Bob Kidd came over around five. Who poured the drinks?"

Lisa stared up at him, eyes wide. She shook her head. "Why, I did. I always do. I have since I have been here. I serve them the drinks, and they toast each other—and me, and the show, and the old country. Then they talked about the old days in Hungary—in some Magyar tongue that I don't even understand. They always laughed a lot. And they laughed together today."

"They didn't argue—even in Magyar? Did they look angry as they talked?"

"No. No. I'm sure they didn't."

Longarm left the caravan wagon and strode through the lighted circus grounds to the first-aid tent. The place was deserted except for Cy Slimer, who slept with a pillow over his head. Dr. Lawson Bennett was gathering up his things, closing the black medical kit he carried.

Dr. Bennett said, "I had the body removed to my office. I'll make as decent a post-mortem as I can. As you might suspect, I am the county coroner as well as the physician in these parts. I don't know how much more I'll be able to tell you, but I'll let you know. As of now, I'm convinced that Mr. Begovic died of a caustic poison."

"That somebody got him to drink?"

"Obviously."

"But you think this particular poison, whatever it was, would taste or smell bad?"

"That's right. That's why, as coroner, I'm ruling out murder."

Longarm stared at the exhausted medic. "You're not going to call it murder?"

"You knew the man. The size and build and temperament of him, the strength of him... You're a pretty fair-sized spec-

127

imen—do you think you could have made Begovic drink a bad-tasting, bad-smelling poison?"

"Maybe in something that hid the taste—or killed the smell—long enough to get it past his nose?"

The doctor shrugged. "Not likely."

"Even if the drink was a drink he had regularly—with someone he drank with regularly?"

"It's remotely possible, Mr. Long. But only remotely. I'd be lying to you if I said it was at all likely that Marko Begovic would sit idly and let even his mother poison him with a caustic poison that seared his mouth and throat."

"Yet he did drink it."

The doctor nodded and yawned. "That's why I'm ninety-nine percent inclined to call it suicide on the death certificate. You see, Mr. Long, anybody who wanted to murder another person would have to disguise the smell and taste and burn of a poison. Any of those things would arouse immediate suspicion. On the other hand, a man wanting to commit suicide badly enough will take any evil-smelling and evil-tasting poisonous substance. And as I said, this was a caustic substance, already creating changes in the appearance of the skin around the mouth and the anus. No, I've been as thorough as I know how, Mr. Long, and I think it's poison—but I'm also certain it was taken purposely."

"Dr. Bennett, I don't agree with you."

The doctor yawned. "That's your privilege, Mr. Long. I am only a physician. I do my best. But if I suggested I might be infallible, I did so unintentionally. I can be wrong."

"Oh, I ain't saying you're wrong. I'm sure, just like you say, Begovic must have been poisoned. But let's look just one step further. Would he have taken a poison and then gone out there in that ring—before all those people—to die?"

"I don't know. He might have. He did."

"Yeah. He went out there tonight. But whether he knew he was going to die, that's something else. He acted confused...."

"Drowsy?"

"Yes. You could say that. As if his mind was blurred, and he wasn't even right sure where he was. Then he seemed to have cramps. He fell. He clutched at his throat. He was immediately unconscious, and he died quickly. Before any of us got to him, I reckon."

128

"Those are classic symptoms of several kinds of ordinary poisons, Mr. Long. But they don't prove the poison was administered by another person. That remains unlikely."

Longarm chewed for a moment at the cold cheroot. As Dr. Bennett started to move past him, Longarm stopped him with a hand on his shoulder. "Let me ask you one more question, Dr. Bennett. I know you're not a vet, but—"

"I've been called worse."

"You do know active poisons that people are allowed to buy to treat things like horse skin diseases—sitfasts, tumors, mange, warts, fungus, collar tumor?"

"Yes. Antimony, strychnine, zinc . . . there are several."

Longarm exhaled heavily and nodded. "Thanks, doc. You've helped me a lot."

The doctor nodded, then smiled. "Maybe I'm not as much help as you tell yourself, Mr. Long. As a lawman, you can see things I can't see. I see a man dead of a poison, I figure he either had to be forced to drink it—or he drank it of his own free will—because he *wanted* to. Somehow, as a doctor, that's easier for me to believe. I don't have to imagine a man big enough to force a fellow like Marko Begovic to drink a foul-smelling, evil-tasting brew. And then, not being a lawman, I'm not naturally suspicious."

"I reckon I am," Longarm said. "Begovic didn't seem like a man that wanted to die. That makes me a mite suspicious, doctor. Hell, I don't know. Maybe lawmen are born suspicious. Maybe it's part of their nature. Maybe that's why they take the infernal job in the first place."

Chapter 11

Longarm awoke in the hottest hole beyond hell. He felt as if he were on fire. His cot was a bed of crimson-hot coals. Sweat marbled and ran down his sodden body. His nightmare raged so hideously that he was almost afraid to face waking reality. Yet devils prodded him with fiery pitchforks, and yelled his name.

He struggled for a moment and then opened his eyes to the brilliant lances of morning sunlight. A young circus errand boy leaned over him, shaking his shoulder. "Got a telegram for you, Mr. Long."

Longarm shook away the last sticky wisps of nightmare and swung his legs around, sitting up on the edge of the cot. He ran his tongue over his teeth and shuddered. He found his pants, tossed the boy a nickel, and took the folded yellow sheet of paper.

He didn't have to read it to know its message, but he read it anyway, as a formality: "RETURN DENVER INSTANT STOP EXPECT YOU IN THIS OFFICE TODAY STOP YOU ARE OFF CASE STOP VAIL US MARSHAL DENV"

He sat there for a long time, his mind and his mouth sour. He kept rereading Billy Vail's telegram and hating it more with each reading. He hated to leave anything unfinished. He hated to fail at anything. This yellow sheet of paper was his certificate of failure.

He wadded it in his fist, threw it away. Then he had to get down on his knees to retrieve and destroy it.

Twenty minutes later he came out of the men's baths, shaved, washed up, his mouth clean, but his mind still sour with the sense of failure.

He walked over to the mess tent. Not because he was hungry—he wasn't—but because he reckoned himself a creature of habit. As he walked, he thought back over last night—another failure in his laundry list of trying and falling flat on his face.

It began with the doctor's calling Marko Begovic's death a suicide. Even if Marko were depressed over his expectations of being denied the opportunity to perform before Princess Danica in Golden, that didn't add up to a motive for taking his own life. That was totally out of character with what he knew of Begovic. Begovic was the sort of man who was inspired by obstacles and challenges, not defeated and destroyed by them. Begovic was a man looking forward to being the first animal trainer to work lions and tigers together in one cage. No matter what had happened yesterday, Begovic wasn't a man to kill himself. Yet, one fact advanced by Dr. Bennett remained indisputable to this moment: if Begovic hadn't committed suicide, then somebody had to force him to drink a caustic, foul-smelling poison. And that made less sense than anything else.

After Longarm had talked with Dr. Bennett, he'd waited around until Bronco Bob Kidd's show ended, then he walked over to the Western-style living quarters on wheels.

He'd knocked on the door. A blond woman in her late twenties, and still wearing the cowgirl outfit she wore in the show, opened it and stared at him, her tiredly pretty face gray. "What do you want?"

"I want to talk to Bronco Bob."

She gazed at him as if he'd lost his senses. "You must know better than that."

"No, I don't. Doesn't the Shootin' Kid talk to anybody but God?"

The girl's mouth twisted. "I don't know who you are—some lawman or something—and I don't care. But you should know one thing. Mr. Kidd has lost his closest friend in this world. He is distraught. He is not seeing anyone."

Longarm drew a deep breath. "He did his show tonight."

"Yes. Because he felt he owed that to the people who paid to see him. But he broke down as soon as he walked in this place. He will see no one. He's too ill to see anyone. Perhaps your heart is hardened, Mr. Lawman. But Mr. Kidd's poor heart is broken. You wouldn't want to see him. You wouldn't want to see a strong man cry."

"Maybe I would," Longarm said. "Maybe I'd like to see how real his tears are."

A howl broke the taut stillness within Kidd's wagon. The agonized cry seemed torn from deep inside a bereaved man. Suddenly the girl was thrust aside and Bronco Bob stood framed in the lighted doorway. He wore no shirt, no boots. His muscular body gleamed in the lamplight. And Longarm could see that Kidd's face was swollen, reddened with his sobbing.

"I heard that, you no-heart bastard," Kidd growled, deep in his throat. "I ought to kill you, hombre, but you ain't worth killing."

Longarm retreated slightly. There was no way to doubt the depth or the sincerity of Bob Kidd's grief. He looked mindless with loss and despair. Longarm said, "I reckon you're right. I am a heartless bastard. I'm a lawman. I guess it goes with the territory. You don't feel grief first. You feel suspicion."

"Suspicion?" Kidd's voice shook. "Suspicion of what?"

"Of murder."

"Marko? Murdered? The doctor told me it was suicide."

"Do you think Marko Begovic would take his own life?"

Bronco hesitated. He sniffled slightly and drew the back of his calloused hand across his reddened nose. "He had to. A poison like that."

"But why would he want to do it? Kill himself? Was he despondent? Depressed? Afraid of something? Of somebody?"

"I don't know." Bronco Bob swung his arm. "Come on in, Long. We can't stand here yelling at each other like this, this time of night."

Longarm stepped inside the spartanly furnished trailer. Kidd swung his arm toward a wicker chair and sat in its twin, elbows on his knees, gazing at the floor.

"I don't know," Bronco said again, after a long pause. The tired-looking blond sank into a small loveseat-sized divan covered with a bright Indian blanket. She gazed, eyes chilled with hatred, at Longarm.

"What is it you don't know?" Longarm prompted. "Who he was afraid of?"

Bronco looked up, his mouth twisting. "I know that. Marko wasn't afraid of nobody. Not of the devil. He felt toward all men just as he did toward his lions. He could handle them."

"Fear and trust," Longarm said.

Bronco almost smiled. He drew a deep breath and his eyes brimmed with tears again. "That's right. Fear and trust. Marko trusted everybody as long as he could. He feared nobody. No, he didn't kill himself because he was scared of anybody."

"But you think he did kill himself."

"I don't know. I'm too sick, too torn up to think that straight. In all the years I've known Marko, I never thought of him as a man who would take his own life. But what do we really know, even of the people close to us, when we can't know what we might do . . . if things went bad enough?"

"Were things going bad for Marko?"

"Not that I know of. Things were better for him than they had been, many times in the past."

"He told me that he was expecting to appear before Princess Danica of Hungary at Governor Loving's party in Golden. Along with you."

Kidd continued to stare at the floor between his bare feet. He shrugged. "That's true." He added no more, volunteered nothing else.

"It may be just the suspicious lawman in me again, Kidd. But I get the feeling *you* don't think Marko Begovic committed suicide."

Now Kidd looked up and met Longarm's gaze. He merely shook his head. "I don't know. I told you. I don't know."

"You wouldn't tell me, even if you did think he was murdered, would you?"

Kidd shrugged those wide, thin shoulders again. "Probably not."

"Because you don't trust me?"

Kidd didn't answer at once. He picked up a battered Stetson from a small rack beside his chair and twirled it in his hands for a moment. Then he grinned coldly from his grief-stricken face. "That would be as good as a reason as any."

Longarm said, "We haven't got along good, Kidd. But it seems to me that's because I didn't share your total love of yourself—not a matter of mistrust and suspicion."

"I don't like a man, I don't trust him." Kidd stuck the old Stetson at an angle on his head. It was as if he didn't even know he did it.

"We're not going to get very far, are we?"

Kidd spread his hands. "I've nothing to say to you."

"Would it change anything if I told you that I know you were the last person to be alone with Marko Begovic this afternoon?"

Kidd shook his head.

"Even though that might make you a suspect—a prime suspect—in Marko's murder?" Longarm heard the blond's sharp intake of breath, but he did not glance toward her.

Kidd's voice remained chilled. "You're more than a little addled, aren't you, hombre? Maybe from riding too many unbroken horses with hair bridles." He laughed in cold contempt. "There has been no murder. Remember? Even the doctor said Marko committed suicide."

"But you and I know better, don't we?"

"What we know, hombre, is not important. I don't want to talk about this anymore. If you want to charge me, you do it. If you have authority here, arrest me."

"I'm a deputy U.S. marshal. I have the authority."

"Then arrest me, or get the hell out of here."

"Dammit, I only want to talk to you."

"Rosa tried to tell you. I am too full of grief over my dead friend to talk to anyone—even to my friends. I got nothing to say to you." Then he laughed coldly. "Yes. I have one thing to say to you."

"What's that?"

"Be here at the matinee, hombre. We got a deal to settle, with wild horses."

"Why don't you forget that? If Buffalo Bill Cody is going to be there—"

"That has nothing to do with you, hombre. I'll handle my horses. But I do not forget or forgive an insult. You have insulted me and my career. Everything that I am. I'll show you I am a better man than you, Long. I'll ride wild horses. I'll ride them by your rules. And I'll beat you. You will apologize to me. As to kissing my ass, I don't know that I'd let you *touch* my ass."

Longarm entered the mess tent and sat down at a table alone.

Talk died down at the other tables when he approached, and started up again after he was past. He drank his coffee and pushed his scrambled eggs around on his plate, still without an appetite, still wrapped up in the strange death of Begovic.

Minerva had seated herself across the table from him before he was aware of her. He looked up and tried to smile. There was little warmth in the tattooed lady's face. She could remember their heated hours together, but she could not forget that he was a lawman. This outweighed all other considerations. Anything else she might have forgiven.

She tilted her full lips into the barest suggestion of a smile. She said, "You hear about Vingie?"

Longarm felt himself go taut inside. "What about her?"

"She's been ill—locked in her bedroom in her wagon and won't come out. She's sent word that she's afraid to appear at the show today."

"When did that start?"

"When she heard that Marko Begovic was dead."

Longarm frowned. "Vingie doesn't believe Marko committed suicide?"

Minerva shrugged her picturesque shoulders. "I don't know what she thinks. I haven't talked to her. I haven't seen her. I just thought you might like to know."

Longarm nodded. "Thanks. I'll try to see her before I leave."

Minerva had moved to stand up from the bench that was attached to the pine table. She hesitated, sat down again, and exhaled. "Are you leaving?"

"Yes." Longarm grinned. "A loss I reckon this circus will bear up under real well."

"I thought you were a hell of a nice fellow—once."

Longarm laughed. "I was a nice fellow . . . once."

Longarm left the mess tent and walked to Vingie's caravan wagon. When he knocked on the door, a woman he'd never seen before answered, already shaking her head. "I'd like to see Miss Vingie," he said.

"You the lawman, named Mr. Long, ain't you?"

"That's right."

"I know Miss Vingie's mighty anxious to talk with you. But you can't see her right now. Dr. Bennett was here. He gave her something to make her sleep. Said something about laudanum or something. She's resting now. First time all night."

"I'll come back," Longarm said. "Will you tell Vingie that

I was here and that I'll come back?"

From Vingie's wagon he walked to Begovic's wagon. Lisa welcomed him without warmth. She had thought of nothing new since she had seen him last. She had accepted Dr. Bennett's diagnosis of the cause of Marko's death.

Longarm stared at her. "You don't really believe that, do you? That he killed himself?"

Lisa shuddered and shook her head. "I don't want to talk about it."

He prowled the circus grounds, feeling time running out on him. He believed that somehow the death of Marko Begovic was entangled with the arrival of Princess Danica at Golden. He couldn't say why, but he couldn't shake the conviction, either. Hell, he couldn't even say why Marko had died.

He found himself standing beside the corral where the latest herd of Kidd's wild ponies were penned.

He leaned against the bars, staring at the shaggy-haired, wild-eyed mustangs. He grinned faintly. At least Bronco Bob Kidd was a man of his word. The mustangs had not been touched since their arrival. There were no marks on them. When they threw saddles on the ponies in that ring, it would be the first time. Kidd was observing the rules to the letter.

Longarm was aware of someone's presence, and he turned his head. One of Kidd's stunt riders stood beside him. "They look bad enough for you, lawman? Or do they look too bad for you?"

"I think your boss is a fool to go ahead with this grudge match, with Buffalo Bill coming here to see his act."

"That just proves how little you know the boss, lawman. His honor is more important to him than any job he might get, in any show. I know that. If you knew ol' Bronc, you'd know it." His mouth twisted. "I hear you been recalled from here. Kind of surprised you ain't left already."

Longarm laughed. "Did your boss send you out here to say that?"

"Why, no, he didn't, friend. I thought of that one all by myself."

"You got a hell of a suspicious mind."

The shockwaves of excitement flooded back from the main tent across the corrals and animal wagons: Buffalo Bill Cody and his party had arrived up front. Buffalo Bill Cody in person.

Even the hardest of Kidd's riders drifted forward to get a look at the living legend. General George Custer was dead. So was the man called Wild Bill Hickok. Down south, a homicidal kid named Bonney, but called Billy the Kid, was at large. But none of these names had the hard currency of that of Colonel Buffalo Bill Cody. Ten years ago he'd worked guiding wagon trains; today, his was one of the best-known names in the country.

Though less than impressed with the legend of Buffalo Bill, Longarm drifted to the main tent to witness the arrival of the celebrity.

He stood at the rear entrance and watched Bill Cody enter a specially set up box that would make him part of the show, as well as the most important member of the audience.

People were already arriving, and they gazed in awe and disbelief at the heroic figure.

Longarm grinned. He admitted Buffalo Bill was impressive in person. Surrounded by his hangers-on and helpers and servants, Cody was impressive as hell. God alone knew what his white suit had cost. His Stetson was white and immaculate, with an Indian band. Cody's golden hair touched at his wide shoulders. He was a tall man, and his height had been accentuated by high heels on his glittering new boots.

Buffalo Bill entered the specially built box seats, but he did not sit down. He waved and smiled and nodded at the growing crowd of adoring fans. He even spoke to them in a calm, deep voice about his plans to bring his own real, live, Western show to their town, as well as taking it East—and to Europe.

Buffalo Bill was everything Longarm had heard he was, and more. The frontiersman and Indian fighter was a product of the fertile imagination of an eastern pulp-magazine writer named Edward Zane Carroll Judson, alias Ned Buntline. And here was Ned Buntline's million-dollar creation, in person.

Buntline was a writer who had come West to pan gold, but not in the wastelands, rivers or mountains, but among its frontiersmen. The people back East were avid for any written word on this new breed of hero. And Ned Buntline had discovered and developed for them the ideal Westerner. A young buffalo-hunter and sometime army scout named Will Cody looked like a pure bonanza to Buntline, who named the handsome young rider Buffalo Bill. Buntline himself breveted Cody a colonel.

And after making financial deals, Buntline began writing about Colonel Buffalo Bill Cody in *Ned Buntline's Wild West Magazine*. It proved to be a gold strike beyond belief. People waited in line to read the latest incredible exploits of the young Westerner. Even Will Cody read the magazine and began to believe the fantastic fictions Buntline produced about him. Cody began to dress and talk the part. He washed his hair and brushed it and let it grow into a mane. His soup-strainer mustache gave him just the touch he needed—mature, but not elderly, a real man of the real West. He bought new clothes that made him look like a living legend. And gradually he became one. He began to look the part Buntline wrote for him, a role that fate had meant for him to play—for profit.

By now, ten or so years after Buffalo Bill had been discovered and exploited in a hundred stories by Ned Buntline, Cody was totally immersed and involved in his role. He was everything Buntline said he was. He walked, talked, and lived the thrilling legend. No one believed it more totally than Will Cody himself.

Because the excitement and noise created by the arrival of Buffalo Bill shut out everything else, time suddenly seemed to move out of control—like the wild mustangs. Suddenly the clowns appeared, and the tent was filled to standing-room-only capacity. People who had been to every show before this one, since the circus arrived in Black Lake, returned for this one. Not only was Buffalo Bill himself present, but Bronco Bob had sent out the word that there would be a grudge riding match between the Shootin' Kid and a riding expert. Tension lay thick across the huge tent.

The circus acts came and went swiftly, as if everything were speeded up, racing toward some precipice in time. The master of ceremonies, in his red coat and top hat, strode out into the center ring and spoke through his megaphone, slowly pivoting to face each area of his audience.

"Ladies and gentlemen! The management of Baldwin-Naylor Combined Circus and Wild West Show have asked me to announce that, due to the tragic passing away of our beloved Marko Begovic, there will be no lion-taming act tonight. The management has decided against providing a substitute—a show of less quality and wonder than Marko Begovic's internationally acclaimed performance. We want you all to know that a worldwide search has already been begun, seeking a successor to the incredible Marko Begovic. Instead, we are adding a new feature—for this performance only. It is being presented as a special tribute to our renowned and beloved guest of honor here today, Colonel Buffalo Bill Cody!"

The stands went wild with applause. Colonel Cody stood up and took a prolonged bow. Gradually, quiet settled again and the master of ceremonies continued:

"Besides the thrilling exhibitions of shooting, riding, and roping, Bronco Bob Kidd—your own Shootin' Kid from the Lone Star State—is presenting an extra added attraction, at no additional cost, ladies and gentlemen, and for this one performance only. A grudge wild-horse-breaking contest."

The rear flaps of the tent were raised and a dozen buckskin-clad cowboys and bare-chested Indians raced their ponies into the arena through a thick and rolling cloud of dust. They rode the length of the tent, doing their trick riding, breathtaking spills and remounting on the run, shooting and roping. The battle raged everywhere.

The crowd loved the swift, chaotic exhibition. Following some prolonged moments of tension after Bronco Bob was announced, the horsemen formed their honor guard in two lines near the center entrance to the tent.

The ringmaster shouted through his megaphone, "And now, here he is, ladies and gentlemen . . . the greatest circus cowboy of the West . . . the preeminent sixgun artist, the finest roper alive . . . and, as he will prove in a grudge horse-breaking contest, the world's supreme horseman. Bronco Bob Kidd—your own Shootin' Kid from the Lone Star State!"

In a roaring wave of adulation and welcome, Bronco Bob raced his white gelding into the ring.

He maneuvered the pony in a series of short, sharp-stepping turns, making a perfect circle and letting the world—and Buffalo Bill—see how elegant he looked in silver and white, his golden mane bouncing in the wind.

But something happened to spoil the effect of easy perfection. The horse, in turning, seemed to miss a step, and Bronco Bob had to grab the pommel to keep from falling from the saddle.

Kidd recovered himself quickly. He laughed and removed

his hat and waved it reassuringly. But when he tried to return the hat to his head, his fingers loosened involuntarily and the Stetson fell to the ground. A few people laughed nervously.

Bronco Bob recovered smoothly. He turned his horse in a little, mincing pirouette, then swung down and retrieved his hat.

But as the audience applauded, convinced this was all part of his show, Longarm saw that Bronco Bob was sitting straight and stiff in his saddle, as if hanging on for dear life.

He saw Buffalo Bill applauding and nodding his approval to those around him. Hell, what did Ned Buntline's manufactured Westerner know?

Bronco Bob shook his head oddly and glanced about as if drunk, or in a panic. Then he stood the magnificent horse on its hind legs and began to walk the animal around the center ring.

The crowd shouted, whistled, applauded, but Longarm held his breath, watching and sweating, with a sense of doom enveloping him.

Suddenly, Bronco Bob simply released the bridle. He fell clumsily from the saddle. He made no effort to catch himself or to break his fall. He struck the ground, the thud loud in the stunned stillness. He sprawled facedown, his arms outflung. He did not move.

The stunned crowd came to its feet. Many of them had witnessed Marko Begovic's mysterious death.

A handler sprang forward and caught the reins of Kidd's white horse. The band struck up a tentative tune.

Longarm sprinted into the ring. He was the first one to reach the fallen rider. Other men came running, crowding around, forming a wall to keep the crowd at bay.

Longarm caught Kidd's shoulders and turned him. He knelt on one knee and lifted Kidd, feeling ill. Bronco's mouth seemed twisted in an eternal grimace of agony, his eyes dilated, staring wildly, and unable to focus. It was as if Longarm could watch the life fading from them like wicks turned down and finally extinguished.

Bronco Bob gasped. He stared up at Longarm, trying desperately to speak, but unable to form the words or force them up through his throat. Finally he managed to whisper in a raw, hoarse tone, "Tell . . . Vingie . . . for God's sake. . . . !"

He made one final, fearful effort to speak, but he could not do it.

His head sank back and he writhed as if in intolerable pain, unable to speak anymore. Longarm yelled for a doctor, knowing there was only Dr. Lawson Bennett, and that this overworked medico wasn't even on the grounds.

Helplessly he stared down at Bronco Bob. Kidd's body stiffened and a rattle started low in his chest, shook him roughly, and then died in his taut throat.

Bronco Bob slumped heavily in Longarm's arms. He was dead.

Chapter 12

Longarm went at a run across the runway from the main tent. As soon as the riders had removed Kidd's body on a stretcher, and the clowns had distracted and quieted the terrified crowd, Longarm strode out and headed for Vingie's wagon, expecting the worst.

As he hurried, he kept hearing Kidd's last words inside his mind: *"Tell . . . Vingie . . . for God's sake . . . !"*

Tell her what? Warn her? Was she next on the unknown killer's list? Had Kidd finally realized some truth about Marko's killing and his own death? Too late to save himself and, as it turned out, too late even to relay any warning message to Longarm?

He had no answers. He felt nothing except panic as he ran through the darkened areas and the sudden sprays of lantern light, or places streaked with elongated fingers of light and dark from smoking torches.

The door to Vingie's wagon was tightly bolted. He knocked at the panel hard and jerked at the knob. He called her name, trying to keep the edge of panic out of his voice.

After a long moment in which Longarm held his breath without even knowing he did it, he heard a whisper of movement inside the wagon, and then Vingie's quavering whisper through the door. "Longarm?"

"Yes." The breath sighed out of him. "Let me in."

The key turned in the lock.

Longarm glanced over his shoulder, not even sure what he expected to see in that deceiving darkness where everything promised pleasure and excitement, and where, in the occluding blackness, death stalked. Perhaps he felt he might even find Vingie's "unknown forces" out there. He had restrained his laughter when she spoke to him of those "unknown forces of evil." Now he wasn't laughing. Two murders had made a believer out of him. Suddenly now, it was even easy to believe Vingie's wild accusations that someone had tried to kill her—with a target rifle, a driverless carriage, a broken stair. The notion was no more farfetched than the idea that two big, muscular men had been forced to ingest foul-smelling, bad-tasting poison. Vingie's "unknown forces" were at work, sure as hell.

He was overwhelmed with relief at finding her alive. He sagged against the velvet-covered walls and sighed his relief.

Vingie slammed the door again and bolted it. He saw her eyes swirling with shadows of madness and terror. She teetered on the brink of hysteria.

He found a bottle of Hungarian wine and poured three or four ounces in a glass. He gave it to her. "Drink this," he said.

Vingie took the glass but shook her head. "I could not drink it," she said. "It would vomit from me."

"You're pretty wound up. It might help you."

"I have every cause to be—as you say—wound up. Terrified. I did not appear at my show today. Do you know that this is the first show I have missed in five years? I was afraid to go out of this wagon, afraid to let anyone in. I am in hell."

"What's happened to you?"

"Somebody tried to kill me. Tonight. They tried to get into this wagon to get at me. I crouched in terror and listened to them at my door and at my windows."

When she read the faint flicker of skepticism in Longarm's eyes, she burst out, raging, "You are still thinking I make to lie, don't you?"

"Of course I don't. I—"

"Oh, yes. You think this is all the raving of a hysterical woman. That's what you think. I can see it. Well, I won't talk to you anymore, until you take a lantern. Check outside my wagon. If there are no signs that someone tried to force his way in here tonight, then I lie...and I will let you concern yourself no more from me."

He tried to protest, but Vingie insisted. He struck fire to a lantern and she let him out the door and locked it behind him.

He held the lantern aloft and checked first around the door. He caught his breath. There were signs that someone had chopped at the lock with a chisel or screwdriver.

He circled the wagon. Vingie had not exaggerated. All windows had been tampered with—from the outside—as if someone had tried desperately and persistently to get inside this van.

Next he searched the ground around the wagon for footprints. He found nothing helpful. The ground was hard, covered with wet sawdust, and there were no true prints of shoes or boots. In places it looked as if someone had dug in his heels, but this was the only sign he found.

He blew out the lantern, returned to the door, and rapped on it. Silently, Vingie held it open for him. He merely nodded and walked past her into her exotic parlor. "Somebody tried to get in," he said. "Seems crazy that no one would notice in a crowded area like this."

"Maybe crazy to you—what do you say—suspicious lawman's head? But not to me. It was while the circus show was going on. Who was around to see what was being done to my wagon out here?"

He nodded. After a moment he said, "Who would want to kill you?"

She looked as if she would fly into fragments of frustration and hysteria. "If I knew this, would I need you? Somebody. First Marko and now me. Oh, I will be next. I know that."

"No. There's already been a second victim. Janos Kiidislensco died in the circus tent tonight—almost exactly the same way Marko died—and though the doctor hasn't said so yet, I'm sure it was from the same poison."

Vingie seemed to sag like a deflated doll. She sagged upon her couch, trembling visibly. "Oh, God," she whispered. "Oh, my God, what will I do?"

"I'll do everything I can to protect you," Longarm said, conscious of the presence of Vail's telegram in his shirt pocket.

"How can you stop them?" she said, shaking her head. Her eyes appeared fixed on something in the middle distance. "You don't even know who they are."

"Do you?"

"No."

"Yet, when Marko was slain, you felt you would be next."

"Now that Bob Kidd is dead, I know I am not life long to living."

"Why do you believe that?"

"Did Marko tell you who he feared?"

"Yes, he did. In a way. He said that once he had belonged to a gang of young terrorists—bombers, anarchists, anti-royalists—back in Hungary. He said he had changed in the years since he was a student radical."

"Yes. There has been much of that. People who changed. In political views and loyalties. In the years since Franz Josef has become emperor, it has cost many lives. Such a man—like Marko—faces danger from many quarters. From those who once shared his beliefs, and who remain still enemies of the royalists or of the state. From those who have opposed him forever and do not believe he has changed—except like the chameleon, on the outside. From those who collect a bounty by killing him. His life was not worth much, he knew this. He lived constantly on guard. He trusted no one. And it was much like that with Kiidislensco; no matter how much they protested they had changed, there were many who did not believe them— and who hunted them."

"Somebody found them."

"Yes. This is not new. There have been many changes among people who once shared the same beliefs. People who once worked and fought and died together, and are now mortal enemies."

"You think that's why Marko Begovic was killed—by old enemies, old friends, or bounty-hunters from Hungary?"

"I know it. And I know that is why poor Kiidislensco is dead, and that they will be after me now."

"I buy everything you say. It's almost the same as what Marko Begovic told me. An enemy can come from any side— it can even be someone just looking to collect a bounty. But there's still one thing that don't sit right with me. Who could have forced powerful men like Kidd and Begovic to take poison that could not be disguised in liquor or food?"

She shuddered. "Why do you think such a poison could not be concealed in strong drink—or highly spiced food?"

"Because the doc said any poison that burned the way this

one did would have to taste and smell foul. Only a man bent on suicide would be willing to put up with it."

"Do you believe Marko and Kidd committed suicide?"

"I am telling you only what the doctor said."

"About this, I do not care. Both these men I am knowing for many time. Long seasons of friendship in this show. I don't believe they took their own lives."

"Neither do I. But if they didn't, then somebody—some way—forced both of them to take a fearful poison—and Kidd after he was on the alert because of Marko's death."

"Maybe they did take it. Maybe they did not know it was poison."

He shook his head. "Impossible to disguise—even by someone you trusted."

"There is one way you have not consider. A way I think about all the time. Why do you think I eat alone here in my wagon? I eat only food that I prepare for myself, because, like Marko and Kidd, I trust no one."

"You mean someone could have secretly poisoned their drink?"

"Or their food. They eat their heavily spiced Hungarian foods and they think of it nothing. Why not? All Magyars eat a lot of richly spiced foods and most of them add more spices before they taste whatever it is before them. A small amount of lethal poison, even evil-tasting, evil-smelling. Who would think to find it in the dinner he eats each night?"

"Only you."

The diminutive woman shivered. "Yes. And I eat only what I prepare by my own hand." She came to him suddenly and clasped his hand. "I fear desperately for my life. Promise you won't leave me. I have heard the whisper that you are leaving the circus at once."

"I've been ordered back to Denver."

"What is to happen to me? What is to become of me if there is no one I can trust—no one to protect me? I feel safe only when you are with me."

Longarm shook his head ruefully. "I haven't seemed to do much for poor Marko or Bob Kidd."

"You're on guard now. You believe at last what I have been saying. Nobody believed me. They laughed at my fears and called me a stupid little freak. A fool. At least, they laughed before Marko and Kidd died." She shivered. "Barac most of all."

"Do you suspect Barac? Did he have political ties in Hungary, like those of Marko—or opposed to him?"

She spread her hands. "Who knows what to believe of a man like Barac?"

Longarm waited outside Vingie's wagon until she had bolted her door. He hung lanterns on both sides of the van. Anyone approaching it the rest of the night would not benefit from the concealment of darkness.

He crossed the circus grounds and walked down the incline into Black Lake township. Most of the town was dark, in stunned sleep. Two lanterns glowed in the cavelike blackness surrounding the depot.

Longarm shook the stationmaster awake and sent a wire, requesting a delay in his return to Denver. He was less than hopeful and he walked back up to the circus slowly, feeling tired and defeated.

As soon as Longarm reentered the circus grounds, he headed toward the ornate wagon of Josip Barac. It was well after midnight; he supposed Barac would be asleep. Still, he had to do all he could for Vingie before he was yanked out of here by official order, and Barac's trailer seemed the place to begin.

He had expected the wagon to be dark, as were most of the other tents and vans on the lot. A few watchmen and animal handlers wandered in the dark, but otherwise the circus area was quiet.

He was astonished to find all lights glowing in Barac's wagon, and the front door propped open in an effort to entrap errant night winds.

Longarm crossed the damp sawdust. He saw Barac seated alone at a small table set with dinnerware and heavy with steaming foods. Barac was dining alone, but he was guarded by his three personal sentries. These thick-bodied plug-uglies lounged in chairs against the wall while Barac fed himself noisily.

Longarm climbed the metal steps and paused in the doorway. The three bodyguards sat forward, alert. Barac hesitated for a short interval, stared at Longarm, then belched and continued to spoon thick stew into his mouth, washing it down with Badocsony wine.

"May I come in?" Longarm said.

Barac belched again and squinted nearsightedly. "Why not? Pull up a chair and have a dish of Hungarian goulash with me." He laughed and swung his heavy arm. "My friends here will not eat with me. Too spicy."

"We'd rather sleep the rest of the night," one of the guards said.

"Sleep. What is not to sleep when one eats a good Magyar goulash? The secret, my friends, is simple. One sleeps near an open window so one gets plenty of air. That is all a man needs to digest a good goulash."

Longarm hesitated a moment, then nodded. "Sure. I'd like a dish."

"There!" Barac shouted. "A man I could come to admire!" He jerked his head and one of the guards dished up goulash in a bowl.

Longarm sat across from Barac. He took up a soup spoon and dipped it into the stew. When the spicy meat, broth, and vegetables touched his tongue, he felt as if he were afire internally. His eyes reddened and watered. His nose ran. He grabbed up a glass of wine and drank it down.

Barac roared with laughter and his helpers grinned. It was almost as if they felt revenged upon Longarm for his humiliating them on the day he arrived at the circus at Medicine Run.

"A man takes smaller bites that ain't a born Magyar," Barac advised. Longarm nodded, breathing through his parted mouth. But inside his mind he was certain he had found the answer; he needed now only to learn if Kidd and Marko regularly ate Hungarian goulash. One thing was indisputable: none of his senses reacted except in pain. He smelled nothing, tasted nothing but the searing heat that scorched its way down his throat.

Longarm took a smaller bite. He tried to keep his tone conversational. "You fellows don't seem too upset over the deaths of the two star attractions of your circus."

Barac laid aside his spoon a moment and sipped reflectively at his wine. "These things happen," he said. "Both of them were mixed up in things they knew were dangerous. They had been all their lives. In a way, they were men on the run." He cracked his knuckles and shook his huge head. "Sure, we'll miss them. But we'll find somebody to replace both of them. That is all we can do. In many ways, we have been most fortunate."

Longarm frowned, puzzled. "Two men like Kidd and Begovic are killed, and you feel fortunate?"

"Bad," Barac agreed. "It is very bad. Nobody can't deny that. They were both great showmen. Nobody can't deny that. But their deaths have not caused us a lot of trouble with the law. There have been no troublesome investigations, eh? In that we are lucky. This country-hick doctor has been the biggest help of all. He says both Kidd and Begovic died in suicide. The law accepts that. And so do I."

"You know better."

Barac shrugged and grunted. "Who knows better? I know what the doctor told me."

"So do I. But I also know that during showtime tonight, somebody tried to break into Vingie Vinson's van to get at her. Would that have been another suicide?"

Barac shook his head, glanced at his three bodyguards, and grinned coldly. "Are the goblins after the tiny terror again?"

"They weren't goblins, Barac. I saw where somebody had tried to pry off the bolts or lift the windows."

"For what? Who could force his body through such tiny windows? I'll tell you who. Nobody but Miss Tiny Terror herself."

"A man's arm and his gun would be all he'd have to get through the window, Barac. You're that smart."

Barac belched. "I'm smarter than that. I stopped listening to Vingie Vinson a long time ago. She's crazy in the head about somebody trying to kill her, or cheat her, or exploit her. . . ."

"I haven't been here long, but I'm with her—on all those counts."

"Well. You waste your time if you want to. Just don't waste mine. No goblins are after Vingie Vinson. Nobody threatens her. No way. She goes off like this in her head."

"She's not lying. She's in terror. And I think she has a right to be."

"Well, I don't, Mr. Goddamn Marshal. And I'll tell you why. I know Vingie much better than you. If she's scared, it's in her own conscience, that's where she's scared."

"Even so, she's powerful scared. But of what?"

"Would I know? How would I know? Maybe she ain't scared of nothing. I know Vingie a long time. I never saw her scared of nobody. Not me. Nobody. Most people say that proves she's crazy. They say if she had one bit of good sense, she'd be just one little bit scared of Josip Barac. I know better. She ain't scared of nobody."

"She didn't appear at her show tonight. She's scared to do her shows."

"Then let her sell out."

"Just sell out? Leave the only friends she has—her side-show—all she has?"

"She don't have that many friends. She could sell out to me, at a nice profit."

"I still don't see why she would do that . . . unless she was scared into it."

"You goddamn accusing me of trying to scare her until she sells? Is this what you say? That's bull, Mr. Marshal. For goddamn money, that's why she could sell out to me."

"Would one of those reasons be the way you and your bully boys put the spurs to her—and her people—every chance you get?"

Barac pushed back from the table as if he'd suddenly lost his appetite. "Whatever I do, it is for the goddamn money. Money, Mr. Goddamn Marshall. That's the American way. It don't matter what you do, just so you get the money. All of it you can get. Any way you can get it. You don't believe me? Look at Mr. Rockefeller, Mr. Morgan, Mr. Carnegie. In my country they would be criminals against the state. In America they are barons, loved and respected."

Longarm laughed. "So that's what you're doing, eh? Just making your money the American way, eh?"

"That's right, Mr. Marshal. I am American now. I have no other country. No other politics. I have found my own heaven, where men are worshipped if they steal and cheat and rob the big American way. You try to make something else out of it, you are full of the bullshits."

Barac got up from the table and prowled like a rhino, squinting. He bumped his way to a small safe set against an inner wall and bolted to the flooring. He cracked his knuckles a couple of times, as if marshaling his memory, and then worked at the combination with knockwurst-like fingers.

Longarm sat still, watching the circus owner. A streamer of light fell across the big man, the wide shoulders hunched forward, the thick mat of hair.

Barac opened the safe, quickly removed a sheet of paper, and in the same movement slammed the door. It was as if Barac not only didn't trust Longarm and his own bodyguards; he didn't even trust himself.

Barac stood up. He turned and faced Longarm in the silent wagon. He clutched a folded legal foolscap in his hamhock fist.

He shook the paper out and lumbered forward. He extended the document toward Longarm. His hand shook, as did his thunderous basso voice, but the trembling came from his righteous indignation, not from any weakness.

"Read this, Mr. Marshal. It is the American way. That's Josip Barac's way. Yes. Sure. I want to own Vingie Vinson's sideshow. For a long time I try to get her to sell. For cash. For discount. The American way."

"No pressures? No threats?"

"Not from me, Mr. Lawman. Maybe Vingie Vinson she got her own goddamn pressures, Mr. Marshal—but not from me. I want her sideshow and her freaks. I freely admit this. But that is all I want. And I offer legal to buy them legal. Legal. Cash. The American way. There it is. All clear and upstairs above the boards. The American way. You can no way mix me up in any other way with these troubles the little freak claims to herself." He sat back down at the table and wiped his napkin across his mouth. "Just don't try to mix me up in any Old World terrorism or anarchy or any other fool thing that don't make nobody no profit. Profit. That is what I learn. I am now one-hundred-percent American now. Everything I do is one-hundred-percent the American way. For profit."

A man rode out from Black Lake depot with Billy Vail's reply to Longarm's request for extension of time on the present assignment. As usual, the chief marshal wasted few words and little of the taxpayers' money:

"YOU CRAZY QUESTION MARK HELL NO STOP LEAVE FOR DENVER NOW TONIGHT STOP REGARDS VAIL U S MARSHAL DENV"

Carrying the wire crushed in his fist, Longarm walked toward Vingie's van. Shouts and weeping struck like sudden rain in his face, and he ran between the tents and wagons.

The freaks were gathered outside Vingie's van. They wailed, gesturing toward Longarm, all of them talking at once.

He pushed his way through them. The first thing he saw was that the door had been torn loose from its bolts. It swung back like a bird's broken wing.

The inside of the van had been ripped apart. Chairs were overturned, windows smashed, and tables broken. It looked as if someone had taken an axe to the exotic carriage. It was a total wreck.

Wee Vingie was nowhere in sight.

Longarm thrust his way through the small rooms of the wagon. He found only destruction everywhere.

He walked back outside to where the freaks stood, numbed, helpless.

He hated to ask because he dreaded the answer he knew he was going to get. "Where is she?"

"She's gone," Ljubo said.

"Somebody broke in. Didn't anybody hear anything?"

"By the time we got here it was too late. She was gone. Whoever it was, they had taken her away."

His heart sinking, Longarm stared silently at each of the faces of the freaks. They could tell him nothing except of their own terror. He tried to tell himself that it had not been the one-hundred-percent American Josip Barac or his henchmen . . . unless they had invited him in, fed him, and kept him occupied while somebody in their pay wrought this havoc.

He searched the ground around the van for signs, but any tracks had been obscured by the milling feet of the freaks.

"Don't any of you know who her enemies were?" Longarm pleaded. "Who hated her?"

"Many hated her," Minerva said.

"But not to kill her," Fatima said.

Ljubo frowned with the strain of thinking. "Maybe Cy Slimer. Cy knows her best of all of us. He would know her enemies."

Longarm strode away, going between the darkened tents toward the lighted first-aid tent. When he walked into the clinic, he hesitated just inside the vaguely lighted structure.

He stopped, staring. Cy Slimer was not in his bed.

At first, Longarm thought the tent was deserted. Then he saw the clown, Felix, sit up on one of the beds. Longarm said, "Where's Cy Slimer?"

The clown shrugged. "He was lying there when I came in. One of those damned burros bit me. I came over for treatment. Decided to spend the night. These beds are a lot more comfortable than my cot in the clowns' tent. And it's a hell of a lot quieter. Nobody here but Slimer, and him asleep. I finally dozed off, and then one of them freaks run in, yelling that something had happened to that midget Vingie Vinson. She was gone and nobody knew where."

"And Slimer got up?"

"Sure as hell did. Gun wounds and all. I tried to talk him out of it. But he went running off. Said something about how Wee Vingie couldn't do anything without him. She was helpless without him, he said."

"What made him think he could find her?"

"That's what I asked him. He didn't make sense. He only kept saying he had to find her. He grabbed up a big carpetbag and ran out of here. That's the last I saw of him."

Chapter 13

Marshal Billy Vail was prowling his outer office in the federal building when Longarm arrived. Vail gave him only a glance, then resumed prowling. Tired, and feeling sick with loss and failure, Longarm sagged against a wall and watched the balding lawman.

Billy kept bending over Frank's shoulder as the young clerk painfully and slowly pecked out Billy's latest report.

Billy tapped Frank's shoulder and pointed at the paper in the bail of the newfangled typewriter. "Period goes there, boy."

Frank looked up, sweated and frustrated. "You got to give me a chance to find the key before I can hit it, sir."

"Hell, you ought to know where the period is on that infernal machine by now," Vail said. He snorted in disgust and turned away. "Government's always coming up with machines to save time, for God's sake. Could have written this report by hand and had it in the mail by now."

"I'm doing the best I can, sir." Frank's voice shook.

Vail shrugged. "That's what all you bureaucrats say." He turned and jerked his head toward his inner office. "Come on in, Longarm."

As Longarm walked past Vail into the inner office, Billy said to Frank, "You keep at that damn thing. We got to get it out today, and I don't want it looking like you wrote it with an eraser and corrected it with a typewriter, either. You understand what I'm saying?"

Marshal Vail glanced at Longarm as he strode past him, going around his desk and sagging into the swivel chair under the framed, tinted photograph of the President. His head jerked up and he stared at Longarm again. "My God, boy," he said. "You look like hell. Worse even than usual."

Longarm exhaled. "Little gut-sick, that's all."

"Still off your feed because I yanked you out of that circus? What were you doing, laying the bearded lady?"

"I might as well have been, for all the good I did."

"You did your job."

"Two murders and a kidnapping. Right under my nose. And I'm as much in the dark now as I was when the crimes happened. Maybe I got a few ideas, but they won't do me any good now."

"I assigned you to the case, Longarm. I took you off. Forget it."

"I don't like to fail, Billy."

"Hell, nobody does. But we got jobs to do—different jobs. Right now, we got a different job."

"Just like that."

Vail's head jerked up. "That's right. Just like that. You don't like the way I run this office, you write a letter. If I like the way it sounds, I'll have Frank type it up and I'll mail it in to headquarters myself. Meantime, I'm the boss."

Longarm winced. "I'm here, Billy. As per orders. Now, if you're going to tell me I've got to like following every order you give me, you can cram it."

Vail smiled. "You're right. Whether you like your jobs or not ain't my concern. But bellyaching—even under your breath—can affect the way you work on a new job, and I make that my concern."

Longarm walked to the window. Then he turned. "Billy, tell me one thing. Ain't you still interested in a plot against the life of Princess Danica?"

"You can bet on it."

"Well, that's what's eatin' at me, and you might as well know it. I got this terrible notion, Billy, that somebody is going to try to kill Princess Danica, likely at Governor Loving's shindig. And they might be able to get away with it, first because I failed, and second because you yanked me off the case before I could figure what went wrong."

Vail shrugged. "You're just one deputy marshal, Longarm. You did your job. I needed you and I had to call you in. That don't mean we're not using the information you provided from the circus. And it don't mean that we ain't on our toes more than ever, because of what you found out. We got marshals coming in here from as far away as Washington, D.C., Chicago, New York, and San Francisco. We're alerted. We're ready. If anybody gets close to Princess Danica, they're going to find a wall of marshals they got to get through."

Longarm shook his head. "I might have been able to figure it out and stop them, if that stupid robbery hadn't blown my cover."

"But it did blow your cover. And that robbery was one of the biggest breaks this office has had in years. Because of it, and what you fellows did in breaking it up, we found out why Texas Bill Wirt is up this way, and what he wants."

Longarm's head came up and he watched Vail intently. Vail nodded emphatically. "That's right. Texas Bill pulled the circus job because it looked easy and because he needed financing to stay hid out up here so far from his own stomping grounds and all. But the circus job was just peanuts—just keeping his hand in, and trying to pick up working capital. He didn't even send in his best men. He didn't go along himself. But we know for damn sure he'll be in on the next job. We even know what he's doing up here so far north of the Brazos. First, it's got too hot for Wirt in Texas—the weather and the law. And second, he's planning to pull a job that I wouldn't believe if I hadn't got it from the horse's mouth. Would you believe he's after a bullion train in the Burlington yards—a train on its way to the Denver Mint?"

"No."

"Well, I'm telling you, he is. We got it from a thug named Atwood. This Atwood was bad wounded in the shootout at the Black Lake circus heist. One of you fellows got him. Drilled him good. In the gut. He managed to ride, but not too far. He tried to get medical aid, and that's when our men picked him up. So you see, you did us some good up there with the circus.

"This Atwood was so near dead that we had the doctor here in Denver sign his death warrant. It was in the newspapers that Atwood croaked. We wanted word to get back to Wirt that Atwood was dead because we don't want ol' Texas Bill to suspicion that Atwood turned bright yellow when he thought he was dying, and talked his little heart out."

Longarm sweated profusely in the darkened freight car. Empty cars like this one strategically dotted the yard, encircling the

157

U.S. bullion train, though the government's plan was predicated on the slim hope that the placement of these cars wouldn't alarm Texas Bill Wirt, arouse his suspicions, or change his plans. The government wanted Texas Bill. They'd spent a lot of money preparing this reception for him. They were betting that the lure of that bullion would be too much for the greedy bandit to resist.

From where Longarm stood in the shadows beside a slightly opened door, he could get a pretty fair view of the rails, maintenance sheds, sidings, and towers of the Burlington yards. Behind him, three bored deputy marshals—two of them from the Chicago area office and loudly contemptuous of this hick operation—played cards, swatted at flies, and perspired.

Longarm held back a yawn. No stakeout was ever easy. This had been a long, unpleasant wait. The deputies—he didn't even know how many were assigned to this case—had all come into the yards inside empty freight cars, and they had not left them, even under deepest cover of night. Cold cans of pork and beans provided provisions. A cutaway gallon drum half-filled with lime offered the only toilet facilities. And the flies multiplied.

Longarm's beard itched. He and the deputies in the cars were assigned one job: jump Wirt's riders when and if they approached the bullion train. They had no horses. They could not hope to pursue the bandits, or engage in any kind of running battle with Wirt's men. The chase, if there had to be one, would be handled by other deputies, hidden with their saddled mounts outside the yards.

Dusk was settling in, a thin gray cloak tossed from the high shoulders of the Front Range, off to the west, when the long wait suddenly ended.

From beyond the soot-blackened buildings rimming the railroad yards, huge orange, green, and red plumes of fire erupted. The sudden brilliance was so fearful and intense that the inside of the freight car was illuminated with crimson shafts that licked at the shadows.

The deputies dropped their cards and leaped to their feet. They crowded around Longarm at the slightly cracked door.

They could hear the bells and the clatter of distant horse-drawn fire fighting equipment rattling uphill. "Might be something we can do to help," somebody said.

"Hell, yes. Let's get over there."

"Stay." Longarm's voice crackled in the sweated car.

"Who the hell are you, giving orders? I'm from Chicago. I don't take my orders from some backcountry deputy. Who the hell you think you are?"

"Push me and find out, Chicago. I shoot the first bastard that tries to leave this freight car."

"Hell, Long. That fire looks like it could wipe out half of Denver."

Longarm swore. "Maybe it can. But whether it does or not ain't up to us. Running off to fight a fire is just what Texas Bill Wirt would love to have you do. If he's within twenty miles, he's figuring you'll do just that. You fight the fire— and he takes the gold."

"Shit, cowboy," Chicago said. "There ain't going to be no play for that bullion."

"There better be. I ain't sat in this sweat and flies and stink to watch a fire."

"Hell, nobody's stupid enough to attack an armed bullion train—not even out here this far from civilization—"

"Shut up," Longarm rasped. He glimpsed movement along the tracks. Holding his breath, he watched the first shadowy horsemen moving beside the rails, passing the farthest cars, taking their time, but heading toward the bullion train. He would not have spotted them, they moved so stealthily in the darkness, except for the bright fireglow. "Here they come."

The other deputies fell silent.

Longarm moved his gaze along the tracks. The deputies stationed in the other cars made no move, either. Men on horseback seemed to appear from every direction and in the same instant. Texas Bill was a smart field general.

"Son of a bitch," Longarm whispered. "He must have brought half of Texas with him."

"Lots of cheap guns from down that way these days," one of the deputies whispered from behind him. "The Texas Rangers are doing a pretty fair job, heatin' up the border country. Lew Wallace's men are running the gun thugs out of New Mexico. Lincoln County's quieted down. Wirt could of recruited quite an army."

"It's Texas Bill's men, all right," Longarm said. "This is his method of operation. First he stakes his lookouts—see them, all along the tracks? They won't move unless there's trouble. Next he posts guards along his exits. He don't go in anywhere that he don't leave his backtrail covered—with guns. Bastard never leaves nothing to chance."

"Hell, let's take the son of a bitch," Chicago said. "We surprise the sucker, we stop him before he gets set."

"You make a move now, you're the sucker," Longarm said.

Suddenly, Longarm heard the low, steady thud of hooves. He couldn't tell how many horses were closing in on the car where he and the other deputies waited, but he saw at least four riders encircling each of the other freight cars. Either Texas Bill had figured out the setup or, being naturally cautious, he was taking no chances.

The other deputies heard the horsemen too. None of them spoke. They breathed shallowly, watching the men outside, armed with Winchesters, sitting their mounts in the shadows of the cars, waiting for a door to open, or for a lawman to show himself.

Checkmate, Longarm thought, feeling ill. They had only to vent that door as much as an inch and the horsemen outside would open fire with their Winchesters. They were pinned down in here, helpless to do anything but watch Texas Bill Wirt pull off the train robbery of the century. The hell of it was, the lawmen in all the other cars were just as impotent. Wirt had sealed them off in these cars, unable even to help each other. They could not even fire a gun to alert the mounted lawmen outside the yards. They could only wait, and sweat. Breaking this door open and leaping out was too much like ejecting clay pigeons from a trap.

In the very dim light from the distant conflagration, Longarm saw the main body of Wirt's legion, coldly businesslike and self-assured professionals, totally prepared in advance, armed with rifles, riding slowly between their own lines of waiting sentries toward that bullion car where three armed guards waited—like fish in a barrel.

Longarm sweated. Marbles of sweat formed under his hatband and leaked into his eyes. Jesus, this car stunk. The flies were unbearable. This was just no place to die.

He eased back from the doorway. Chicago took his place, gun drawn, itching to fire down on any moving target in the yards, but finding none. The riders guarding this car were pressed close in against it, using it as a shield as they waited for any movement at that door.

Longarm looked around. The door on the far side of the car was tightly closed, and even if it hadn't been, he knew Wirt's men were guarding it. In one way, fighting Wirt was easier than fighting a stupid foe. With Wirt, you knew in advance what to expect—total professionalism and careful planning. All the odds were stacked against you; Texas Bill had lasted so long primarily because he left nothing to chance. He figured all angles ahead of time, and prepared for them.

Longarm's gaze touched at faint wisps of light winking at the far end of the car roofing. Signaling the deputy nearest him to silence, Longarm pointed toward the skylight trapdoor.

After a moment, the other deputy understood and nodded his head. Silently, he alerted the others to the trapdoor in the roof. The deputies agreed with the proposed strategy—hell, anything was better than waiting in here. They removed their guns cautiously from their holsters, wincing at the faint whisper of metal against leather.

Longarm took a long time traveling the length of the car. He crept along on his toes, setting each foot down solidly between steps.

He paused at the iron ladder and glanced back. The other deputies watched him tensely. Suddenly, Chicago waved his arm frantically.

Longarm got the message. Wirt's men were at the bullion car. It was now or never. Either somebody made a move or it was too late and Wirt rode out of here a rich man, while twenty deputy U.S. marshals watched helplessly.

In the taut silence, Longarm climbed to the skylight. He eased the cover aside, aware of the sudden kiss of fresh air, fireglow, and the first stars just breaking out like measles beyond the timberline.

He removed his Colt from its holster and set it out on the car roofing. Holding his breath, he hoisted himself up into the opening. He pushed his head over the top, checking the yards. He counted five horsemen lined up along the car below him and at least five horsemen guarding all the other cars grouped around the yard. He saw men dismount and approach the bullion car under protection of a dozen rifles held at the ready by mounted gunmen.

He chewed at his underlip. He had to move fast or one of Wirt's lookouts would spot him in the firelight. But he had to move carefully or somebody from out there would pick him off before he could set himself ready to fire.

He pressed facedown close to the roofing, practically kissing the wood, and took up his Colt in his right fist. He slithered out onto the rooftop, trying to hide his outline against the firelit sky.

As soon as his boots cleared the opening, he located a target, a thin man in a Texas sombrero and leather chaps, on a piebald pony. He set the gun, taking his time, and squeezed the trigger. The piebald lunged upward, squealing, the sound carrying in the taut silence. The rider dropped his rifle and toppled from the saddle—and all hell broke loose across the railyards.

Far across the webbing of tracks, mounted men rode, firing, out of the big maintenance sheds. The gunfire was a signal for every planned action, on both sides. The men at the bullion car went on working. Their horsemen turned, looking for foes, ready to fire.

From within the bullion cars, the armed guards opened fire.

Below where Longarm lay pressed against the roofing, the outlaw riders hesitated in one moment of shock and panic. This hesitation gave Chicago and the other two deputies their single chance to hurl open that door and lay down a barrage of gunfire.

There was a simultaneous explosion from all the rifles of the outlaws. But they were forced from the cover of the train. Inside the car, the deputies found whatever cover they could and fired at anything that moved.

The owlhoots were firing at Longarm on the rooftop now. Bullets whipped past his head. Longarm admitted what he had a hundred times before. When somebody's shooting at him, a man can hunker down behind a pebble or a piece of soot. He sprawled low on the curved roofing, grabbing what concealment he could.

From where he lay, Longarm saw and heard something that gave his heart a lift. The gates to the yards swung closed on all sides. Wirt was not the only field general who planned in advance. The high fences, topped with barbed wire, enclosed them all now, friends and foes.

Longarm realized that whoever had been shooting at him had been taken out of action. Exultant, he lifted his head and almost lost it. A bullet bit into the wood next to his shoulder.

Longarm jerked up his head and stared at the outlaw at the other end of the train roof. Extending his pistol ahead of him, Longarm lay unmoving, without breathing. All he wanted to do was to lure that gunman all the way up on the roof to give him a better target.

The man suddenly sprang up on the roof. Longarm pressed the trigger.

The gunman staggered, turned all the way around. He dropped his gun, fell to his knees on the edge of the roof, and then fell, headfirst, outward into the darkness.

The two remaining horsemen retreated and Longarm lifted himself slightly, firing after them.

Chicago and the other two deputies leaped from the train and crouched in the deep shadows beside the wheels, firing at the retreating bandits.

The piebald remained unmoving near where his master had fallen. Longarm took one quick look around. He found that their gunfire had decoyed some of Wirt's men from their posts beside other freight cars. Suddenly those other car doors were thrown open. Deputies dove outward toward the ground, firing as they leaped.

Longarm crawled to the edge of the boxcar roofing. Setting himself, he sprang outward, hoping to land in the piebald's saddle and praying to miss the pommel. It was either that or sing soprano for the rest of his life.

He struck the saddle, and the frightened pony was already running, as if trying to run out from under him. Longarm grabbed reins, mane, and pommel, holding on. His boots found the stirrups and he slammed his feet into them. He fought for and caught his balance, bringing the terrified piebald under control.

The railyards were a place of chaos. The robbery at the bullion train had suddenly broken down and was abandoned. The riders there were looking for cover and finding none.

At several places across the yard, outlaws, some wounded and others suddenly religious, were yelling, "God, don't shoot." They threw their guns away, dismounted, and stood beside their horses.

Near the bullion train, a tall thin man, his hat blown off his head and held at his throat with a thong, was yelling at them in a baritone voice that was used to commanding attention amid the sustained roar of gunfire.

For a few minutes, Texas Bill was able to rally his forces. His riders, those who had not thrown down their weapons or were not wounded or slain, tried to ride to where Wirt and his men were holing up at the bullion car.

Longarm was conscious of someone riding beside him in the firelit darkness. He glanced over his shoulder and saw Chicago grinning at him. "Nice going, cowboy," the deputy said. "Looks like you saved the day."

"Hell," Longarm said, "it's plumb easy when you learn how."

The firing intensified at the bullion car. Longarm and Chicago rode across the tracks, going toward it.

The shooting stopped abruptly before they reached the bullion car. Even in the smoke and dust, Longarm could see why. Texas Bill Wirt's big horse stood riderless. The fight was gone out of Wirt's legions. They threw down their guns.

Billy Vail appeared, shouting orders. The gang members were to be cuffed together. They were to take no chances. Each outlaw was to be searched closely for any weaponry. Then Vail said, "Count the wounded. See if any of our men need medical attention. Doctors will be in here as soon as the gates are opened."

The marshals crowded around to get a look at Texas Bill Wirt. Few of them had seen the infamous Texan except on wanted posters.

Texas Bill was dead, there could be no doubt about that. It was as if every marshal in range had fired at a single target, each wanting to be the man who killed Texas Bill Wirt. His body was bullet-riddled.

Chicago swung down from his horse and stood beside Vail, gazing down at the dead outlaw leader.

"Ugly brute dead, ain't he?" Vail said.

"Don't look like he won any beauty contests alive," Chicago said.

"Them reward dodgers flattered hell out of him."

"He don't look like so much to me," one of the Eastern marshals said.

Vail jerked his head around and glared at the deputy. "No," Vail said. "He wasn't much. Just outlived most of the other wild bunch. And it just took twenty of us, and every trick in the book, to get him."

Longarm slumped tiredly in his saddle. The yard gates were thrown open and medical men in carriages, with male nurses along, entered the area.

Vail let the deputies stand around until a body count was made and until all marshals who required it had received medical attention. Then he said, "Men, you did a good job. I wish I could say, well done, so go get drunk. But that ain't the way it is. Most of you men, you know, came out here on another assignment, and that job opens up tomorrow when Princess Danica of Hungary arrives in Golden. That's when your real work begins. Hope this was a good warmup for what's ahead of you."

Vail got into one of the doctors' carriages and rode out of the yard. Longarm grinned coldly. Another day, another dollar.

Chapter 14

Longarm rode into the village of Golden in the fiery glow of false dawn. There wasn't much to see: a mining town in the foothills of the Front Range, fifteen or so miles northwest of Denver. He had seen a hundred towns just like Golden, but nobody had to tell him this settlement was different today, totally unlike any he'd ever known before.

Except for the unusual number of carriages, wagons, and coaches parked in every vacant lot, Golden didn't look very different, a typical little Rocky Mountain crossroads town with false fronts, railroad depot, a couple of paint-thirsty churches on its one long main street. This thoroughfare climbed up out of the timber and writhed off into it. Distantly, he saw the dark sheds of the mines, while closer in were the ornate signs of the saloons where the cowhands gathered from the nearby ranches.

Longarm rode slowly into the town, studying the place and memorizing it. Golden hunched down in a saucer between Lookout Mountain, which rose to its west, and Castle Rock, the big red butte that partially cut it off from the High Plains stretching toward Denver. In the clear, crisp atmosphere, one could see all the way to Denver from either Lookout Mountain or Castle Rock.

Longarm glanced over his shoulder. The road from Denver was becoming crowded. The good people of the city would be arriving, guests of Governor Loving at his mansion. Longarm supposed the state official lived in his grand estate near the mines because it was from them that he drew his amazing wealth.

The tall lawman looked forward with no enthusiasm to the long day ahead. He dreaded this assignment for many reasons.

First, he still felt cold and guilty that he had failed little Vingie Vinson; there had been no trace of her since he'd left the circus. Not even the fact that he'd been praised for having broken the impasse between Wirt's legions and the marshals in the Burlington train yards lifted his spirits. Praise has a way of diluting itself in the truth one knows deep inside oneself. But guilt and failure can haunt you and keep you awake nights. And he had failed.

Second in his list of discomforts was the prospect of spending the day riding herd on Princess Danica and her party of royalists among the Denver swells who would gather at Loving's reception. No doubt, all the elite from the luxurious brownstone homes of East Denver would be at that party. No matter how snooty the Boston Back Bay Brahmins were, the Colorado First Families of Sherman Avenue were as elegant. And they'd all be there, all the names out of the society columns: the Evanses, the Loves, the Browns, Tabors, and Zietzes.

Longarm shrugged his jacket up on his shoulders. Damn it, he was tough. Ten times tougher than the Good Lord made most men. And he knew how to handle himself in trouble— let his foes draw guns, knives or clubs and he could take care of himself. But damn it all, he felt out of place and awkward among society swells. They made him as sweaty and ill at ease as a gun muzzle poking in his back.

And there was more. He had the sure instinct that trouble lay ahead. It was like an arthritic toe acting up before a rain. They were in for it, and there was no way to call it off. Trouble was going to strike, like a coiled sidewinder. Only nobody knew from where—and their not knowing came partly from his own failure.

He found a cafe open and sat over scrambled eggs and steak medium, watching wagons roll past in the street out front. Other marshals drifted in, trying to look casual, trying to melt into the crowd. But Longarm had no trouble recognizing them. He could not believe any anarchists would be fooled, either. A man smart enough to assemble a bomb would spot these fellows anywhere. As far as Longarm was concerned, the deputy marshals stood out in Golden like tits on a bull. Another bad omen.

The cafe proprietor said something. Longarm jerked his head up. "What?"

"Just said, big day ahead. Biggest in the history of this town."

"Yes. Big day," Longarm said in a dull voice.

"Reckon it'll be as big as the day when Jeb Loving became governor. That was a big one too."

Longarm prowled the boardwalks from one end of town to the other. There was no certain way to stop a determined assassin, but one took all precautions. He found the alleyways and nooks where a man could conceal himself, or make a fast exit. He mostly found other deputies making their own rounds, their checks and surveys, as they policed the area.

By nine that morning. the streets were filling with people bringing their own stools and kitchen chairs and lining the parade route where Princess Danica would pass on her way to Governor Loving's mansion.

The curious had come from distant towns. One bearded man was telling a new acquaintance, "My family and me. Came all the way from Black Lake. We seen the circus. Hell of a show. Lot of excitement. But like my good lady says, ain't every day people get to see a real live princess from the middle of Europe."

"That's right, by God. A real princess."

Longarm exhaled and walked on past. The farmer was right. Danica was a real princess. Maybe a doomed princess, keeping a date with destiny today while the world watched helplessly.

"Howdy, Marshal Long."

Longarm stopped dead in his tracks and turned, recognizing Felix the clown from the Baldwin-Naylor Circus. It was on the tip of his tongue to demand what Felix was doing here in Golden, but he caught himself in time. Felix had every right to be here, more even than the Coloradans who'd never seen royalty. Danica was Felix's own princess, from his distant home.

"You look like you seen a ghost, bub," Felix said.

"Just surprised to see you, that's all."

"Surprised? Why? Why wouldn't I want to see Princess Danica in the flesh, bub? They say she is one of the loveliest women that ever lived. That makes her worth seeing. After all,

she comes from one of the ugliest royal familes in all Europe."
He laughed. He swung his arm and indicated others from the
circus. "Lot of us down here. All the Magyars, Croats, Serbs."

Dismayed, Longarm recognized Josip Barac and his bodyguards sitting in an open carriage. He saw other clowns, as
well as some of the freaks. He felt sweat form in his armpits
and ooze along his ribs.

"Great," he heard himself saying. He slapped Felix on the
shoulder and moved away along the street.

Governor Loving's mansion was unlike anything Longarm had
ever seen before. The massive stone chalet was set like a gem
in the bright setting of formal gardens, pools, ponds, hammocks, and emerald-green lawns. There was breathtaking
beauty in the turrets, gables, and gingerbread of the four-story
home. Tall windows caught the sunlight and glittered, jewellike. On the east lawn, colorful striped tents had been set up
for the reception. There was a raised dais for the distinguished
guests and a lectérn waiting for the governor's welcoming
address. Over a hundred chairs had been set in rows facing the
dais. Beyond them, tables, richly decorated with flowers,
awaited the food and drink that would be served. The place
was primed and waiting for a gala party, but all Longarm could
think was that the house, grounds, and parks provided a
hundred potential hiding places for assassins.

He whistled between his teeth. The town was bad enough,
but this place of topiary gardens and shadowed parks was
almost impossible to police.

The deputy marshals were gathered in the first two rows
of chairs. After a brief wait, the governor's executive secretary,
a man named Marvin Wilson, appeared, carrying a stack of
papers and wearing an unflappable smile.

"Gentlemen, the governor wants me to welcome you, and
to express in advance his appreciation for the task you'll be
called upon to perform today. Without men like you, international affairs like this would be impossible to put on. Un-
fortunately, the world is filled with people motivated by hate,
people who believe that violence will help to solve our problems. Whether we agree with them or not, we've got to deal
with them. But I don't have to tell you that; that's your job.

"First, there are coffee and doughnuts there at the first tent.

You're invited to help yourself as soon as this briefing is over. And I'll try to keep it as brief as possible. I'm not going to try to tell you your job. What I want to tell you is that Princess Danica is due to arrive at the station in Golden within the hour. Our latest information is that, for some reason, the train is running precisely on time." He waited for the small laugh and then continued, "You will be there—except those assigned to remain here at the mansion. There will be a parade through town. There are hundreds of people in Golden for this occasion. The princess will ride in Governor Loving's open carriage. We will—as your superiors have advised—keep the procession moving as steadily as possible, but the princess—and Governor Loving—will not want to insult the many onlookers by racing through them. We promise to take every precaution possible.

"The parade will proceed from town, up the road there, and through those iron gates at the front wall. From there, the carriages will follow the drive to the front of the mansion. The princess will be briefly inside the house and then will appear on this dais with her party and the governor and other distinguished guests. The only formal events will follow. The princess will be welcomed. Children from the Golden primary grades will present bouquets of wildflowers to the princess. This will be followed by the governor's welcoming address. Then there will be entertainment, followed by food and drink.

"I am sure if we are all alert and aware of the *threat* of possible danger, even in a gala surrounding like this, our party will be successful and memorable. Are there any questions?"

Longarm's first view of Princess Danica was much like being kicked in the face by a mule—one didn't recover quickly.

Felix the clown had not exaggerated—if anything, he had erred on the side of understatement—when he called Princess Danica one of the loveliest women that ever lived.

Longarm stood in the sun on the station platform as Princess Danica emerged from her private car and paused for a moment, smiling on the steps.

Longarm's mouth gaped and he forgot the first rule for a good sentry: to look at everything and everybody *except* the person you're guarding. He stared openly at Princess Danica, as did everybody else on the elevated platform.

Longarm had never seen a real princess. He was unaccustomed to royalty. But he needed no yardstick to know that Princess Danica was incredible and exceptional.

There was about her a fragility that was more palpable than the Dresden china of the small statuettes he had seen in Vingie's van. There was a regal air about her, but it was inborn and innate and a part of her, so that she could seem natural and unaffected and yet somehow removed, all at the same time.

Her hair was a shimmering, rich red-gold. She wore it brushed and shining about her delicately featured face. That hair caught all the sunlight and gleamed like a scepter.

It was a hell of a thing to think at a time like this, but she was that kind of dream woman that a man would go through hell for—and pray for no more reward than an hour in her bed.

Her lime-green dress was simple and unadorned, from small lace high-standing collar to elegantly full bust, to eighteen-inch waist, slender hips, and lace ruffles, spilling about her slippers.

There was a stunned, awed silence the length of the freight platform. Longarm permitted himself that one luxurious moment of admiring Princess Danica to the exclusion of everything else. For that brief instant he was dazed. When Governor Loving stepped forward to greet the princess, the reverie ended and Longarm snapped back to reality, staring about him alert and suspicious, trusting no one, and savagely resolved that no evil would befall such a lovely creature as long as he lived.

He stood aside, watchful, head and shoulders above the crowd. Princess Danica's dazzling smile warmed the governor and rewarded the crowd for coming. Her party emerged from the private cars and they all moved with the local and state dignitaries to the waiting carriages outside the depot.

Longarm strode around the small, soot-streaked building and took his place at the right rear wheel of the governor's carriage. His gaze raked the street ahead, where hundreds of people stood expectantly, smiling and waving flags.

Princess Danica came out of the depot. People applauded. She smiled and waved. One of the governor's footmen touched the royal elbow to help her into the rear of the open carriage.

For a moment, Princess Danica paused. Her gaze touched at Longarm, standing directly behind the carriage, and moved on. Then her eyes moved back. He swore they did, lingering on him for a moment.

Hell, don't flatter yourself, old son. Every man she looks

*at thinks she is looking at him as she never looked at any other
man.*

Still, Longarm could not deny that when the governor was
seated in the tonneau of the carriage at Princess Danica's left,
the royal beauty bent toward the official and whispered something. Loving looked up, twisting his neck and staring at Longarm for a half-second. Then he smiled and said something to
Princess Danica.

The procession moved off along the main street.

People along the boardwalks, in windows, and on shaded
stoops, gawked and waved as the carriage rolled slowly past.

Longarm felt his heart slug oddly. Princess Danica waved
back at the onlookers, smiling, as friendly and natural as a
cornflower.

Longarm forced himself to avert his head from the carriage.
He swept the crowds ahead of the open vehicle, watching them
as the driver moved through, then let the marshal behind him
take over that sector while he jerked his gaze ahead again.

His gaze touched at an old man, bent, dusty, looking like
a desert rat without his burro. Longarm never knew what
snagged his attention. God knew, there was nothing all that
unusual about the slumped figure—he wore a battered bonnet,
with its floppy brim shapeless about his bearded face, his hair
gray and straggly about his shoulders. His coat was buttoned
tightly and his hands were thrust deeply into the pockets. His
Levi's were ragged and salty. Only his shoes looked as if they'd
been purchased as recently as the last year.

Longarm started on past; then, pausing, he stared again at
the crouched figure of the wanderer. Maybe it was nothing
more than that natural suspicion that made a man turn to law
enforcement in the first place.

But the old man was aware that he'd attracted Longarm's
attention. Longarm saw him stiffen and withdraw into the
crowd. Maybe some drifter whose guilt upset him.

Longarm shrugged and was just training his gaze ahead
when the old man suddenly heeled around and tried to force
his way roughly through the crowd that was four deep on the
boardwalk.

Longarm turned, jerked his head at the marshal directly
behind him. The deputy nodded and strode forward, taking his
place.

The old man was fighting his way to the rear of the crowd.

Longarm still had no idea why he pursued him. There was something faintly familiar about him, but it was nothing he could put his finger on. Still, he kept his gaze on him.

When the old man thrust a child aside and the child toppled, crying out, two farmers, angered, snagged at the old man's arms. They jerked him around, straightening him and pulling his hands from his pockets. The old codger fought like a wildcat.

Longarm's gaze focused on the old man's right hand, mutilated, the fingers missing between thumb and pinky.

"Excuse me," he said, pushing his way into the crowd. Trying to keep his voice pitched low and casual, moving as unobtrusively as possible, Longarm said to the farmers, "Hold him. Don't let him go."

"He ain't going nowhere, mister," one of the farmers said.

Cy Slimer stared at Longarm, his thin ferret's face twisted, his eyes glittering with madness.

Longarm snapped handcuffs on Slimer's wrists and thrust him ahead of him through the crowd, toward the sheriff's office and town jail.

"What you doin'?" Slimer said. "You got nothing against me."

"I *had* nothing against you, Slimer. Until you ran from me."

"Is that against the law now—running from a big ugly cuss like you?"

Longarm grinned coldly. "It is now, Cy, on a day like this. It is when you look like a desert rat instead of a carney rat. You're trying to hide from somebody, Slimer. And that's against the law—today of all days."

Cy Slimer shrugged. "I just didn't want Felix and Barac and them others to recognize me, that's all."

"No time to argue with you about it now, Cy. If you got nothing to hide except your face—from your circus friends—you won't mind sitting in the local jail until after Princess Danica leaves town."

By the time Longarm rejoined the royal party, the procession had reached the far limits of Golden and started up the incline toward Loving's estate.

Sweating, Longarm plodded in the wake of the royal parade; the morning sun was growing hotter, the white road glared.

He walked through the iron gate in the five-foot-high brick wall that enclosed the vast estate. He supposed people like Loving erected walls for safety, but this one simply added hiding places for any anarchists, and there were already enough hiding places in the gardens, hammocks, and richly luxuriant parks.

He paused inside the gates and watched the carriages pull into the shaded drive outside the front veranda. In the distance he saw the governor step down from the open carriage and extend his hand to help Princess Danica alight. They stood for a moment on the steps, then entered the house, followed by members of the immediate royal party. The others drifted around the lawn to where the dais, tents, and serving tables were set up.

Carriages and smartly dressed people on foot passed Longarm, entering the grounds and flowing in a colorful channel toward the reception area. Soon every chair was occupied. Harried servants ran to set up more rented seats, but at last surrendered. There was standing room only for the latecomers.

Longarm crossed the grass, studying the faces of the people in the crowd. How did you find an anarchist? What telltale sign did an assassin reveal? He knew the answer to that too. There were not any. Some of the most angelic-looking boys he had ever seen turned out to be the kind who smiled in your face and shot you in the back. You stayed alert, and this was the only magic.

Easily, Longarm picked out the watching deputies in the crowds. These men looked as awkward and out of place as he felt. In chairs near the front he saw Josip Barac sitting with his bodyguards. Near them, Minerva had found a chair among the socially elite, and Felix the clown sat in an end chair. Even Ljubo the Giraffe Man had appropriated a chair near the dais.

Long before he was ready, the crowd came to its feet as one person. The band, in bright red uniforms, struck up the Hungarian national anthem. People began to applaud as Governor Loving, Princess Danica, Mrs. Loving, and the other dignitaries marched out of French doors, crossed a sunlit veranda, and climbed to the dais.

The music ended and Longarm hoped the audience would be seated. Some of them did fan themselves and settle toward their chairs. But at that moment the band struck up "The Star-

Spangled Banner" and everybody stood silently at attention as the music reverberated against the hills. This was followed by the Colorado state song. Finally the crowd was permitted to sit down on chairs or upon the sun-dappled lawn.

Longarm exhaled heavily. If there was going to be an attempt to assassinate that lovely young girl up there today, the assassins had missed one hell of an opportunity to strike in the midst of confusion and noise, to take advantage of a natural diversionary action. Texas Bill Wirt last night had set fire to a meat plant to assure himself easier access to the Burlington yards. Diversionary action was a hoary trick, but it had always been good, it would always work to some degree.

The crowd grew quiet, the buzzing whispers faded. For a long time people went on nudging each other and nodding toward Princess Danica. Longarm couldn't blame them. She was so lovely, lighted by the sun gathering in her red-gold hair, that she might as well have been alone up on that dais.

Longarm stood at the far rim of the crowd. He tried to discipline himself to remain alert and to keep his gaze from straying like a stallion with the scent toward that incredibly lovely girl on the dais. But he could not help gazing at her for one long moment.

From where he stood, Longarm swore that Princess Danica had tilted her delicately sculptured head and moved her gaze across the horizon of the crowd until she found him. For one moment she met his gaze.

The hell she did, he thought. At this distance? Wishful thinking. It made no sense. He warned himself to keep his mind on his job, which was to protect the princess, not to graze over her like a hungry ram.

The schoolchildren sang next. There must have been a dozen little girls from six to ten, ramrodded by a tall, stringy, prim, narrow-faced old maid of a schoolteacher. She herded the girls along in their new, ruffled, lacy, ankle-length party dresses. Each child carried a large bouquet of flowers which she would present to the princess after they had sung and the governor had welcomed the royal lady to Colorado.

The children sang, some of them on key, all of them with energy and enthusiasm, a few even gazing toward their teacher, who swung her arms as choir leader.

The princess smiled. The crowd laughed and whispered about how adorable the children were.

Longarm thought the mindless little song would never end, but mercifully it did. The little girls curtsied, straightened up, and turned around to return to their first-row chairs.

As they walked, Longarm checked them idly, for want of something better to do. Suddenly his gaze struck one of the children, a little girl with black curls almost to her shoulders, a beautiful little thing carrying a large bouquet and keeping her eyes demurely to the ground.

Longarm's gaze leaped back to that face as the girl turned and took her place among the children.

He felt stunned, for that moment unable to move. It was as if he were caught in one of those nightmares in which he had only to cry out and all would be well—only he could not utter a sound. His throat was constricted, his limbs weak and useless.

God in heaven, I've found Wee Vingie Vinson.

He stared at that midget among the children. He didn't know how she'd managed to be accepted among them, but that seemed less than urgent at the moment. She was there.

He knew a lot of answers suddenly. He knew who had made the bomb. He knew where it was. And he knew how it would be presented to Princess Danica.

Vingie waited down there, a tiny incarnation of evil, carrying a lethal bouquet.

Chapter 15

The band played a musical flourish and Governor Loving got to his feet. He smiled and bowed to Princess Danica. He kissed her hand gallantly and many men in the audience hooted in derision. Then Governor Loving walked to the lectern.

Longarm stared at the little figure sitting angelically among the other little girls. From where he stood, her shoulder-length black curls looked real. Hell, *she* looked real. She'd fooled everybody until this moment.

Longarm watched Vingie, feeling helpless and afraid that the intensity of his gaze might alarm her.

He was certain of only one thing. Vingie hadn't seen him yet. If she had, she would not be sitting so calmly with that lethal bouquet in her lap. The irony was that she hadn't seen him earlier because he'd been delayed in arriving up here when he'd stopped to arrest her accomplice, Cy Slimer.

If she had not seen him, he had to make certain she did not see him until he was near enough to grab her. He remembered in a flash the way she'd eluded him that night in her van, like quicksilver, like a hummingbird, like grabbing one's own shadow.

He exhaled, watching her. She sat with calm assurance in what she could do. Maybe she had spotted him. Maybe she just didn't give a damn because she believed he could not get near enough to stop her in time to save Princess Danica, no matter what he did.

In a kind of daze, Longarm heard Governor Loving's voice in the humming silence of the morning garden. The governor welcomed the "lovely and gracious" Princess Danica to God's country. He thanked the schoolgirls for their "lovely and an-

179

gelic" singing. He observed that a man who got to be his age might grow cynical, but any man would have his faith restored when he looked at a lady as lovely as Princess Danica and little girls as beautiful as these children. The world was a good and pure place in which to live, after all.

Following prolonged applause, the governor continued. He thanked God for the unmatched beauty and glorious bounty of Colorado, for its High Plains and vast mountains, for the riches from the heart of its earth and from its fields. There was more and wilder applause, and then the governor added his thanks to God for the safe arrival and the continued safety of their guest and her royal party.

Keep talking, Longarm urged the Governor deep in his mind. *For God's sake, don't stop now.*

Sweat marbling along his face, Longarm looked around in desperation. He spied Chicago, the tall, bulky, barrel-chested deputy who'd sided with him last night in the Burlington yards. After a shaky beginning, a kind of mutual, gibing camaraderie had grown between them.

Longarm motioned Chicago to him. Chicago scowled and formed "Who? Me?" with his lips. Then, at something he saw in Longarm's face, he nodded and pushed his way forward to where Longarm stood in a wide aisle between the two sections of chairs.

The governor continued to speak. He knew all the right things to say to this party crowd and he said them and they responded happily and noisily. In fact, everybody in the huge garden was smiling except Longarm.

"What the hell you want, cowboy?" Chicago whispered.

Longarm placed the bulky deputy in front of him, keeping the heavyset man between him and the front rows of chairs.

Chicago stared at him as if afraid the heat had affected him.

Longarm spoke as softly as he could, but his voice crackled with intensity. "If you ever did anything right in your life, Chicago, do it now."

"What are you talking about?"

"I want you to listen good, mister. I want you to start walking—right now—up to the very front row of chairs in this middle section. Up to where those school kids are sitting with their goddamn flowers. I'll stay as close behind you as I can get. But there's one thing I want you to do, no matter what

180

happens. See that kid—she's the fourth one in from this aisle—the one with the long black curls?"

"Yeah. What about her?"

"If for any reason I don't make it, if I don't get to her in time—I want you to shoot her before she can get near Princess Danica with that bouquet."

Chicago's gasp was the loudest sound in the garden, bouncing against the easy voice of the governor. People turned, staring at them. "Are you loco?"

Longarm gripped the thick, muscular arm in viselike fingers. "You want to save Princess Danica—and your job—you do what I tell you."

"I think you're tetched."

"We'll talk about that sometime, mister, but not here."

"In the federal pen. I'm not going to shoot a little girl."

"Maybe you won't have to, if you'll shut up and get me up there as quickly and quietly as we can go."

Chicago's wide-eyed glance consigned Longarm to the maximum-security cell of the nearest funny farm, but he moved forward with Longarm concealed as much as possible at his right shoulder.

Moving two big men quietly or quickly through a crowd was easier planned than accomplished. People hissed at them when they cut off their view of the smiling Governor Loving. There were muted catcalls and hisses, and people rasped, "Down in front!"

As if trying to obey them, Longarm crouched down behind Chicago and prodded the big man forward.

They were not yet near the front row when, in a torrent of applause and approving shouting, Governor Loving ceased speaking and sat down beside Princess Danica, mopping at the sweat on his forehead with an immaculate white handkerchief.

"Faster," Longarm hissed.

Instead, Chicago slowed, like a stubborn mule. "You're attracting more attention than a flag-raisin', dude."

"Move."

The band played a happy and mindless Stephen Foster tune about Jeannie and her light brown hair. People clapped and tapped their feet in time with the music. The prim schoolmarm stood up and clapped her hands. All the little girls stood up, carrying their flowers.

"Oh, Jesus," Longarm whispered. "Move faster, you mule."

"We both look like jackasses," Chicago said.

Longarm had forgotten Chicago. He watched the first of the little girls move out into the aisle and mince toward the dais, followed by the others as the teacher twisted her vinegary old-maid face into a beaming smile of pride.

As Vingie reached the aisle, she glanced up for almost the first time. As Longarm had known she would, she spotted him instantly.

Something happened in her face. He saw everything there in that flash of time, except fear. Wee Vingie wasn't afraid of anything or anybody. She stared at Longarm, she looked at the crowd, and then jerked her gaze around to her prey on that dais. All of this happened in the blink of an eye. She studied the odds, made her decision.

Longarm read her mind. She was going to do the one thing he could not let her do. She was going to run toward that dais and try to reach the princess before he could stop her.

She pushed the girl ahead of her aside and ran, as Longarm thrust Chicago aside and lunged toward her.

The little girl fell to her knees, screaming in shock and outrage. People yelled around them. Vingie stumbled over the little girl's outstretched arm.

With one hand, Longarm grabbed at Vingie's hair. It came off in his hand, and a shocked gasp flew across the stunned audience.

On the dais, Governor Loving and Princess Danica leaped to their feet. "Stop that man!" the governor yelled.

As Vingie eluded him, Longarm's left hand closed on the fabric along the spine of her dress. He straightened like a fisherman with a catch, and she wriggled, kicking like a gaffed fish in his fist.

He tucked her under his arm and heeled around in one movement. He was vaguely aware of Chicago's gaping mouth and wild eyes as he passed him.

He ran along the aisle, with Vingie screaming and kicking under his arm.

People sprang to their feet, knocking over chairs. The prim schoolteacher fainted, toppling like a felled pine. Women screamed and the governor shouted again, his voice imperious and wrathful, "Stop that man! Stop him!"

A well-dressed man in an aisle chair lunged out into the aisle and barred the way.

Longarm stiff-armed him and the man crumpled. The sight of a man being brushed aside so easily, of a wild man running with a screaming, crying, cursing little girl under his arm, held the other people at bay.

The other deputies drew their guns, as did the state and local police. But they recognized Longarm and hesitated. They heard Governor Loving's raging voice ordering them to shoot the madman and they hesitated.

With Vingie clutched, squirming and cursing, under his arm, Longarm cleared the outer ring of spectators and sprinted toward the nearest wall ringing the property.

"Put me down!" Vingie raged, twisting under his arm. "You're smarter than this, Long. You know she dies or you do."

Longarm kept running. "Turns out I'm smarter than you, Vingie."

"Then you're smart enough to know—"

"That you're a Croatian terrorist?"

"That you can't hold me—" She spun her lithe body inside his arm like a pinwheel, though he held her with all his strength. She had twisted all the way around, an incredible contortionist. Suddenly her tiny slipper caught him in the crotch, three times, rapidly and painfully. "—unless I want you to."

Fire exploded in the crown of Longarm's skull. His eyes watered. His mouth gaped open. For one instant his arms went numb, paralyzed. He felt the walls of his stomach give way, and only by extreme exercise of will was he able to keep from pissing his pants.

Vingie kicked him again. In that brief second while he was incapacitated, with the howling mob bearing down on them from across the lawn, Wee Vingie spun in his arms again, and using his belly as her personal trampoline, as she had done that long-ago night in their happier times, she thrust outward.

He was unable to hold her. Vingie flew from his arms as a mosquito might escape an open fist. It was not a small girl, but a weightless sprite who struck the ground on her toes. He sprang for her, but she was gone again, lightly touching the boles, the branches, the stems of wall vines. She poised for one split-second on the top of the wall, and her eyes touched at his, and he grimaced, agonized at what he saw in them.

Longarm watched her vaguely as if through occluding clouds around some remote planet. She was gone beyond his reach. He saw her only indistinctly through the swirling stars and moons and Roman candles that sparked, crackled, and glittered in the circuitry of his brain.

"Vingie," he moaned, reaching out for her. "Vingie. Don't."

Crouched over like a senile old man with belly cramps, Longarm stared up at the beautiful, miniature woman on that wall, with her bouquet clutched in her tiny, fragile hands.

For that one brief instant, she stared down straight into his face. He saw that she was crying now, sobbing. She didn't speak, and with the caterwauling behind them, he wouldn't have heard her if she had.

His own eyes brimmed with tears that had nothing to do with the agony twisting his groin. Longarm leaped up the wall. But it was no good. He was too late, and anyway, he was helpless to catch her, unable to stop her.

The elfin figure sailed lightly outward, disappearing on the other side of the wall.

Longarm fell heavily against the brick wall as the explosion shook the earth under him, rattled windows in the mansion, broke glasses, and set the women to screaming louder than ever and sent strong men scrambling for cover.

After a moment to recover their wits, most of the deputies sprinted toward the iron gate and the pillar of smoke rising beyond that wall. Longarm stayed where he was. His legs felt too weak to support him. Anyhow, he had no will to move just now. And he did not want to see what Vingie had done to herself.

He stayed pressed against the wall for some moments, hardly aware of the crowd swirling around him like bats in a dark cave. That was what the world was for him just then, a deep and bottomless dark cave.

"Jesus," he whispered to no one, "she could have dropped that bomb—and taken me with her."

She could have, but she hadn't.

He kept seeing her as she had looked down at him for that briefest space of time from the wall. Her eyes would haunt him. He shivered in the warm, midmorning sunlight.

Longarm sank slowly to his knees, doubled over in agony, though there was no longer any pain in his groin, no memory of physical pain. The sound of the explosion reverberated in the still atmosphere of the hills, rolled and echoed and died away. But he went on hearing it inside his mind.

Longarm sat on the edge of a cot in a Denver federal detention cell. He watched Cy Slimer pace the small cage, a human jackal. Slimer bent forward slightly, still pulled out of shape by the agony of ill-healed bullet wounds.

"Before you told me, I already knew she was dead," Slimer said. He nodded and then stared at the floor for a long moment as if trying to reconcile himself to the truth.

"Did you? In this cell?"

Slimer drew a deep breath and held it. "Didn't matter where I was. I heard that bomb go off up in Golden. Before they brought me here, I heard that Princess Danica had escaped unharmed." He sighed heavily. "I knew right then that Vingie was"—his voice cracked—"was dead."

Longarm's voice was charged with guilt and self-hatred. "Vingie didn't kill herself. Not purposely. I caught her. I was trying to get her and her bomb out of there."

Cy shook his head. "No matter what you did, you couldn't have made it. It was a time bomb. We had it timed so in case Vingie was stopped at the last minute, or couldn't get to hand the flowers to Danica, she could throw it at her and it would go off anyway."

Longarm held in the anger that threatened to engulf him. "Vingie didn't throw it. She held on to it. She exploded with it. I should have taken the damn thing away from her...I could have saved her."

"For what?" Cy turned and pressed his thin shoulders against the iron bars. That old familiar simpering smile twisted his ferret-like features. But this smile was different, a smile of contempt. "You feelin' sick in the belly, eh, Long? 'Cause you had her, and she got away from you?"

"Yes. She jumped over a stone wall."

Slimer's mouth twisted. "And you think she did it to save you, eh, lawman?"

"I know if I could only have gotten that damned bouquet away from her—"

Slimer shook his head, eyes dead with cold hatred. "No. I don't want you to have some stupid notion that Vingie did what she did to save you. She didn't."

"She could have let that bomb blow both of us up. But she didn't."

"Hell. Because she was afraid you *would* get it away from her. She knew. We both knew. If she was caught and failed to kill Danica, there was no way she could go on living."

"What kind of crazy idea is that?"

"Not as crazy as the idea that she was trying to save *your* stupid life."

"She saved it once."

"When that bandit was going to kill you? She thought then that you could help her get this job done. She thought you could keep our enemies away from her until she could get to Danica with that bomb."

Longarm felt a shudder wrack his body.

"That's right, lawman," Slimer went on. "For the past months—hell, years—all we been living for was to get near enough to that high-living Danica to hand her a bomb. And we knew we were suspected by people who were loyal to that murdering, bloodsucking emperor."

"Like Marko Begovic?"

Slimer shrugged. "Marko was one. A dangerous one. Because he had once been one of us. But he had changed. He was suspicious of Vingie. But she had been only a little girl at the time of the bombing death of Danica's uncle, the Grand Duke Bojdan."

"But you were there."

Slimer straightened, pride glinting in his eyes. His smile was chilly. "I made the bomb."

"And lost most of your right hand."

"That's right. Everything has its price. The bomb that killed Grand Duke Bojdan was not timed. It was built to explode on impact."

"But it went off ahead of time."

"That's right. The explosion killed a few innocent people, but it got most of the grand duke's stinking royalist entourage. So it was worth it. It killed some of our most loyal party members, and those of us who were not killed were maimed

186

one way or another—lost eyes, legs, arms, testicles. I was lucky, I lost only part of my hand."

"And Marko Begovic was among the rebels that day?"

"In the crowd. He and Kiidislensco. They were not in the inner party, as I was."

"Only the bomb went off too soon, and almost killed you."

Slimer moved his shoulders in a casual gesture of dismissal. "I do not see it as a bad loss. Or error. Or failure. We accomplished our goal. At a heavy cost, yes. But everything costs. The bombing was a good thing for those of us fighting the cause of true Croatian freedom. If it had not exploded prematurely, looking back now, we know we would have missed our chance at the grand duke. We were being driven back away from him, and he was passing to safety when the bomb suddenly exploded. As it was, that way we killed the ruthless Bojdan and most of his hated hangers-on, those decadent nobles. It was bloody. Costly. But we hit our target."

"And so you always use bombs."

Slimer nodded. "Always. For many reasons. There is nothing the police can trace, and we can assemble our bombs from materials that—separately—are harmless. They are purchased singly, one element at a time. In different places."

"And then you put the parts together into something lethal. You and Wee Vingie had planned all along to dress her as a little girl so she could get close enough to hand the bomb to Princess Danica, or to toss it."

Slimer nodded coldly, smiling in that strange, empty way. "And we knew that if we failed, prison for life would be the easiest sentence we could expect. Vingie could not endure the thought of this. She meant to die with the bomb if she failed in her mission."

Longarm felt some of the heavy depression lift. "It almost worked."

Slimer shrugged. After a moment he said, "Vingie was the smart one. She made all the plans, even to her own death if she failed. She kept all our enemies at bay until we could get to where we had a chance at Danica—the evil daughter of a villainous oppressor."

Longarm exhaled a long sigh between his teeth. "So, when Vingie disappeared from the circus and made it look like she'd

187

been killed or kidnapped, everybody was willing to believe it. Hell, she even pried at her own windows and door lock in the darkness to make it look like somebody was trying to kill her. And those heel marks I found were what they most looked like—prints of the small ladder she used to climb up to her own windows."

Slimer's voice shook. "Like I said, Vingie was smart."

"And you. That's why you followed her. That's why you told Felix she needed you—she could do nothing without you. Sure. She needed you to make the bomb."

"Felix is a fool. I didn't go looking for Vingie, I took her with me."

"In the carpetbag!"

Cy Slimer smiled. "In the carpetbag. Vingie simply sneaked out a small trapdoor in her van, hid in my carpetbag, and then I asked Ljubo to bring the bag to the medical tent to me. And I walked away—carrying Vingie in the bag."

"Very clever."

Slimer shrugged. "Often I took Vingie places she needed to be—without being seen—in that carpetbag. Little Vingie was an unbelievable contortionist and could fold herself up and hide in places no one would ever even think of looking for her. That way she overheard secret conversations. Knew what people were saying about her. Knew everything that was going on among her enemies. She knew their plans as soon as they spoke them aloud. Most of all, she could get into a room full of people, silently and stealthily, and poison a drink or food, then leave—unseen and unsuspected."

"She heard Begovic talking to me?"

"That's right. She was concealed within a few feet of you and Marko. She was afraid Marko would betray her—or me—to you. She had to stop him."

"With strychnine in his goulash."

Slimer shrugged again. "Then, when Begovic was dead, she knew it would be only a matter of hours until Kidd figured out who had killed his friend Marko. So then she had to kill Kidd." Slimer stared at Longarm, his face twisted with malignant fury. "She did not want to do these terrible things, but we could not be stopped in our crusade. Nothing could be allowed to stop us. She meant to kill you if you acted suspicious of her, or tried to stop her. You were useful to her only as

188

long as you helped her and kept anyone from betraying or delaying her."

Longarm exhaled heavily. "Well, one thing you've done, you've removed one hell of a lot of guilt I was carrying around."

Slimer's face twisted, full of jealousy and contempt and a lifetime of hatred for authority and its servant, the law. "She never cared for you, Long. Never. Nothing for you. Like me, she lived only for the liberation of Croatia. When you stopped her at Loving's mansion before she could get to the hated Danica, she wasn't trying to save you. She was trying only to escape you and the horror of life in prison. She knew all along that if she lived—and was caught—you would soon tie her into the murders of both Kidd and Begovic. She died because she would rather die."

Chapter 16

Marshal Billy Vail stared up at Longarm from across his desk. He didn't bother to smile. "That's an order," he said. "She wants to see you."

"Why?"

"Good lord, Longarm. Are you really that dense? You been working too hard? She wants to thank you."

"I get paid."

Vail wadded a sheet of paper in his fist. "This is protocol, damn it. Foreign affairs. International relations."

"Right. A job for diplomats."

"She wants to thank *you*."

"People thanking me gives me the hives," Longarm said. "You go."

Vail still did not smile. "I'd be glad to go, Longarm. Ordinarily, in fact, I'd even say I *should* be the one to get the reward from the princess—"

"Reward?"

"That's right. Her exact words. She wants to thank you. In person. She wants to reward you. In person. But, of course, as you say, I *am* chief U.S. marshal in this district. Whatever happens in this jurisdiction is my responsibility. The good *and* the bad. I sure catch hell for everything that goes wrong. So when something goes right, by all lights I ought to get such thanks and rewards as there might be."

"Then go."

Vail uncrumpled the wad of paper in his fist and smoothed it out on his desktop. "She asked for you. You. Personally. Definitely." He nodded, eyes cold. "You'll go. That's an order. From Washington. From me. You'll be on your best behavior. You'll do nothing—nothing—to embarrass or compromise this great nation. And I want no complaints coming down on my head from Washington about your behavior in the presence of Princess Danica. Do you savvy?"

Longarm was totally ill at ease in the presence of royalty. Princess Danica's people had transformed a Denver hotel suite into a royal reception chamber. The place glittered with gold and silver and with all the sable-soft trappings of royalty. A dozen high-backed Sheraton chairs had been placed in the center of a Persian rug, and each chair was occupied by a stiff-necked personage in dress clothes.

Longarm's starched collar choked him. Sweat trickled along his forehead, into his eyes, stinging. His borrowed evening clothes were too small, and pinched at his armpits and crotch. He wanted a smoke, but knew better.

And finally, when he'd resigned himself to standing at rigid, miserable attention forever, Princess Danica appeared.

She was even lovelier than she had seemed at that tragic party in Governor Loving's garden. She was just as regal, but far more human, close up like this. Her radiant red-gold hair, skin like quicksilver, delicately hewn features set jewellike upon the slender column of her throat, would have inspired Leonardo.

She looked expensive. Wars had been fought, intrigues executed or exposed, thrones toppled, fortunes forfeited, democracies dissolved to make her possible, a true princess, down to her elegant, dainty fingertips.

Her pale yellow gown of unadorned silk, classically tailored to caress the supple lines of her body, spilled in breathtaking folds from thin gold shoulder straps to pointed gold slippers, winking at its hem. She not only looked untouched, she looked untouchable.

He could not relax during the brief ceremonies in this magnificently refurbished parlor. It did not help that he and Princess Danica were the focus of all eyes.

A mustachioed man in black dress suit handed the princess a small, velvet-covered box. From it she drew a gold cross that glittered almost garishly in the vaguely illumined room.

She came close to Longarm, the crown of her regal head

192

at his chin. A faint, elusive, but unforgettable fragrance assailed his nostrils. The memory of this haunting scent would trail after him through all the beer-wet saloons and dung-smeared corrals and lonely trails, and would harry his dreams as long as he lived.

"This is my country's highest award for valor," she announced to the people in the room in a lovely, lightly accented voice. A brief smattering of applause. Then her head tilted and she looked up at Longarm and spoke directly to him. "I pin this poor medal on you in gratitude, in admiration—and in great humility."

She attached the brilliant little cross on the lapel of Longarm's jacket. Then she reached up and cupped her lovely, fragrant hands on each side of his head. She drew him down and kissed his right cheek and then his left. It was all very decorous, impeccably correct—except that her sharp nails dug into his neck until he had to bite his lip to keep from wincing.

Smiling in that regal, cool, and impersonal way, Princess Danica released Longarm and stepped back from him. "Thank you," she said.

Longarm sighed and nodded. It was over. It had not been too stuffy after all, and Princess Danica had proved herself quite human with her little byplay while she kissed his cheeks. Now he was free to go, as he saw the other guests leaving.

"Your Serene Highness," he said as he had been instructed. He bowed, also as he had been taught. "In the name of my government, I thank you for this generous award. It is far more reward than I deserve, and I appreciate it deeply."

She met his eyes levelly. "This is not your reward," she said tautly and between her teeth, her lips unmoving, so that only he heard her. "I have thanked you publicly. You will stay for your reward—after the others have gone."

His heart seemed to constrict for a moment and then to pump crazily. He could almost convince himself she had not really spoken. No one had heard her except him, and he was not sure he had not fantasized the words. She stood before him, waiting as the guests bowed to her and departed.

He felt her penetrating gaze fixed on him, and he managed to nod and went on standing ramrod-straight, while the room emptied. Tantalized by the almost imperceptible fragrance that rose from her, by her ethereal beauty and by the quality of passion in her tone, Longarm found that his legs, shoulders, and arms were not the only parts of his anatomy standing erect and at attention. He felt his face burning.

At last they were alone in the elegantly furnished suite. Longarm was hotly aware of the silences, of her cool nearness, her upsetting beauty, her unattainability.

"And now for your reward, Mr. Long," she said with a faint smile, her voice oddly breathless.

"You've done enough, ma'am. Too much."

"Too much? I've done nothing. Yet." With a sigh, the slender princess turned and walked to a closed inner door across the room.

She paused there, her delicate fingers on the knob, astonished that he had not moved. "Your reward," she said. "It's in here."

He felt the blood pulse in his temples as it was already pounding in his loins. If he misunderstood her, he could disgrace his service, his country, and cause an international incident. But there seemed no confusion in the way she held open the door of her bedroom. Beyond her, he could see silken covers and sheets gleaming their own kind of invitation. And yet, since it was hard to imagine her even going to the toilet as ordinary people did, her asking for sex was doubly incredible, unlikely, and unreasonable. He warned himself to tread easy.

"Please, Mr. Long," she said. Her deep eyes were veiled, her accented voice gentle, with a faint edge of steel glinting in it.

Longarm entered her bedroom.

She stood in the doorway for a long moment. Then she said, with a surprisingly warm laugh, "Stop pretending, Mr. Long. I saw it in your face when I stepped off that train in Golden. I saw you look at me. I read your thoughts across that crowd of people. You thought, 'I would give anything to go to bed with her.'"

Longarm grinned, slightly more at ease. "Not exactly, Your Highness. I never thought about going to bed with you. I thought you are the kind of dream woman that a man could go through hell for, and pray for no more reward than an hour in her bed."

"Close enough," Princess Danica said, laughing. "I got your message."

She closed the door behind her and turned the large brass key in its lock. Then, smiling, she straightened and tossed the key across the room. It clattered into the shadows.

Shocked, but intrigued, Longarm smiled with her. "Suppose there's a fire?" he said.

"I'll be disappointed if there isn't," she said.

"I don't think we are talking about the same thing."

"That is always the problem with different languages. But if we don't talk at all, we'll understand perfectly, eh?"

She came slowly across the room toward him, walking like a princess, like a ballet dancer, like a female lynx on the prowl. He had the distinct feeling that she was stalking him.

He drew a deep breath, held it.

"Why do you go on pretending you do not understand all this?" she said in that cool, lovely, accented voice. "You've got an erection. You had an erection out there. I saw it. Didn't you? Haven't you?"

His face burned but he grinned. "Yes, Your Highness."

"My informal name is Marie Therese."

He nodded. "Fair enough. *My* informal name's Longarm, and yes."

She looked puzzled. "Yes, what?"

"Yes, I've got an erection."

She didn't even blink. "And you've had it ever since I kissed your cheek out there, isn't that right . . . Longarm?"

He smiled and spread his hands. "I hope you can forgive me, Your Highness."

"Forgive you? Why, I'm flattered. Very flattered."

"Thank God."

"God? What's God got to do with it?"

"Nothing. It's just that I've very likely had a hard-on since the first time I saw you, on that station platform. I wouldn't want to cause an international incident."

"Oh, I hope it will be more than an incident, Longarm. Much more. For both of us. After all, I saw *you* on that station platform, too."

"You're the princess."

"Yes. And you know what the princess wants. What are you waiting for?"

Longarm exhaled. "It's just that I never made love to a princess before..."

"I assure you, Longarm, I am as human as any other woman you ever knew. When I look at you, I'm human as hell."

"Yes, Your Highness."

"Stop that 'Your Highness' nonsense, Longarm. I am disappointed. I'd thought a man like you would know what to do. I thought perhaps I might have trouble stopping you. I had no idea I'd have so much difficulty getting you started."

She came close, stood on her tiptoes, and pressed her lips upon his. Her mouth was heatedly scented now, her breath fevered and ragged. She caught his head in her hand and dug her nails into the nape of his neck and the base of his skull. "There. How was that?"

"Habit-forming."

"Are you afraid of me, Longarm?"

"No, ma'am. Yes. In a way. If this goes wrong, I could be in a hell of a lot of trouble."

"Aren't I worth it? Isn't that what you thought—on that station platform?"

"My exact thoughts."

He slipped his arms about her at the small of her arched back. He drew her against him. He caught his breath when Marie Therese—Princess Danica—rose upward on her toes and pressed her pubic bone upon the eminence throbbing at his groin.

"I do understand, Longarm," she whispered. But she undulated upon him maddeningly. "A princess. A woman who soon may be head of her state. It must make you uncomfortable. But forget Princess Danica. Think only of Marie Therese, for there would now be no state, there would be anarchy and chaos in my poor country but for you, Longarm. I should be dead now. My death may not have been too important in the grand scheme of things, but when I died, it would have been the death of my poor, dear country too. I owe you far more than my body, Longarm. I owe you my life."

He held her close but spoke honestly. "I get paid for doing my job."

She smiled drowsily up at him, working her hips upon him, tantalizing him. "What you did was far beyond the call of duty, and to reward you, I want to go far beyond the call of reason, of sanity. You drive me out of my mind, Longarm, and that's where I want to be driven, and I shan't be content until you are as insane as I."

He swallowed hard at something in his throat. "I see."

"Do you?" She slid her hands along his biceps, pressing at the rigid musculature savagely. Her breath quickened. "Do you? You are so strong and tall. Built as the Greek gods of antiquity might have wished to be built. There's life and power and poetry and savagery in you, Longarm, and I want it all. I need it all. My body is weak and empty and sick with longing—and I need your fierce, wild strength drained from you into me—I need to suck it all out of you."

She lifted her fevered face to his. In the wanly lit room, her porcelain flesh glowed, her eyes glittered, swirling with fires and shadows. He kissed her.

He felt her sag submissively against him, and in that moment she was no longer a princess. She was a woman with fierce needs. She opened her lips to his tongue, and when he thrust it between her teeth, she nursed it frantically.

At last she drew away. "Undress me, Longarm." Her voice shook. "It's been a long time since I first saw you at that train station. I've wanted you for such a long time. I want you to undress me."

He nodded. There was far less to this task than one might have supposed in that age of buttons, bows, laces, chemises, corsets, bodices, and underdrawers. Under the soft watered silk of her dress she wore none of these impeding articles of clothing. She stepped out of her golden slippers, standing nude and lovely before him.

And now, panting, she yanked at the buttons of his vest and shirt. His heart pounding erratically, he shrugged out of his jacket, tossed his vest behind him, and pulled the tails of his shirt from his trousers.

She went down on her knees before him. She reached up and loosened his belt buckle. Her slender fingers worked at the buttons of his fly and then peeled his trousers down along his legs.

When he was trapped, helpless, with his trousers around

his ankles, she laughed, tearing open his underclothes. She knew what she wanted and she found it unerringly. She caught his throbbing staff in her hand and fell backwards across the silken covers of her bed, still clinging to him.

He managed to kick off his boots and to worm out of his trousers. She had unbuttoned his underclothes and, still holding him possessively, she suckled at his paps, traced her tongue over the hard musculature of his chest.

Then her head fell back on the covers and she lifted her legs, parting them wide. "Do it to me, Longarm," she pleaded. "Please. Do it to me. Now."

He found her fiery hot, bubblingly liquid. As he penetrated her, she was already working her hips involuntarily. He thrust himself into her and she cried out in sweet anguish.

"Oh, my God," she wept, laughing at the same time, "how will I ever let you go? Push, Longarm, push. Just a little bit more . . . all the way . . . there . . . there . . . oh, my God, there . . ."

Her head stretched back on the delicate column of her neck, her red-gold hair loose and wild upon the sheets, she thrust frantically with her hips. She locked her long legs about him. She closed her eyes tightly. She moved her hips like horses, arching her back and lifting herself to him.

His mouth covered hers. She opened her lips wide and he probed her mouth with his tongue. She breathed helplessly, gasping, as if, in her paralyzing pleasure, she forgot to breathe.

He felt her body stiffen and thrust upward. She cried out and writhed against him, thrusting with all her strength. He held himself rock-firm while she reached an explosive climax.

She clung to him, sagging suddenly, spent, but unwilling to release him.

For a long time they lay close together. Then he felt her hot tears splash on his cheeks. "What's the matter?" he whispered.

"You waited . . . you let me . . . first . . ."

"I wanted to."

"Yes. I tried to reward you, but instead I got rewarded—for being a woman. It's my turn to reward you, truly reward you, Longarm. What do you want of me?"

"You. All of you."

"No. What do you want me to do? For you? Whatever it is, tell me—I'll do it. I want to do it for you . . . your way . . . as much as you like . . . as long as you like . . . there's nothing I won't do to reward you."

"You've already rewarded me."

"For saving my life, yes. I'm not talking about that. Now I owe you new rewards—which I insist upon paying—for your bringing me to life. You brought me to life as I never was alive before. I know I can never really repay you, but I must try— with all my heart and soul."

And she did try. Again and again. And Longarm thought she succeeded right well.

SPECIAL PREVIEW

Here are the opening scenes
from

LONGARM AND THE LAREDO LOOP

thirty-third novel in the bold
LONGARM series from Jove

It was never easy to get to work on time, but this one old morning was a pisser. Longarm rose early with good intentions. He'd struck out the night before with that snooty little redhead from the Black Cat Saloon. So, waking up at dawn with a clear head and a hard-on, he decided to get to the office early and tell his boss he'd reformed.

He washed down his goosebumps with a wet string rag dipped in cold water. He woke up some more when he brushed his teeth with Maryland rye. He'd shaved his jaw the evening before, not knowing then how the redhead felt about gents who didn't own at least a silver mine. So Longarm ran a thumbnail along the angle of his jaw and decided the hell with it. He didn't expect to meet anybody at the office prettier than the prissy young dude who played the typewriter in the front room, and Longarm had never been that desperate yet.

He put on a fresh hickory shirt, even though it was the middle of the week. The shirt he'd worn the night before was still reasonable as far as clean went, but he knew his boss, U.S. Marshal Billy Vail, liked to play at detective work, so he'd likely comment on the violet stink. Longarm had told that infernal barber he only wanted bay rum to spruce him up for that match with the redhead, but the romantic Eye-talian barber had conviced him that gals liked stronger stink-pretty on a man. So here it was, the middle of the week, and he had to change his shirt.

As he buttoned up he growled, "A lot you know about redheads, you damned old gondolier. She'd have let me smell like cowshit if I could have told her I owned the Diamond K. We were getting along just swell until I told her what Uncle Sam pays a deputy marshal these days!"

He caught himself scowling in the mirror and suddenly laughed. He nodded to his reflection and said, "Morning. That was close, old son. You know no gal is interested in a man's salary unless she has dishonorable intentions."

He sat down and hauled on his tight tweed trousers and stovepipe boots as he pondered the infinite treachery of womankind. It was getting so a man couldn't feel safe with any of 'em, these days. You'd think a saloon gal who painted her face would be less anxious to rope and hogtie a friendly old boy. But they were all the same. A man figured the game was won and over about the time he got a gal between the sheets. But that was where the game just started getting interesting to a gal. They didn't figure *they'd* won till they could show their girlfriends a diamond ring.

He stood and strapped on his cross-draw rig, checking the five rounds of .44-40 in the chambers as he did every morning. Nobody had ever stolen his bullets while he slept alone, but a man in Longarm's line of work couldn't afford sloppy habits.

He put on the sissy string tie they made him wear around the Federal Building in Denver. He'd never gotten used to the new rules of President Hayes's reform administration. He buttoned his brown tweed vest over the ends of the tie and took a long gold-washed chain from the dresser top. There was an Ingersoll pocket watch at one end of the chain and a brass derringer at the other. The watch kept fair time and the derringer fired two .44-caliber rounds on occasion.

He put the watch in the left pocket of his vest and the gun in the other, leaving the chain draped across his chest sort of elegant-like. He put on his dark brown frock coat and smoothed the collar where it was a mite frayed. He'd been wearing his federal shield pinned to the lapel more than usual, lately. Billy Vail had been using him over at the federal courthouse as a prison-chaser since the suit had last been cleaned and pressed. He'd had his badge pinned in his wallet the night before, of course, but the redhead had likely noticed the threadbare lapel while going over his accounts with those knowing green eyes. They'd been getting along like fury till she'd gotten around to his job and how much it paid. He'd been caught off-guard, thinking he was among friends. If he had it to do over again, he'd tell her he hadn't had time to change, coming from his mine up in Leadville. For treachery deserved the same in return, and he was willing to bet she'd settle for being the play-pretty of a rich old married gent, even if an honest working bachelor wasn't her notion of a bright future.

Longarm put on his flat-crowned Stetson and left the rooming house on the unfashionable side of Cherry Creek. It was a bright sunny morn, and as he crunched along the cinder roadway, a meadowlark perched on a fence cocked its beady eye at him and whistled saucily. Longarm said, "Aw, shut up. It ain't that pretty out, and I face a long hard day at the office."

He was almost to the Cherry Creek bridge when he heard the sound of gunshots—a *lot* of gunshots—coming his way from somewhere near the Burlington Railroad yards to the northwest.

Longarm knew better. He was a federal lawman and the Denver Municipal Police had ears. He took out his watch and consulted it. The office wouldn't open for almost an hour, but he'd intended to eat some chili con carne for breakfast on Larimer Street. What was happening yonder was none of his business.

Another shot rang out. It sounded like a ten-gauge scatter-gun. The first shots had been .44s or .45s from a handgun. He heard the whipcrack report of a Winchester, making it at least three folks shooting over there. This was getting sort of interesting. So, though he knew better, Longarm started legging toward the sounds of gunfire. Longarm legged good. He was over six feet and long of limb, with a mile-eating stride most men had to trot alongside to keep up. Working more on foot than the average cowhand, he favored low-heeled army stovepipe boots without spurs, so he moved cat-quiet, too.

But there was no need for pussyfooting this morning. He spotted the police line a full block away as he rounded a corner. They had the Burlington yards covered, and their blue backs faced him as he approached. Longarm knew most of the local coppers, but not all, and there was a fool city ordinance about wearing public guns these days. So he took out his wallet and pinned his federal shield to his lapel before he moseyed up to them, .44 double-action in hand, to ask pleasantly and politely what the hell was going on.

A police sergeant he knew turned with a frown, saw who it was, and said, "Howdy, Longarm. You remember the Terrible Tracy Twins?"

Longarm nodded. "Yeah, they ain't really twins, but they sure acted terrible the last time they held up the Drovers Savings and Loan."

"Well, they just tried to do her again."

"Do tell? It's a mite early to make a withdrawal, gun or no. The banks ain't open yet, are they?"

"Nope. The Tracy boys grabbed the head teller at home, aiming to make him open early, I reckon. Teller spotted one of our patrolmen on Lincoln Avenue as they was frog-marching him down Capitol Hill. He was either a brave or foolish man, for he let out a holler and it's been sort of interesting ever since."

"You say *was*?"

"Yeah, the poor teller was killed on the spot. Our patrolman took a round in the leg, but hit one of the Tracy boys as he went down. They must have lost interest in our fair city about then, for, as you see, they headed for the tracks out. Another copper swapped some shots with them as they run across the schoolyard of Evans Elementary, and now he's on his way to the hospital too. Them Terrible Tracys are right good shots."

Longarm traced a mental route from the old brownstone school to the nearby railyards and observed, "Interesting is a mild word when you consider one damn long running gunfight, Sarge. How the hell did they ever get this far, still standing?"

"They run and fight pretty good. We figure they've both been hit a few times, and as you see, we've got 'em boxed in the yards now. Our orders are to keep 'em there whilst the captain figures out the next move. They can't get out and we don't aim to lose any more men this morning."

Longarm moved to the tipped-over wagon the police were using as a shield. He stared into the railroad yards beyond. There was nothing to be seen but the maze of tracks and stationary rolling stock. Way up the track a switch engine stood quietly, venting an occasional plume of steam. He asked the sergeant, "Who fired that shotgun I heard?" and the copper said, "Railyard bull. He ain't with us no more. See that caboose yonder? He fired from there as the Terrible Tracy Twins ran betwixt them other boxcars. One of 'em nailed him with a lovely offhand shot. They swapped a couple more shots with another railroad dick before the fellow decided he'd feel safer somewhere else. Now the ornery sons of bitches are anywhere among all them railroad cars, and it figures to be a waiting game."

Longarm glanced at the sky and commented, "Well, you have a full day and at least one of them's wounded. What happened to the yard bull they put on the ground? I fail to see him over by yonder caboose."

"Oh, a couple of yard workers carried him out. We yelled at them to take cover, but they must have been fond of him. The Tracy Twins never shot them. Don't ask me why."

"Don't have to," Longarm said. "They've moved up the line between the cars. You boys have the whole yard surrounded, huh?"

"Of course. The yards is big and sprawly, as you can see. But there's no way out we haven't got covered. We can't go in and they can't come out."

Longarm looked at his watch. "Damn," he said, "I meant to beat old Billy Vail to the office this morning, too."

The sergeant asked, "Why don't you, Longarm? You can see this figures to take all day and what just happened wasn't a federal crime."

Longarm replied, "What happened earlier *was*. The Terrible Tracy Twins are wanted on a couple of federal warrants too. They sure shoot good, but the brainless bastards *will* hold up post offices when they can't find a bank open. Killed a federal employee, last time they did it."

He put the watch away, but not the .44, and stepped around the end of the wagon bed. As he started walking toward the tracks, the police sergeant yelled, "Come back here, damn it!" But Longarm didn't have to obey any old local lawman. So he didn't look back.

"Goddamm it, that's suicide, and suicide is agin the law, Longarm!" called the copper behind him. He eased over to the caboose they'd been discussing. He saw by the blood on the ballast rock at his feet that they'd told him true about the yard bull. He had a good view up the line from here. The cars stretched in a broken line to some loading chutes a furlong north. He couldn't see what lay beyond, but there was nobody shooting at him between here and there. He hadn't expected there would be. The open stretch was covered by the coppers infesting the jagged line of fences, buildings, and such that were facing the cars on the track.

Longarm made his way into a slowly settling cloud of dust inhabited by some Denver cops, railroad men, and a herd of sheep penned in a loading corral beside a halted string of stock cars. The critters had been spooked by the gunplay and were still milling and cussing in Sheep, but they'd started to settle, some, so you could talk. Longarm nodded to a Denver P.D. captain he knew and asked what they were doing, if it wasn't herding sheep.

The captain said they'd chased the Tracy Twins this far and lost them in the infernal dust. He added, "It looks like they ducked under the wheels of this stock train and now God knows where they are out yonder."

Longarm stared thoughtfully at the halted rolling stock in the vast yard and said, "They couldn't get in any of the sealed freight cars. But the railroad sends empty reefers back down the line unlocked and regular. If I was a Terrible Tracy, right now, I'd be hunkered in some empty car, hoping for a free ride out before anybody got to it."

"Hell, ain't no cars going in or out until we catch the bastards."

A railroad man nearby said, "The hell you say! We got melting ice and uncared for livestock to think about, even if we didn't run this here railroad on a time table."

The captain looked at Longarm, who shrugged and said, "It ought to be safe to let sealed cars through your cordon. Might clear the field of action, too, if we could narrow her down to the empty rolling stock the owlhoots figure to be hiding in."

The police captain turned to one of the civilians nearby and asked him, "Do you Burlington gents have a list of empty, unlocked boxcars?"

The railroad man said, "Not on me. But we'd have one at the dispatcher's." He turned to one of his helpers and added, "Owens, run over and get today's orders." Then, as the other man sprinted away, he turned back to Longarm and the copper to say, "I can tell you they ain't in that string of stock cars there. So what about it?"

Longarm glanced at the nearby string of cagelike stock cars, then turned to study the milling sheep penned beyond them all, at the base of a loading chute with its gate closed. He didn't answer. The police captain said, "I don't know." "Damn it," the railroad man said, "we got a timetable to keep, you know. Them sheep should have been on their way to K.C. half an hour ago!"

The police captain asked Longarm, "What do you think?"

"I'll take a look," Longarm replied as he drew his gun again and stepped over to the short line of stock cars. The sides of the cars were made of horizontal slats with wide spaces between them, and he could see clean through to the far side. He hunkered down and had a look at the undercarriages. Nobody was riding the rods. He'd have been surprised if he'd seen anyone, considering.

He walked back to the fence and said, "Short train, all stock cars with no caboose or tender at either end. I reckon it's safe to get those sheep out of the sun, but how do you aim to move 'em anywhere worth mention?"

The railroad man said, "Oh, this here's a special order of spring lamb."

"Yeah? Some of those sheep look as old as the lamb I was fooling with at the Black Cat last night. But what the butcher won't tell 'em, they likely won't know. I see no reason not to load 'em on board. That switcher is standing by to haul 'em out of the yards, right?"

"Yeah, we're fixing to run this short string around to Fitz-simmons, northeast of town, and add 'em to an eastbound UP freight. That other train will be leaving *without* these here sheep if we don't get cracking, too!"

Longarm stared over into the tightly packed woolly-backs. "I'll move up and make sure nobody we're interested in is hiding in the coal tender and such," he told the captain.

He climbed over the loading chute, not touching his boots to the sheepshit-covered bottom planks as he forked his legs over the rough rails on either side. He moved up the short line, checking each empty stock car as he passed. Someone must have signaled the engineer in the tender, for it started backing as he walked to meet it. He hunkered down to peer under the moving wheels as the tender's coupler snapped onto that of the forward car. The colored fireman was staring down curiously. Longarm walked over and mounted to the cabin, putting his gun away. He told the two crewmen who he was and what was going on. They said they doubted like hell he'd find any outlaws hiding back in the coal, but he looked anyway, and, seeing they were right, dropped off to rejoin the others back at the chute.

They'd already started loading. A yard rider on a bored-looking pinto cutting horse was hazing the woolly-backs by riding back and forth along the far rails as a couple of Mex kids poked them up the chute into the first car. It took little time to fill the car and drop the gate. But Longarm knew his office would be opening about now, and if Billy Vail believed this story, he'd believe anything. Had Longarm known he'd be spending the morning this close to sheep, he'd have left his old shirt on. You couldn't get near the critters without walking away smelling like a sheepherder. They were heated and sweated up from being packed so close. They bitched and butted each other to crowd away from the pony that was hazing them, which added floating, fuzzy lumps of lint to the dust they were stirring up. Longarm figured there was no sense brushing himself off until the last of 'em were aboard and out of his way. Moving this line of cars might simplify the search, but he knew they had a lot of work ahead, and the damned day was starting to be a hot one.

They got the last sheep loaded and the switch engine slowly started to move them off to market, poor critters. The man they'd sent for the papers returned with the list of empty, unlocked cars. As they were going over them another uni-formed copper ran up the now-empty line the stock cars had been standing on. He called out, "We got one, Captain. Old Tinker Tracy bled hisself to death just down the line. One of the boys noticed blood running out of a door. So Colson and his men moved in. They found the rascal as dead as a turd in a milk bucket."

"What about his brother Tiny?" the captain asked.

"Not a sign of the other twin, Captain. He must have left his brother to die. He sure ain't in any car near enough to matter. Old Colson's sort of encouraged, and he's been look-ing."

The captain snorted. "Well, run back and tell Colson to move careful. We only got one to deal with now, but Tiny Tracy is mean as hell."

He turned to Longarm and said, "We'll get us some boys and start at this end, slow and easy. There's just no way he's

210

gonna slip through us, but old Tiny's desperate and he might try anything."

Longarm nodded as he fished out a cheroot and lit it. He flicked the match stem into the trampled sheepshit of the now-empty yard. Then his eyes narrowed as he stared down at the countless hoofmarks and he muttered, "Son of a bitch! I just wasn't awake yet!"

The captain asked him what he meant, but Longarm was moving too fast to answer. He called after the stockyard rider who was walking his pinto away. The man reined in, and as Longarm caught up, he told the stockyard man to get the hell off that mount, adding, in a politer tone, "I'm on federal business, and you'll be paid if I bust your brute up."

The other man made no move to dismount as he asked Longarm what the hell he was talking about. Some men were like that. So Longarm swore, grabbed him by the belt, and hauled him off bodily. He forked his own leg over the saddle as the former rider sat up, spitting dust and cussing. Longarm heeled the pinto into a flat run without looking back to say he was sorry.

The pinto had seen better days and was surprised as hell to be tearing through the streets of Denver at a full gallop, but as Longarm had suspected, he was an old cow pony, and the day was young, so what the hell.

The old plug's hooves struck sparks as they pounded on the pavement when they reached the politer side of Larimer Street and kept going. Longarm started lashing with the rein-ends as they tore past a streetcar heading east on Colfax. The folks riding inside stared out like they'd never seen a fast rider before.

A dray wagon was blocking the way near Broadway, so Longarm rode up over the sidewalk, nodding politely to a couple of surprised-looking gals walking along with parasols. A man in a derby jumped out of the way and shouted, "Damn drunk cowboy!" as Longarm flashed by. The pony caught a shoe on the streetcar tracks running along Broadway. For a scared split-second, Longarm braced for an ass-over-teakettle fall. But the good old horse recovered his balance and made it across. Longarm guided him off the paving of Colfax to lope up the grassy grounds of the State House atop Capitol Hill. A boy mowing the lawn with a quartet of sheep called out, "Hey, cowboy, you ain't allowed to ride on the grass!" But Longarm kept going without looking back.

Capitol Hill was really the edge of a vast mesa, with its far side too far off to worry about. So, once they'd made the top, it was flat running. Longarm whipped the pony faster, snapping, "Come on, damm it, let's *move,* you useless mess of crowbait!"

The trouble with Denver was that the streets atop Capitol Hill were laid out in a grid running east and west and north and south. Longarm wanted to head northeast. So he did. He tore between two houses and busted through a clothesline, yelling back that he was sorry as a woman came out waving a broom at him.

There was a solid wall of housing along Seventeenth Avenue—running east and west, goddamm it. He swore and loped toward Aurora, where he didn't want to go, till he spied another gap and tore through to Sixteenth, swerved around a house and across a vacant lot to Fifteenth, where he was once more forced to ride due east for three damned blocks before he came to a water-filled construction site and splashed through, cursing, at a northeast angle.

He left an awful lot of housewives cussing in his wake. The kids on their way to school thought it was neat to see a cowboy gallop by, and waved at him as he passed. That meant it was nearly nine o'clock and he was in trouble with his boss, too. It was sobering to think what might have happened had the Terrible Tracy Twins crossed that schoolyard down yonder a mite later in the morning!

He saw a mess of little kids ahead and cut sideways through a yard to avoid them. A woman watering her garden out back gasped, "What on earth...?" He saw that the rear of her yard was fences, and jumped his lathered pony over the pickets without taking time to tip his hat to the lady.

The houses were spread thinner now, so he was able to make better time as he zigzagged between them. Chickens scattered and dogs chased him, snapping at the pony's heels, which was all to the good, as it encouraged him to keep moving.

The old stockyard horse was only good for eight or ten miles at this pace. So when Longarm spotted a gent sitting in a carriage by a house he reined in, tapped the federal badge on his lapel, and said, "Howdy. I need that perky-looking chestnut pacer, friend."

The man shot a startled glance at the carriage horse between his own shafts and gasped, "This here's not a saddle horse, officer."

"Sure he is. Help me saddle him up, goddamm it!" Longarm said as he dismounted and proceeded to unhitch the fresher animal. The man made no move to help, although he knew better than to resist an obvious lunatic as big as Longarm. It took a few minutes to unhitch the carriage horse and saddle it. So he told the man what was going on while he did it. A worried-looking woman in a sunbonnet and Dolly Varden dress stuck herself out the side door of the house to ask what was going on. Her husband said, "Get back inside. I'll tell you later."

Longarm told him where to ask about his chestnut, if he never saw it again, and told him to hang onto the pinto. Then he mounted the chestnut and saw that the man had been right. It wasn't a saddle horse and it had no intention of being one. So, by the time they got that settled they'd made a mess out of the front lawn and flower beds with its bucking hooves. But when he finally got the chestnut settled down and headed the right way, he saw he'd still gained some time. For the fresh mount was fast as well as ornery. Longarm admired its long-legged pace. He didn't try to lope it. He saw they were making smart time at the pacer's comfortable gait and, praise the Lord, the houses were thinning out and spread far enough apart so he could set a beeline for Fitzsimmons Siding.

The small town of Fitzsimmons was planning to be a Denver suburb one of these days, but Denver still had some growing to do, so they were soon riding over open prairie, navigating by the sun in the sky and the smoke of the locomotive dead ahead. Longarm didn't think the smoke was moving, but he lashed the pacer into a full run anyway, and as he raced into Fitzsimmons he saw he'd timed it close.

He tore through the yards to rein in the lathered chestnut by the UP Baldwin just as the engineer was sounding his departing whistle. He yelled up. "Hold your steam, old son. This here train is under arrest. I'll tell you all about it directly. Right now I'm busy."

He dismounted and tethered the chestnut to a grab rail. As he started down along the tracks, another man wearing a badge came to meet him warily, and said, "Morning. Did you have some reason for riding through my salad greens just now?"

"I did," Longarm said. "I'm after Tiny Tracy, who just left Denver after committing crimes too numerous to relate. You'd best stand clear unless you take that badge serious, pard. He's in one of those stock cars down the train."

The Fitzsimmons lawman drew his antique Patterson Conversion .45 and said, "Whither thou goest, so shall I follow, Uncle Sam. But how come you boys let him get this far?"

"The Denver P.D. was dumb. I was asleep or I'd have remembered a story I read when I was a little shaver. Let's keep it down to a roar. Stay back and cover me while I play Bo-Peep."

Longarm eased in on the first stock car. He hunkered down and peered through the slit closest to the straw and the sheepshit-covered decking. He nodded and moved to the next car to repeat the process. Then he motioned to the man backing him to stay put as he crouched even lower to crawl for the door. He turned the handle and slid the door open as he called out, "All right, Ulysses. It worked on Cyclops and it worked on Denver, but it never worked on *me*! Come out of there with your hands held high and we'll wash that sheepshit off you before we lock you up with our less imaginative prisoners."

Tiny Tracy didn't see things Longarm's way. Sheep exploded out the door to leap, bleating and running, in every goddamned direction. The outlaw followed, cussing and shooting.

Longarm had sort of expected it, since one of the few tiny things about the big bastard was his brain. He'd moved away from where he'd spoken, so, as Tiny Tracy put a couple of bullets through the side rails of the car and the space Longarm had vacated, Longarm fired back, taking more time to aim. Tiny Tracy came out anyway, not getting the message that he was dead until he'd landed facedown in the trackside dust.

Longarm rolled him over with his boot and told the awed town constable, "He must have read the same story. It was writ a long time back. Lucky for the rest of us, I noticed the drag marks in the Denver stockyards. He hunkered down amid a herd of sheep being loaded. Lay on his back and held two together, clinging to their wool as they was hazed aboard. It was sort of slick. Who in thunder would ever think to look for a rogue cowboy under a mess of sheep?"

The town law said, "You did." and Longarm shrugged and said "Well, I read books from time to time. I always admired them Greek gents for the slick way they snuck out of that giant's cave. We'd best get some help and round up them scattered woolly-backs. If we herd 'em into those pens down the way and have the train back to the chute, we ought to see them safely on their way again."

"What about this owlhoot you just shot, Uncle Sam?"

"He ain't in shape to herd sheep with us, now. Later, I'd sure be obliged if you can scout me up some water to pour over him and a tarp to wrap him in. I got enough explaining to do, back at the office, without coming in smelling even worse than I already do."

What with one thing and another, it was well past noon by the time Longarm faced the thunder of his boss, U.S. Marshal Billy Vail, across the desk in Vail's office at the Denver Federal Building. Longarm had never been quite this late to work before, but the pudgy older lawman wasn't really sore. He'd heard about the morning's events before Longarm left the morgue, and had already given a statement to the newspapers about the brilliant law enforcement of his top deputy. He likely wouldn't get the complaints and demands for damages for a day or so.

He waited until Longarm had settled back and lit a smoke before he said, "Well, old son, you've had your fun. It's time I put you back to work for the taxpaying public gain."

Longarm blew a smoke ring and said, "That sounds fair, Billy. I'd best change my pants and shave if you want me to ride herd over at the federal court the rest of the afternoon."

"Never mind. You're a mite gamy, but you can freshen up aboard the train. The Denver & Rio Grande has washrooms on their coaches now. Will wonders never cease?"

"So I heard. Am I supposed to be going somewhere on the D&RG, Billy, or do I just climb aboard and marvel at the wonders of the modern age?"

"Oh, I forgot. You were out amusing yourself when the wires came in. Some sons of bitches stole some government beef off the army at Fort Bliss. I want you to go to Laredo and check it out."

Longarm studied the end of his cheroot as he said, "Billy, the last time I looked, Fort Bliss was right outside El Paso."

"Hell, everybody knows that."

"Laredo ain't. Laredo is over five hundred miles southeast of both El Paso and Fort Bliss."

"Everybody knows that too. Mexico is just a spit and a holler south of all the places you just mentioned, old son. Army chased the banditos who lifted their cows as far south as the army is allowed to go, and they were last seen raising dust in the land of hot tamales. Surely you know about the Laredo Loop? I sent you down along the border to check it out a short while ago, remember?"

"Yep. It was sort of interesting. Billy, I told you then and I'm telling you now, the so-called Laredo Loop is a notion of some Wild West writer like Buntline. That other case had nothing to do with this Laredo Loop stuff. I met up with a self-elected sheriff who had to be taught some constitutional law."

"Yeah, they say his funeral was well attended. Forget that side issue you got mixed up in the last time. This time I want you to pay attention and do the job you're sent to do!"

"I'm willing, Billy. But I'm already mixed up. Let's go over that Laredo Loop business again."

Vail sat back and ran a hand over his bald dome as he replied, "It ain't complicated, to me. You know the Díaz administration down Mexico way don't allow folks to steal Mex cows."

Longarm grimaced distastefully. "Porfirio Díaz don't allow much more than breathing, and he'd tax that, if he could figure how. *You* may call his dictatorship an administration, Billy. Me and a mess of decent Mex folks call it hell!"

Vail waved a pudgy hand as if brushing a fly away. "Whatever. The point is that while the *rurales* will blow you out of your pants for running a Mexican brand, they ain't too particular about what happens to a cow calved on this side of the border."

"You mean they hate our gringo guts, don't you?"

"Some Mex lawmen *can* get sort of sullen. Anyway, the way the Laredo Loop works is like so. An American cow gets

216

stolen. It's spirited down to some Mex ranch and given a new brand. A legal brand, in Mexico. The *rurales* ain't interested in the old brand, as long as it ain't on their list of stolen cows."

"Don't you mean they're in on it, Billy?"

"Whatever. What they're pulling is legal, in Mexico. The new Mex owner keeps the cow for a time. Then, when its new brand heals, he sells it, legal, to a licensed buyer passing through."

"Licensed by Mexico and working with the cow thieves," Longarm said.

"Of course, but try telling that to the folks running things down there. Anyway, the buyer moves the beef sideways in a big sort of loop through old Mexico, where nobody can question a trail herd's lawfully registered brands. It's called the Laredo Loop 'cause Laredo is the port of entry where the cows come back across the border to be sold with a lawful bill of sale. You know the price of beef is up, back East. So there's many a buyer for the meat packers waiting to get a good buy on slightly cheaper Mex cows."

Longarm snorted derisively. "Yeah, and who's about to let his conscience stand in the way of a good buy? But what about the Texas Rangers? Last I heard, they were still fairly honest. How would you flimflam a ranger with a fancy new brand and some pretty papers writ in Spanish? What about the old brand they can still read on the critter, if they take the trouble to look? Don't they keep a record of stolen cows, Billy?"

"Sure they do. Stolen *Texas* cows. No cows stole in Texas are ever sent back through Laredo. *They* wind up getting sold in Arizona. That's the other end of the loop. Cows stolen west of the New Mexico line don't have brands registered in Texas. Lawmen out in New Mexico or Arizona don't keep tabs on Texas brands. This loop, trail, whatever, shuttles American cows stolen in one part of these United States to some other parts where it's safe to sell 'em, see?"

"I see some of it. Not all. How come they call it the Laredo Loop if Laredo's only one end of the secret passage? Where do they unload the Texas cows?"

"Nobody knows for sure. We've only found out recent about the plentiful Mex beef crossing at Laredo. The Western territories ain't as settled as old Texas. So they likely smuggle them through more than one border crossing out there. What you *call* the racket ain't our problem. Our problem is to find out who's doing it and make 'em stop."

Longarm took a drag of smoke before replying, "That sounds reasonable. But you're still sending me the wrong damn way, Billy. If those last cows were snitched near El Paso, they'd have Texas brands, wouldn't they?"

"No, and the army is sort of sheepish about that. Fort Bliss is a supply depot. So they furnish beef for smaller posts all over the southwest. You don't exactly get a top hand for thirteen dollars a month and beans. The government herd was run sort of, uh, informal."

"Jesus, you mean they didn't even have the usual U.S. brands?"

"Some may have. Most had just been purchased and had whatever old brand they came with. The fool purchasing officer didn't keep a record. So the stolen herd could be packing just about any brands, or none at all."

Longarm whistled silently and said, "Billy, you are wasting my time and the taxpayers' money by sending me all the infernal way to Laredo! In the first place, those cow thieves might have run them west, the other way. In the second, I wouldn't recognize one of those particular cows as stolen if I had it for supper! What in thunder am I supposed to do, stand on the corner in Laredo and ask every cow I see if she's new in town?"

Marshal Vail looked down at his desk blotter and said, "Well, you're a sort of ingenious cuss, and they're expecting me to do *something*."

"That's another question I've been meaning to ask. How come *us*? Don't they have a district court and a U.S. marshal down El Paso way, Billy?"

"They do," Vail said. "Washington asked us to handle it because the matter is sort of delicate. They, uh, ain't sure about the federal men along the border."

"You mean Washington suspicions them of being in on it with the other crooks?"

"Damn it, Longarm, I sure wish you'd learn to talk more polite about our fellow peace officers! Nobody's saying any border lawmen are working with the crooks. They'd just feel safer about it if they knew for sure. This office is far enough from the border to make us above suspicion. I don't want to swell your head, but you might as well know, certain folks in Washington have heard about your habit of getting results. So they told me to put you on the case, and that's what I'm trying to do, goddammit."

Longarm nodded and said, "All right. But going to Laredo for openers is still dumb. Why don't I just run down to El Paso and start looking for signs where the cows were stolen?"

"Uh, I sure wish you wouldn't. You remember Colonel Walthers?"

"Sure, that asshole army man I can't seem to get along with for some reason."

"I noticed. He's in charge of the investigation at Fort Bliss. He runs the military police there."

Longarm laughed and said, "Shoot, Colonel Walthers might be able to get his socks on without help, but whatever he might think he's doing for the army down there, he sure ain't *running* it! I'll stay out of his way, Billy. I'll stay off the army post and just sniff for signs along the border."

Vail shook his head and said, "No, goddammit, I don't want you anywhere *near* El Paso! We know where the cows crossed the Rio. I want you to head 'em off, not chase 'em."

"Hell, Billy, you ain't listening. Those cows could come back anywhere! I ain't tall enough to see the whole infernal border from any one spot. If I went down into Mexico and found the hideouts where they change the brands and all—"

But Billy Vail was rearing up behind his desk, red-faced, as he cut in. "Goddammit, Longarm, you are the one who isn't listening! I ain't sending you to Mexico. I want you to stay the hell *out* of Mexico! That's a direct order, damn your eyes! The last time you were south of the border you caused all sorts of problems that ain't quite died down yet. You may be a lawman in these United States, but in Mexico they still have papers out on you for murder!"

Longarm shrugged and grumbled, "Hell, I never murdered anybody down there, Billy. Maybe shot up some asshole *rurales* who were acting truculent, but—"

"But me no buts," Vail interrupted. "This time you're to

go where I send you, and go after the folks I send you after. You're to do your whole and entire investigation on this side of the border. Is that clear?"

Longarm puffed his cheroot and said he'd catch the 8:15 south. Billy Vail sat down again and said, "Right. You change at Alamosa for the train to Laredo. And Longarm?"

"Yeah, Billy?"

"Please don't get us into another war with Mexico."